'Grainne Murphy's third novel allows a death to ask questions of life, of three lives in particular, those of Helen, Annie and Laura. This is a thoughtful meditation on what happens to old friendships when you make yourself a new life. Insightful, believable and raw, there are questions here about all of our lives.'

JOANNA GLEN, the Costa First Novel Award shortlisted author of
The Other Half of Augusta Hope

'Set in the latter days of the pandemic, *Greener* is a quiet yet powerful novel which examines the nature of friendship and the compromises that people make in their lives. This is a beautifully-written and emotionally engaging work.'

MADELEINE D'ARCY, author of *Liberty Terrace*

'What a gorgeous novel! I've been a fan of Gráinne's books for a while now, and it was a treat to find myself absorbed once again by the worlds that she so deftly creates. Gráinne Murphy's keen-eyed exploration of the complexities of adult friendship brims with warmth and humour.'

DANIELLE MCLAUGHLIN, author of *The Art of Falling*

'Murphy is an accomplished writer with the gift of transferring everyday life onto the page, assuredly.'

'In *Greener*, Gráinne Murphy reveals depths in the seemingly everyday. By turns heartbreaking, philosophical and funny, this book makes us question the changing and unchanging nature of ourselves and of friendships, new and old.'

GREENER

Gráinne Murphy

Legend Press Ltd, 51 Gower Street, London, WC1E 6HJ
info@legendpress.co.uk | www.legendpress.co.uk

Contents © Gráinne Murphy 2024
The right of the above author to be identified as the author of this work has
been asserted in accordance with the Copyright, Designs and Patents Act
1988. British Library Cataloguing in Publication Data available.

Set in Times.
Print ISBN 9781915643377
Ebook ISBN 9781915643384
Cover by Rose Cooper | www.rosecooper.com

Gráinne Murphy grew up in rural West Cork, Ireland. At university she studied Applied Psychology and Forensic Research. In 2011 she moved with her family to Brussels for 5 years. She has now returned to West Cork, working as a self-employed language editor specialising in human rights and environmental issues.

Gráinne's debut novel *Where the Edge Is* was published by Legend Press in 2020, *The Ghostlights* was published in 2021, and *Winter People* was published in 2022.

Visit Gráinne
www.grainnemurphy.ie

Follow her on X
@GraMurphy

and Instagram
@gramurphywriter

CONTENTS

For Rachel and Sylvia, who always ask the right questions

Goose says just be born to it.
Dog says roll yourself in it,

be governed by fear of loss of it.
Cat says you can always leave.

[...]

Bowerbird says go to great lengths for it.
Penguin walks hundreds of miles for it.

Firefly burns very bright for it.
Frog just holds on. Tight.

Taken from 'What the Frog Taught Me About Love', from the collection
Towards a General Theory of Love by Clare Shaw (Bloodaxe Books, 2022)

TIME RATHER THAN SPACE

A whisker over fourteen hours, two in the air and twelve in her head, and Helen was at the narrower side gate, looking at the house through the iron bars, like a Dickens orphan. Same view of the drive. Same gravel underfoot. Same code for the gate. As if she had never left. As if the trains and planes and taxis had conspired to move her through time rather than space.

Her hand on the gate told her that time had passed. She extended her fingers to their fullest and watched the flesh pucker and gather. Her skin cross-hatched like tweed. Her nails with their little half-moons that, despite frequent manicures, always looked like they were struggling. She had watched the moon rise one night and sure enough its own edges were ragged. No crisp lemon-rind distinction but a trailing off of pale into dark. She liked it more after that. Ragged as it was, determinedly hanging in the sky above her. Who hung the moon? Wasn't that a song or a poem? A story. Something.

Hello, Annie, she would say.

She could say that much with ease. Then leave a space that Annie could fill with whatever she liked. Professional distance or gushy catching up. It was all the one to Helen.

Her hand on the garden gate, pushing it open. Waiting for the squeak – a long moment when change seemed possible, but then, there it was. Hearing it and feeling … what? Sick, maybe, or starving. She held her emotions in her stomach, every therapist and healer and alternative remedy specialist had always told her. Every conventional medic, too, albeit in weightier language. She had to peer past the money to see it.

Hello, Annie, she would say. *How is he doing?*

Her hand on the garden gate. Ahead of her, the house was greyer than usual in the cold late-winter light, the Virginia creeper reduced to dull spiny fingers. The trees along the drive – *the avenue*, her mother used to call it, always eager to shore up her husband's notions – were a weary brown, their bare branches leaving the house exposed and self-conscious.

Hello, Annie, she would say. *Long time no see* and *Aren't you looking well* and *I came as soon as I could, had to wait for the PCR result. You know.*

Inside the gate, the air smelled white. Air couldn't smell of a colour, yes, yes, whatever. She was foolish enough to say out loud once that the air smelled green and Conor told her it was really wild garlic she was smelling. That, or her imagination. His fanciful Helen. His Hell-in. A years-old tease that had outlived whatever fun or humour it once held. Sometimes she pretended not to hear him, on days when the prospect of a laugh, or even a smile, felt it would cost her her sanity. On those days, she imagined them ending up in court one day, repeating these small personal atrocities in front of a judge. *He teased me, Your Honour. He mispronounced my name on purpose.*

If she thought the garden smelled white then it smelled white, dammit.

No swearing, Helen.

Hell-in.

She should have let Conor come. If he were here, she could look at him and see her present instead of her past. She could put her hand in his and dispel the notion that the gate was a portal. That she was twenty-two. Seventeen. Eleven. Four. That everything was still ahead of her. The magic and the misery and the mistakes.

Hello, Annie, she would say, as airily as if Annie were just anyone. As if it hadn't been almost forty years since they were put sitting beside one another on the first day of primary school. *Hello, Annie. I'm Helen. I like your purple pencil case.*

At Mass, years ago, the priest gave a sermon about making the world a better place. He had been working on a jigsaw at home, he told the rustling crowd. A difficult one: a map of the entire world. So difficult, in fact, that he despaired of ever finishing it and picked it up to return it, half-finished, to the box. As he lifted it, however, it fell from his hands and landed upside down, which was the point at which he discovered that the back of the jigsaw was a picture of a man. All he had to do to complete it, the priest told them, was to get the man right and then the world would be right, too. It didn't seem that profound to her at the time – certainly not enough to warrant carrying it with her through all the relationships and life events that had happened since. Neither the emptiness of atheism nor the filling-up of alternatives had managed to shift it. Some things were unshakeable. She would be one hundred and two, toothless, wordless, in an adult nappy, in a corner, in another world, and see a picture of a jigsaw on TV and think 'fix the man, fix the world'. Some part of her holding on to the belief that things were simple. *I like your pencil case.*

She took a fresh mask from the wipe-clean pouch in her handbag and sealed the one she had worn in the taxi into a freezer baggie.

Hello, Annie. I'm sorry it took me this long.

If you could do it all again. Another great therapy favourite. She couldn't. None of them could and to pretend otherwise was for fantasists. Perhaps for that earlier fanciful *Hell-in* that Conor was so determined to hold on to.

If the gate had taken twenty-five years from her, ringing the doorbell gave it all back. She had to remind herself to straighten her shoulders. To smooth down the stray hair in her left eyebrow. To twist her wedding and engagement rings so that they faced out.

Hello, Annie, she said in her head. *Hello, Annie. Hello, Annie. Hello, Annie.*

Everything else she might say vanished.

'Helen.' Annie opened the door and her smile was about seventy per cent of what it used to be. She stood aside. 'Come on in. Jack is in the living room.'

And there was neither time nor need for her *Hello, Annie* at all.

TUCK IN YOUR HEELS!

The double doors to the living room were open and Annie disappeared inside. 'Look who's here,' Helen heard her say, and imagined her father turning towards the door in happy expectation, yet somehow her feet wouldn't carry her out of the safety of the hallway.

She unwrapped her scarf and hung it carefully on a hook in the little cloakroom, then took off her coat, turned it inside out and placed it over the scarf. She had done the same thing at least once a day for the past twenty-five years in her own home, yet here it became, once again, her mother's habit.

She pressed hard on the floorboard outside the living room door and it obliged her with the same reassuring creak as always. She stepped inside the room to find her father had turned towards the door and she was greeted with the reality of him.

Later, she would think about how, in movies, when the hero sees their age-transformed loved one, they superimpose the memory of youth and vigour, looking past the shell and recognising the unchanged soul within. Self-aggrandising nonsense. Show her someone generous enough to effect that immediate a shift in the midst of their own shock and she would consider them halfway to a saint.

He had already been old the last time she saw him. Now, however, he was the kind of old that shrank the skeleton and stretched the skin so that it looped and folded and jowled. She had the urge to reach into her handbag for a hair bobble so that she could gather the loose skin and tie it back neatly at the nape of his neck.

Everything within her – stomach, throat, breath – tightened in response. 'Hello,' she said from the doorway.

He appeared to be trying to get up, rocking back and forth in the wing-back chair as though to gain enough momentum to lurch towards her. *Tuck in your heels!* she wanted to urge, the way he did when the swing set was installed in the garden and he needed her to learn to do it on her own, his patience for pushing quickly exhausted.

Helen waited to see if Annie would help him to his feet but she had retreated into the bow of the window and was looking out into the front garden. For Christ's sake. If she was trying to be discreet or to give them their space, she should leave the room, not stand there as if suddenly rendered deaf and blind. As if she wasn't absolutely aware of exactly how much she had hidden.

In the chair, the jerking continued and there seemed no way to stop his efforts other than to go to him instead.

Annie looked at Helen frozen in the doorway and moved to stand beside the chair. 'Stay where you are, Jack,' she said, her hand firm on his shoulder.

For a second – no more – Helen believed that Annie's touch might be magical. That her hand would transform this old man and deliver up her father's voice in all its power and warmth and certainty. The rich voice that was his calling card. Drifting up the stairs at night in low, fond conversation with her mother. Rising from groups of women at parties. Flowing from the school gates when there was a break in filming and he came to collect her. Emerging from Dr Danny Furlong on television at seven thirty on alternate week nights.

Who was her father without his voice?

But the sound that came out was something entirely alien.

'He's delighted you're here,' Annie said. 'Aren't you, Jack?'

Helen straightened her shoulders and took off her mask. If they weren't going to wear them, she wouldn't either. She had her negative PCR and, besides, she wasn't a guest here. She placed her handbag on the old green sofa and tried to breathe all the way into her stomach. His eyes were the same, she told herself, as she crossed the room to him. She could look at his eyes.

'I'll leave you two to catch up,' Annie said, smiling at them both and moving past Helen to the door.

Having wished her gone, Helen was seized with the urge to go after her, to beg her to stay, to help, interpret, whatever. But she was gone, closing the doors noiselessly behind her. Helen sat down in the wing-back chair opposite her father – perching on the edge as though she might have to go at any minute – and waited for words.

ASK ME AND I'LL TELL YOU

The longest hour of her life later – and who would have thought the final throes of Rex's birth would ever be usurped for drawn-out torment? – her father closed his eyes and Helen went to find Annie.

She left the living room doors open and walked across the hall, behind the imperial staircase and into the kitchen. Annie was sitting at the table, reading the newspaper.

'He fell asleep,' Helen said apologetically, then was annoyed at herself for feeling she had to justify anything to Annie, much less her failure to keep her father entertained enough to stay awake. 'I left the doors open so we can hear if …' She didn't know how to finish. 'If he needs anything.'

'There's a baby monitor in the room,' Annie said, nodding her head towards the dresser. Helen's panic must have shown on her face because Annie added quickly, 'I switched it off when you were in with him.'

She got up and turned it on, and Helen saw her father appear in his chair, his chest rising and falling as she watched.

'Would you like tea? I was going to bring one in to you but I thought you might prefer to catch up, just the two of you.'

'I can make it,' Helen said. It was, after all, her home.

She took a mug from the dresser and spooned coffee into the French press. *Cafetière,* she corrected herself. It was no longer the nineties. It amazed her that her brain could do this, could focus on the tiny things instead of figuring out what to say. What line to take. They had been friends, after all – *such* friends, as Helen's mother used to say. *Helen and Annie are such friends.* And Laura, of course. But her mother pronounced Laura's name with no discernible tone.

While she waited for the kettle to boil, she stacked the boxes of herbal tea by flavour and faced out the glass bottles in the spice rack on the windowsill. It was a terrible place to keep them, the sun would leach out all the flavour. She lifted the rack and moved it into the far corner of the worktop. The dead corner the sun never reached. There.

Annie got up from the table and went out into the hall. Helen could hear her shoes – those wide Crocs, worn with socks – slapping gently as she moved. She watched on the monitor as Annie bent over her father, angling him slightly in the chair and propping a rolled-up towel between his head and the wing of the chair. Her adjustments were gentle and confident. She moved, Helen thought, like someone who didn't see a body as a battleground.

Helen took a sip of her coffee and texted Conor. *Don't forget Ruan is going to Dimi's house after school. Pick-up at 8pm.*

She took another sip of coffee. She would be tossing and turning later, her blood fizzing, her legs twitching in the bed. Like Jack in his chair. The thought was enough for her to spill the remainder of her coffee down the sink. *Hope everyone else home safe,* she added. Conor hated chains of texts, the irritation of several interruptions where one would have done. Being far away granted her an exemption.

Outside the window, the garden was a dull winter green. The garden had always been her mother's domain. She fussed over every little thing out there, from the first and last cut of the grass, to the soil pH that would yield the colour hydrangeas she wanted, to the precise location of each bedding plant. Everything impeccably maintained and controlled. Unkempt, to her mother, meant poor.

The last time Helen stood at this window was when her mother died. She had looked out at her mother's garden while

21

a houseful of people cooed about how brave her father was and he told them what a support Lily had always been. A rock, really. Especially with a demanding career like his.

A rock. Helen had nearly laughed out loud. That was her mother exactly. A rock. No personality, no colour, unless draped with someone else's. That was what happened when you had a child at twenty-one. When you had little idea yet who you were.

The funeral itself had been equally devoid of personality. That was no surprise, she supposed, as nobody appeared to have the faintest idea who her mother had really been. Was she the stalwart the priest spoke of? Lover of ostentatious hymns and dinner parties and her husband and daughter? Or was she someone else entirely? Some secret person who held herself tightly within, beholden to nobody? Helen, made mean with whiskey, railed at her father about the generic funeral he had okayed, about identity and wishes and longing.

'Anyone would think you hardly knew her, *Danny*,' she said, an insult she hadn't used for years but that still made him flinch.

'What would you propose instead, Helen?' her father asked, fixing her in place with that voice, knowing – *knowing* – she had nothing. 'What would you have chosen for Lily?'

It was a relief to leave. To point to her flight. To mutter about Réiltín and the boys at home, needing her. To remind people they didn't travel well. No need for anyone to know they had travelled happily on cars and trains throughout the rest of Europe, if not this particular corner of it. Neither she nor her father ever brought it up again. Both times she came back to Ireland since then, he travelled to meet her in Dublin. She pleaded work meetings, he claimed a happy overlap with the need to catch up with old friends.

Her children had yet to see where their mother grew up. How passive that sounded, when the truth was that she had yet to bring them here.

She walked into the utility room and unlocked the back

door. Outside, the sun had all but disappeared and she shivered in the cold.

The boys would love this garden. At eleven and ten, they would delight in the hide-and-seek options. Réiltín might even be tempted outside. Helen could picture her sitting on the grass, leaning against the base of the bronze sundial, her phone glinting in the sun. The old croquet set could be dragged out of the shed. Or the badminton racquets. They would spread their arms to the world and revel in the space. So different from their chic city terrace, with its planters and paving slabs. She took her phone out of her pocket and took a photo.

She walked to the sundial and ran her fingertips over the cold metal. This was where she used to play when her parents told her they wanted to chat *just themselves*. If she arranged her dolls around the foot of the sundial, she could hear them talking. They must have realised it too because suddenly there was a bright yellow playhouse a little further away and she had to take her dolls there.

In the light from the kitchen window, she saw Annie sit down at the table again. Was that her seat? *Annie's place.* She could almost hear her father saying it.

Back in the kitchen, she ran the hot tap and heated her hands in the warm stream of water. 'Cold out there,' she said.

Annie wasn't looking at her. Nor was she flipping through the paper in the sort of pseudo-nonchalance that might have given her away. She was simply sitting, one hand on the handle of her mug of tea. Not looking into space or picking her nails or biting her lip or one of the hundred things Helen could picture her doing. Had seen her doing a million times. Annie's hair was different. A ponytail still, yes, but lower and neater. A darker, more grown-up shade of auburn than the shades of red she used to favour, when the sun catching her hair flamed like the head of a match. Her clothes were different too. Annie didn't wear a carer's uniform exactly, but her own version – grey cotton trousers, wide-legged and cuffed at the ankle, with a long-sleeved cotton T-shirt. It made

Helen feel overdressed in her tailored trousers and fine-knit jumper over a white shirt. At least she had worn trainers rather than her low-heeled boots.

'So you finished your nursing training, after all,' Helen said, to remind herself of the present. 'I'm glad.'

Annie shook her head. 'Actually, no. I intended to, it just never quite … Timing, you know.'

It would be rude to ask how, then, Annie supposed herself qualified to care for Helen's father, but it took her several swallows to be sure the words would stay put.

'I qualified as a care assistant after my mother died,' Annie said.

'They must be very similar, I imagine,' Helen said.

'In some respects.' Annie looked at Helen directly. 'If you'd rather take over his care, that's no problem. I can show you what you need to do. Check in every day to make sure everything is okay. If you like. Or it doesn't have to be me. The agency can arrange for someone else to help you or to care for Jack.'

Her voice was even. There was nothing objectionable in her words or tone, but nor was there much warmth.

How did they get here? How were they suddenly, within a handful of sentences, in this place of cool words and stiff strangerhood?

If she had hugged Annie at the door, would it feel they were in this together?

Hello, Annie. I'm so glad he has you.

But that wasn't possible. If she had held out her arms, all that time would have pushed in between them, forcing them into the kind of hug that bespoke sadness and false intimacy. A sad, hopeless hug with the cobwebs of years on it.

Over Annie's shoulder, the monitor showed her father asleep in his chair, his cheeks sunken above his slack mouth. Helen had a brief mental image of having to feed him, like trying to spoon cream into a sagging piping bag.

She would never get past it. Whatever memories she had of him should not be overwritten by the day-to-day.

'I'm booked to fly back on Monday, so it might only end up being disruptive for him,' Helen said.

'Let me know if you change your mind. Or I can give you the number of the agency and you can talk to Monica.'

'I've arranged to meet her while I'm here, actually,' Helen said, already hating herself for that *actually*. If they were still friends, Annie would ask her straight out why she was being such a bitch. *Ask me,* she thought. *Ask me and I'll tell you.* But what would she say? More to the point, what could she bear to hear in return?

'I might take my things upstairs,' she said. 'Freshen up a bit.'

But when she pushed open the door to her room, the thought of dealing with her suitcase was exhausting. Instead, she lay fully dressed on top of the quilt and fell into a dreamless sleep.

ENTER AT YOUR OWN PERIL

When Helen woke, the sun had slid towards the horizon, the slurred light making a dark spidery heap of her chair legs and dressing table on the white floorboards. She reached for her phone and saw that it was after four in the evening. Still afternoon really, despite the failing light. She should get up, unpack, shower, sort out food of some kind. Make herself useful. She didn't even know what time her father ate dinner (assuming he did), having forgotten to ask any of the two pages of questions in her notebook. She had been too busy engaging in self-indulgent one-upmanship with the woman who was caring for her father. She ran the phrase around her mind and liked it. Yes. It was easier to think of Annie in those terms: *her father's carer.*

She opened the family WhatsApp group. *Safely arrived. PCR fine. Grandpa Jack sends his love. Hope school was good and you don't have too much homework! Miss you loads. Mum. xxxx.* She attached the photo she took earlier. *Grandpa Jack's garden!* she captioned it, adding a tiny tree and a tiny bird before pressing send.

The boys would be quick to reply, she knew, having got their first phones recently enough that they responded to every message with heartbreaking enthusiasm. Rex would be first, she bet herself. Her baby. Who still sometimes kissed her instead of simply offering his face at bedtime or through the car window.

She put down the phone and stretched. Now that she was

awake, she was starting to get cold. The kind of cold that could only be shaken off with a shower. How long had it been since she slept three hours without waking?

She lingered in the bed. The sheets were crisp and smelled fresh and she imagined Annie making up the bed knowing she was coming. What did she think as she was wrestling with the duvet cover and pillowcases? Warm reminiscing, maybe, about all the Saturday mornings after Friday sleepovers, when she helped Helen to strip this very bed, stuffing everything into one of the pillowcases and leaving it on the landing, ready to go to the dry cleaners.

Or maybe she resented the extra work. Maybe Monica forwarded a list of additional jobs to Annie each week, the way Helen did for Thea, along with a suggestion of the extra time or payment that might be applied. *Skirting boards* or *shower grouting* or *hoover out top kitchen cupboards,* then the following week, *hoover out bottom kitchen cupboards.* Maybe Annie was on her best behaviour. On edge. Or simply house-proud, in this, Helen's house.

Her phone buzzed and she picked it up. Ruan, rather than Rex. The sunny centre of their household, who hadn't even balked when his ten-months-younger brother was given a phone at the same time. *Cool garden! Miss u2,* his message said, accompanied by a pizza emoji. She frowned. Conor shouldn't be giving them midweek treats. She typed out a quick text, then deleted it without sending. Her voice in the message thread was a litany of reminders, nudges and questions. *A machine gun of instructions,* Conor called her once in front of their friends, his warm smile doing nothing to relieve the sting of truth.

The room – her room – was the same colour she had picked out all those years ago, although she would bet it hadn't been repainted since the passing of her mother and her mother's careful three-year room-refreshing rotation. Seafoam, the colour was called. She had picked it purely because her mother kept bringing her samples of pinks and purples, but then fell totally in love with it when it went on her walls, her delight deepening when the dark brown floorboards were stained white and her heavy old furniture was taken away and returned to her in a scrubbed, faded white. Her mother insisted on hanging white linen curtains on both windows, despite Helen's protests that she didn't need them and would never close them.

'I want to feel like I'm sleeping outdoors,' she told Annie, who came over to admire it as soon as the workmen were gone.

'But you hate going outside,' Annie said.

'Exactly,' Helen said. 'Now I don't ever have to.'

And the pair of them fell around laughing.

The large claw-foot bath still held pride of place in the bathroom, but had been joined by a shower cubicle that spoiled the sense of space and luxury Helen had always felt in this room.

A few minutes later, however, she changed her mind. The shower cubicle might be ugly and generic, but it was wonderful in the way a hot shower on demand always was. As she stood under the stream of water, Helen found herself wondering if the shampoo and shower gel were Annie's or if they were here for guests. She picked up the shampoo bottle and examined it for clues: *healthy hydration,* it told her. *Endless shine.* She weighed it in her hand and estimated there was about one third gone. The conditioner matched the shampoo, with about the same amount gone. Unusual. In Helen's experience, the conditioner lasted longer. But that was with both her and Conor using them. Annie hardly had gentlemen callers, not here at her workplace. *I've already arranged to meet Monica, actually.* Helen heard her own voice and felt a squeeze of shame.

The shower gel was almost full. *Specially formulated for sensitive skin,* it proclaimed. She sighed and poured a measure into her cupped hand. No matter how sensitive it was, human skin wasn't designed to be presented with its own raw self.

Helen smoothed on body milk, then dressed in a fresh T-shirt and trousers.

There. She felt equal to seeing her father again. Almost.

She paused outside her bedroom door. Steam wafted lightly out of the bathroom, reminding her of those *Ghostbusters* movies they watched as children. Steam from under a door definitely meant creepy goings-on. Enter at your own peril and so on.

The third door on her side of the hall was closed. It used to be the spare room, but now maybe it was Annie's. She would hardly have taken the master bedroom, would she? Surely not. Whatever else Annie could be accused of – and Helen wasn't sure yet what that might be – crassness would be entirely out of character. She crossed the central landing, glancing down the stairs as she passed. No sign of movement, although the living room doors were open. She went up the three little steps to her parents' room, which spanned almost the length of the house. After her mother died, her father no longer slept upstairs, preferring to put a bed in his study. That worked out well in the end. These old houses would be murder when it came to modifications and things like stairlifts.

She turned the handle slowly and eased the door open, her body remembering the move precisely, her weight shifting to her left foot, giving her enough lean to see into the room. So often had she done this that something within her was certain she would see her mother lying on the bed in her slip. Her dress taken off and hanging neatly over the back of the armchair in the large window that looked over the back garden, her shoes lined up beneath it. Helen was never sure if her mother actually slept during her afternoon rest – always a rest, never a nap – but she didn't come to understand the restorative power of an uninterrupted afternoon hour, sleep or otherwise, until she had children of her own.

There was no evidence of Annie in the room. Nothing to disturb the memory of her mother. In fact, the room was exactly as she remembered, minus her mother on the bed and clothes draped on furniture. Despite the tracks of a Hoover on the thick carpet, there was a musty smell and Helen opened both sets of windows.

She thought of her own town house, the neat, narrow rooms filled with clothes and clutter and life. This was so much house to let go to waste.

She left the bedroom door ajar to remind her to close the windows on her way to bed and made her way downstairs to the living room.

The dining room table was set for two. Properly set, with napkins and a jug of water with ice and lemon. Was this for her? Or for her father and Annie? Was this how they had dinner every night? With some kind of creepy quasi-restaurant formality?

'Sorry to start without you. Jack gets impatient when he's hungry, don't you, Jack?'

Helen startled and turned to see Annie sitting on a stool beside her father, spooning food into his mouth, expertly catching excess with the corner of the spoon.

'I thought maybe you and I could have dinner together. Catch up on Jack's progress,' Annie said.

'Alright.' Helen's tone was stiff, she knew, but how else to respond when she had little idea what such a catch-up might reveal. 'What can I do to help?'

That was somehow worse than the stiffness. Implying as it did that she would sit here and wait for Annie to finish feeding her father and then switch seamlessly to serving Helen. Maybe Helen had misread the situation entirely and she was supposed to start dinner? But the table was set and the water jug, which surely meant that everything was nearly ready?

'May I?' she said, instead moving towards Annie with her hand out for the bowl and spoon. She was relieved when Annie stood and handed them to her. Here was a job she could do.

'His right side is weaker so he manages best if you can—'

'Aim for the left,' Helen finished. 'Got it.'

She was about to add that she had raised three children and knew how to feed someone, when she realised Annie had already left the room.

A few minutes later, she was glad she hadn't said anything. It was as if her father didn't want to eat, so little effort did he make to keep the food in his mouth. Helen tried to mimic the napkin flick she had seen Annie do, but succeeded only in dripping greenish mush onto her clean trousers. She tutted in annoyance. At least Annie wasn't watching her. Then she remembered the monitor. And the fact that her father could hear and understand her.

'We're making a bit of a mess of this, aren't we?' she said brightly. It was the kind of thing she had heard people say in hospital dramas, she realised, and was suddenly grateful to her mother for dying suddenly – quietly – of a heart attack, with no need for such awkward intervention. 'There,' she said, wiping his chin. 'We'll have the hang of it shortly.'

Her father's response was to mumble (oh God, she could see the food in his mouth) and wave his good arm, coming dangerously close to knocking the bowl from her hand. *He gets impatient when he's hungry,* Annie had said, as if Helen had never met him before. As if she hadn't been in charge of making sure there were olives, batons of carrot and cucumber, crackers or thin slices of bread and butter laid out on the table half an hour before he was due home on Friday evenings. Her mother trying to be fancy, she thought dismissively at the time, but of course it was simply her mother safeguarding his good humour.

Helen sighed and looked down at herself: bowl in one hand, spoon in the other. How many more meals before she too had a good arm and a bad arm?

When it seemed he had had enough – the arm stopped waving, the bite fell fully out onto his chest, his eyelids drooped – Helen wiped carefully around his mouth and looked around for somewhere to put the bowl. She didn't want to leave him here on his own so soon after eating, but nor did she want to sit here as though she had no idea what came next.

'I'll take that from you,' Annie said, coming into the room on noiseless feet.

Helen startled for the second time that evening. The woman needed a fucking bell around her neck. Had she been watching on the monitor? There was no way to ask that didn't sound accusing.

'Thanks,' she said, tucking the napkin into the bowl. 'I didn't like to leave him.'

'Do you want to eat now?' Annie said. 'Vegetarian pasta. Nothing fancy.'

'I don't expect you to cook for me,' Helen said.

It must have come out ungrateful because Annie smiled tightly. 'I was making it for myself anyway. It was no trouble to add some extra.'

It was extremely good. Wholewheat pasta, Helen noted approvingly, tossed lightly in good oil, with sun-dried tomatoes, juicy olives, black pepper and freshly grated Parmesan, with slices of focaccia thickly spread with home-made garlic butter.

'Are you vegetarian?' Helen asked, indicating her bowl.

'No,' Annie said. 'I wasn't sure if you were.'

For a second it seemed possible that they might laugh together, but then Annie hurried on.

'I do meat or fish once or twice a week. Jack needs the balance and it's easier to make the same thing for us both.'

'And then puree his,' Helen said. She meant it to be factual but it sounded snarky. As if Annie were giving her father the leftovers of her own meal.

Annie smiled politely, then got up and crossed the room to check on Jack, leaving Helen alone at the table. The crunch of her garlic bread was loud in the silence and she was reminded of long hours at Mass and the rustle of old women trying to open their Murray Mints quietly. If asked, they claimed low blood sugar. Never had a small town had so many undiagnosed diabetics.

'Is he asleep?' Helen asked when Annie slipped back into her seat.

Annie nodded. 'He usually naps for an hour or so after dinner. Then we watch a bit of TV. The soaps, you know. He likes to keep up to speed with the competition.'

The competition? Hardly. It seemed more likely that he hated being forced to watch people he used to work with going about their jobs, their lives. Actors whose skills he used to complain about still getting to be the lead in a particular storyline or a bit player in someone else's drama. Did a character ever suffer a stroke, she wondered, and if so, why not have him play that? Ridiculous thought. Even aside from the insurance implications, nobody would want to see the reality of it. That wasn't what soaps were for. And so they would have a perfectly fit and healthy actor playing a stroke victim, should such a storyline arise, and it would be brief, an episode or two of light medicalisation, then a recovery somewhere far out of sight, before a miraculous return to form. Nothing her father would be able for. Was there a name for that, where someone's own experience directly put them out of the running for something? A sort of reverse-gonzo. Or death, of course.

'Are you alright?' Annie asked.

Helen looked up to find her watching her. 'I'm fine,' she said. 'Just tired.'

'Do you still have trouble sleeping?' Annie asked, and the question was so unexpected, such a direct reference to their shared past, that Helen didn't know how to answer.

She could laugh it off, as she did with colleagues, by saying lightly that parenting was at least fifty per cent exhaustion. That once a person had children, sleep was the holy grail. But Annie didn't have children – that much Helen knew from Monica – and so she might think Helen was engaging in one-upmanship. Or worse, she might not understand that the tiredness that came with children was emotional. After a certain point, the amount a person slept – or didn't – was largely immaterial, made irrelevant by the intensity of the worry in waking hours.

'Work is extra busy since Covid,' she said instead.

'Translator, right?' Annie said. 'Jack never loses an opportunity to mention it. He still notices every time there's a voice-over interpreter on the TV.'

Was this intended to endear her father to her? This glimpse of second-hand pride? Or was it Annie's way of saying that she knew him better than Helen did?

Well, she could have that medal. Helen had long ago given up on trying to impress her father and had no intention of returning to the field.

'Do you work solely for the courts?' Annie said.

'Usually, yes. Sometimes I meet with the client and their solicitor beforehand.'

'What kinds of cases are they? Or is it confidential?'

Helen shook her head. 'It's a lot of asylum applications, visas overstayed, legal arrangements for unaccompanied minors, that sort of thing.'

'Sounds intense.'

The truth was that Helen had learned long ago to disengage her emotions from those situations. She had trained herself to give only her brain, quick as it was to hear and understand broken grammar, to detect nuance. Far better to give too little of herself rather than too much. The people whose lives and circumstances she trapped on paper needed her mind, her exactitude, her attention to detail. Sympathy for her patients might be all well and good for Annie, but it would get Helen's clients nowhere with their indignities and injustices. Her tears would be a self-indulgent waste of everyone's time.

She wanted to ask Annie if she remembered calling her temperamental. How, when Helen had talked about being an actress, Annie would roll her eyes and tell her that she would never be an actress when she could hardly make it through half an hour of TV without crying.

'At least I'm not cold,' Helen had said, stung.

'Who are you calling cold?'

'You never cry,' Helen said.

'How would you know? You're not with me all the time.'

Helen began to count on her fingers. 'Jamie shifted Michelle last year and nothing. You were accused of cheating in that maths exam in front of the whole class and nothing. I broke my arm and nothing.'

'Why would I cry because you broke your arm?'

'Sympathy.'

Annie sat back on her heels and thought about it. 'Maybe I have a tear gland disorder?'

'Maybe you're a sociopath.' Helen made claw hands and zombie-walked towards Annie, gnashing her teeth as if about to bite her. 'That'll make it tricky to pick a career.'

'I'll go up to Sister Bernadette at our next careers class and tell her I need some options that maximise my core skill of heartlessness.' This time, Annie was the one to count on her fingers. 'Newsreader. Lab work. Any kind of science, really. Academic – professors aren't allowed to be human, too much risk of affairs and academic shame, basically. Ooh – the clergy. I could be a nun. They'd go wild for my calm exterior.'

'Sister Bernadette will be beating down your door,' Helen said.

Annie wagged her finger. 'Nope. She wouldn't be allowed. She'll have to suffer her ecstasies alone in her room.'

Their laughing fits used to hurt. After a sleepover, Helen would feel her chest stretched out, as if being around Annie had somehow made her heart bigger.

Now, she looked at Annie across the table from her, spearing individual pieces of pasta and chewing noiselessly. She hadn't asked – wouldn't dare to ask – the question everyone wanted to know: *Do you cry afterwards when you're alone?*

'Do you know the Concorde Effect?' she asked, surprising herself.

Annie looked into the distance. 'I remember hearing about it but not the detail.'

Typical Annie. Never wanting to admit she didn't know something. Everything was something she already knew but couldn't quite put her finger on. Helen felt a flash of the old irritated fondness. 'Basically it means continuing with a lost cause because you've already put so much time and effort into it. That's sort of how I feel about my job, I suppose.'

Annie nodded without saying anything, and Helen was grateful that she didn't rush to ask exactly what Helen meant and whether she was planning to give up her job and, if so, what else would she do and didn't she know that everyone – every single person on the planet – felt that way from time to time and all she needed was a nice weekend away.

Annie waved the water jug at her and Helen held out her glass for a refill. In his chair, Jack gave a small snore.

'Is his speech gone permanently?' she asked Annie. 'Nobody would give me a straight answer.'

'Then you're not going to like my answer much either,' Annie said. 'Aphasia affects people differently. Sometimes it comes back after a few days, sometimes a few weeks. Sorry, I know that's not very helpful, but it's how it is.'

Helen liked both the *sorry* and the assumption she didn't need the word aphasia explained to her.

'It must be so frustrating for him.'

Annie nodded. 'A bit like trying to carry water in a colander, I imagine. Trying to catch everything you're dropping. Anticipating his needs is one way to avoid it, but sometimes I think that must make things worse. Directionless anger, you know. It's better to let him say and do as much as he can.'

'Easier than fighting with him,' Helen agreed.

Annie half smiled and stood. 'I'd better clear these away and wake Jack or he will struggle to get to sleep later.'

'I'll clear,' Helen said. 'After all, you cooked.'

'Thank you.'

'We can do it in reverse tomorrow evening,' Helen said.

And just like that, she was in a temporary house share with her past.

THIS WAS HOW SLEEP VANISHED

Helen woke at three thirty-four a.m.. From sound asleep to wide awake in the space of a single breath. Breathe in, asleep. Breathe out, awake. It was such a habit by now that she had given up wondering what it was about three thirty-four. She had stopped trying to go to bed earlier or later in a bid to trick her body, or, more likely, her mind. Weekdays, weekends, it didn't seem to matter. Three thirty-four and Helen was awake. The only difference was that Conor wasn't fast asleep beside her.

The night before every bank holiday, Conor talked about the luxury of waking at the usual time and realising he could simply go back to sleep. Then the morning came and he got up anyway and went for a run, and she often caught him, sheepish at his laptop, sending emails or reviewing client accounts and tax returns. *To take the pressure off the week,* he claimed, and she was happy enough to believe him, even if the week, when it came, showed no appreciable difference. She was careful to take the time off herself. Just because the children weren't planning to do anything with her didn't mean they were blind to her availability in the kitchen or the living room. It was enough to be present. For them to know they came first.

When they were little, she used to worry about dying while they still needed her. Lately, she had begun to think they would be absolutely fine. It would be briefly terrible for them, of course – they weren't monsters – but then it would be absolutely fine. Annie was thirteen when her father died and she got over it with reasonable equanimity. Children were better at understanding the idea of things being bigger than themselves. It was their everyday reality, after all. Conor would miss her, she supposed. On a practical level, perhaps most of all. He liked to have things settled. The idea of starting over would freak him out.

What if she were the one who had to start over? It was possible to picture, with almost alarming ease, the house without Conor. It was all the other little losses that would bother her. The in-jokes evaporated. The history. Seeing a rabbit on the road without anyone else to point and say, *Look! Bunny rabbit!* to make each other laugh.

This was how sleep vanished: one random thought after another until she was planning what she would wear to her husband's funeral. Her perfectly healthy husband.

She kicked her feet against the sheet. Sleep was so natural, so thoughtless when it was going well, so fraught when it wasn't. In her reading – and Helen had read a lot about it, searching for a cure, a tip, a trick, that would somehow give her what most people had effortlessly – she had encountered so many theories about why humans sleep, how they sleep, its function, its purpose, its joy. Everything from the mystical to the biochemical. From dream theories to dire predictions about what would happen to teenagers forced out of their natural circadian rhythms and into the routine of starting school early in the morning. Yet she was no closer to knowing exactly what it was sleep did, beyond thinking that it was some form of profound magic that transformed the present into the past without making people live through every aching second.

Shorn of that particular respite, was she stuck in an eternal present?

Hardly. Here she was, literally in her past.

In her childhood bed, in her childhood room, in her childhood home.

Downstairs, her father was sleeping his chemical sleep,

having been shuttled off to bed by Annie after two hours of soaps so dull that Helen suspected the medication was entirely surplus to requirements.

She could get up without waking him, she knew. Annie, however, was a different matter. The thought of Annie hearing her walking around so early in the morning– in what was the middle of the night for most people – inferring how poor her sleep had become, perhaps congratulating herself on her insight or, worse, thinking she still somehow *knew* Helen, was unbearable. As if she had paraded naked into Annie's bedroom, flashing her cottage cheese thighs and saggy boobs and beginners' bingo wings. No, it was better to remain in bed and wait.

Even lying in bed was resting, she reminded herself.

Two mornings ago, she had woken to the familiar silence of her own home. The air shimmering with sleep, the house full of night smells. The boys in their rooms, in a tangle of sheets (Rex) and neatly curled with one hand under his pillow (Ruan). Réiltín likely sitting up in bed, her face glowing blue in the light of her screen. Helen had tried (and tried and tried and tried) to confront her daughter's phone use. Taking the phone from her at night (only to find Réiltín had borrowed a friend's 'spare' phone, with all the attendant lack of security *that* implied), buying one of those wifi blockers that shut everything off at nine p.m. (forgetting in her aged stupidity that she could not shut off her daughter's phone network, short of climbing a mobile tower with an axe, and she wasn't quite there yet), and – yes, in a final act of desperation – sitting Réiltín down and trying to have a grown-up conversation about it, which failed in the space of a single sentence when Helen began to speak about the importance of sleep and was met with, *Yeah and how many hours a night do you get, Mum?*

Conor thought she was overparenting. His favourite expression for any hint of hard-line conversation. 'It's not that different to staying up late reading,' he said.

'But she's not reading. It is objectively different. That's the whole point. If she was staying up late reading, I wouldn't care.'

'At least she's in the house.'

'That's your bar? That everything is fine as long as she's not sneaking out?'

'At fourteen? Frankly, yes.'

Nevertheless, he agreed that they should make a production out of putting away their own phones at dinner time and not picking them up again until the children had gone to bed. In exchange, Helen let the arguing go. In truth, she was happy not to take away a means of social engagement, considering how difficult Réiltín's early years of secondary school had proven. The usual issues with girls – whispering, ostracising, judging. Every school holiday, Helen would broach the subject of moving school, but Réiltín always refused. Conor thought that made her optimistic and resilient. All she needed, he said, was to find her own space and then she would – here, he clicked his fingers as though a transformation were imminent. Every time those fingers clicked, Helen looked at his hand and thought that, given the choice, if he were kidnapped, say, and the kidnappers insisted she choose, she would happily sacrifice his middle finger. His clicking finger.

And you think she's optimistic? Helen wanted to ask him, when it came to light that Réiltín was skipping school altogether. 'You must make her go,' the principal told them, and for a while they split the week between them, Helen driving Ré to the school gate one morning and Conor the next. But neither of them could hold out for long against the demands of their workplaces and things soon lapsed back to the way they were before. Ré made it to school more often than not, according to the school's weekly attendance email. She missed a handful of days each month, but if she had bad menstrual cramps she might miss that same amount and nobody would raise an eyebrow. They were on borrowed time, Helen knew with a kind of sick certainty, but she had no idea how to confront someone whose daily problems were so vastly different from her own at that age.

I just want you to be happy, she said, over and over. Always hearing how needy it sounded. And that reductive 'just'! As if being happy was the simplest, most basic wish.

It wasn't even true. She didn't just want Réiltín – or the boys, for that matter – to be happy. She wanted them to succeed at life. There. Was that such a bad thing to want? According to the school psychologist, yes. Success had too many conditions, apparently. It was too subjective. Too determined by recourse to external standards. Too steeped in what others wanted.

'When were you last happy?' she wanted to ask her daughter, who used to dance across supermarket car parks and smile at strangers. 'Tell me how to make you happy.' But her daughter's happiness was, like sleep or time or the moon, something over which Helen had no control.

'Teenagers are never happy,' Conor said. 'That's the nature of the beast.'

She had to remind herself that his matter-of-fact attitude was one of the things she had fallen in love with. That two over-thinkers together would be a disaster that never left the house but sat in darkened gloom trying to out-apocalypse one another.

Of course she knew why she was so focused on Reiltín's happiness. Anyone with the most cursory awareness of humans' powers of self-denial would see that she was projecting. That what she wanted was for someone to sit her, Helen, down and ask when she had last been happy.

It was the kind of thing Annie would do.

Used to do, she corrected herself. The kind of thing Annie used to do.

What's eating you, she used to say, bouncing on Helen's bed. Then, when they were older, *Who pissed in your cornflakes?* Or, in quieter moments, *Who do you think we'll be?*

That was, after all, the crux of things, wasn't it? It wasn't as if her husband was cheating on her or was mean with money or had let himself go or done any other of the standard items on the universally agreed list of marital no-nos. The boys were healthy and happy and reasonably close, although that was most likely due to Ruan's easy-going nature. If pushed, they could each name a best friend, although they squirmed a little at the idea. *Embarrassing, Mum!* Conor said that boys went in less for those sorts of labels and she was happy to take his word for it. And of course they had an hour a day on their shiny new phones. What else did happy look like at ten? At eleven? At fourteen? At forty-four?

When was she last happy?

She made her fist into a pretend microphone and whispered the question aloud: *So, Helen, why don't you tell us what you remember of being happy?*

It was almost embarrassingly twee. Her graduation. Boarding the plane at Dublin Airport knowing that her life and future were waiting for her. Her wedding day. Having her children. Snapshots of holidays bleeding into one another: Helen by the pool with a glass of cold pale-green wine, watching Conor play with the boys while Ré read a book in the shade; eating spaghetti vongole in the cool of an Italian *terrazza*, satisfyingly aware that her shoulders were attractively freckled and that the half-stone she lost over the last month was noticeable.

So far so generic. Where were the specifics that made her a real person? Surely she could come up with at least one or two?

She pushed herself into a sitting position, rearranging the pillows against the headboard, her hands remembering the exact positions so that her neck wasn't resting against the wooden frame of the bed. She clicked on the bedside lamp and pale light warmed the dark. Had Annie checked the bulb? Probably. She was thorough like that.

She opened the notebook that she kept beside her at night. In theory, it was a sleep diary, recording when she slept and woke and how she felt about it, but in practice she used it to make notes when she couldn't sleep. Work stuff. Reminders of things the children had asked her for. At certain times of the year, lists of gift ideas for birthdays and Christmases.

HAPPY, she wrote at the top of the page.

Nothing came to mind. She tapped the biro against her lip for a minute or two, then held it to the paper in case it had ideas of its own.

Nope.

If she were to die right now (something brain-related, she imagined, an aneurysm or a brain haemorrhage, something catastrophic and immediate), whoever gathered her things might flick to the last page she had written on and see the word *HAPPY* in big capitals. Imagine the assumptions! The presumption that she was thrilled (thrilled to death, as it were) to have seen her father once more. She would become the worst of comforts offered to her own children: 'At least you can be certain she was happy – wasn't it the very last thing she wrote?'

She was tempted to score through the word, or add a question mark, but that would be unnecessarily cruel to dead Helen's surviving family.

The thing about happiness was that nobody was ever really aware of it in the moment. They were too busy actually being happy to watch themselves doing it or try to learn how it was done. She thought of the one time she tried drugs, a pill taken on a beach nine thousand miles from home, when there was no chance of stumbling across someone who knew her parents or being forced to get up and go to Mass the following morning. That chemical high was oddly reflective. She was both happy and aware she was happy, standing outside of her body and watching herself simply be happy. It drained away as quickly as it had come and Helen was left moving through time as through water. Or soup. Misty grey soup. Each second stretching into terrifying infinity and then three hours passing in the space of a single song. If that was awareness, then, on balance, she didn't want it.

Was that the sum total of her personal views of happiness as an adult? One ill-advised night of experimentation? Surely there had to be more. As a child and as a teenager, life was full of extremes, happiness included. So many weekends spent in this same room, herself and Annie and, later, Laura, piled on the bed like puppies, watching and rewatching movies, quoting lines to each other, jumping up to rewind and act bits out, to get snacks, to try on the spoils of their latest shopping trip. The night they watched *E.T.*, they slept on the floor between two windows so that they could see the sky. 'Just in case,' Helen said, and although they teased her, they all fell asleep watching the moon. They had seen the film already, of course – it felt almost retro to them, at fifteen. Like watching a piece of their childhood.

How young they were!

On the screen, Elliot hammered on his friend's cocoon and buried his face in his hands. 'That's what I'd be like,' Annie said. 'If anything happened to either of you.'

Laura held up her index finger and touched it slowly to each of their hearts and their laughter sealed the moment rather than breaking it.

Did Annie still sleep with the curtains open? It would be easy to find out – all she needed to do was tiptoe down the hall and peek around the door. She couldn't, Helen knew. Adults didn't do that kind of thing.

They spent so much time laughing as teenagers. When had she ever heard Réiltín laugh like that with anyone?

It didn't mean anything, she told herself. Her own mother had likely been unaware of Helen and her friends at that age, too.

Yes, but …

Yes, but Helen's mother lived her weeks in her own world. Upstairs with a migraine – *I've one of my heads, Helen, maybe you can amuse yourself quietly for a while* – then drifting around the house picking things up and putting them down. Or out in the garden with a distracted 'Hmmm?' to every question, and a large-brimmed hat that hid her eyes. It was only on Friday afternoons that she came alive, a thirsty plant finally watered, in anticipation of Jack coming home and reanimating her.

Her father could do with something similar, Helen thought. Something to reinvigorate him. Maybe she could take him out for a day. To the TV studio in Wicklow, perhaps? They could easily get there and back in a day now that the new motorway was open. For a second, she imagined her father as of old, welcomed like a king, before the reality of him intruded. She pictured him shuffling alongside her, his free arm flapping and slapping, as his erstwhile colleagues covered their distaste with nauseating pretend enthusiasm.

Not the studio, then.

The setting would not transform him. It would not turn the clock back. Nowhere could. People would stare and expect her to explain what he wanted or what he meant with that strange low-level groan that Annie called communication but that to an outsider sounded like distress.

But did that mean *she* was the outsider? And Annie the – what? The insider? The family?

A walk, Helen decided. She would take him out for a walk, on his own two feet if he was able. If he wasn't, then Annie would surely know where to procure a wheelchair.

That was what a carer was paid for, after all.

In all the years and all the conversations about their futures, Annie had tilted towards the medical. While Helen had dithered between being an actress – film? Theatre? – or something behind the scenes, like a director or a producer, and Laura had changed her mind depending on what paid the most. The money was the main thing, Laura said. Enough money for a big, warm house, holidays abroad twice a year, and a new car every two years so she never had to worry about whether or not it would start. Helen and Annie understood, knowing Laura's mortification at having to arrive each day to school in her mother's ancient Yellow Submarine, or, worse still, having to get a lift from Mrs Connolly, the maths teacher, on mornings when the Submarine withstood all efforts to get it going.

Annie alone held firm. She would be a nurse.

Helen and Laura knew better than to say, *Like your mother*. That line was trotted out by every teacher and parent and the girls watched as their friend's lips tightened and she didn't respond.

Were they destined – doomed – to reflect their parents? At eighteen, every decision was a binary: be like your parent or be unlike your parent. In seeking to remove herself so far from her father's life and profession, had Helen put herself in a life she would never have chosen independently?

And this—

this—

this—

THIS

was how a person gave their sleep away.

SHATTERING ONLY BECAUSE IT WAS HERS

It was early, a little before six a.m.. Annie woke to the faint sound of violins coming through the baby monitor on her bedside table. The sound indicator showed one green dot, and every so often, when the music reached a crescendo, it intensified to a greener light, before fading away alongside the music. It was her signal that, downstairs, Jack had woken and pressed the back of his hand against the large flat button that switched on Lyric FM. He was awake and comfortable, he was telling her. He was here and he was fine and she needn't worry.

Annie rose in the dark, pulled on her leggings and a fleece, and stuck a chewable toothpaste tablet in her mouth. The plumbing in these old houses was built to last, but the pipes rattled and she didn't want to wake Helen. Considerate or avoidant? Too early in the morning to try and figure *that* one out.

She tiptoed onto the landing, then down the flight of stairs to the hall. She waved at Jack's closed bedroom door, then curled around to her left under the arch of the stairs, through the kitchen and the laundry room, stopping to pull on her coat and hat, and out the back door into the gloom. In her hurry to tie her shoelaces before her fingers froze, she overshot the double knot and had to start again. Once done, she flipped the fold-out mitten part of her gloves over her fingers and blew gently through the wool as she walked, enjoying the warm damp of it.

With Helen here, she could probably get out for a walk later in the day, but first she needed to be sure that Helen understood the scope of Jack's needs. Her shock yesterday was clear and Annie had spent the evening waiting for the blame to fall. Practising what she would say in response. 'You knew he had a stroke.' 'The hospital was very clear on his prognosis.' 'Whatever you didn't see was because you chose not to see it.'

Until she could be sure of Helen, she would stick to the morning walk that had become her routine. More than her routine, it was her time. She didn't run, because it wasn't about the exercise. It was about the time.

Helen ran, Annie would bet. She had the look of someone who ran miles indoors and then talked about it.

She rounded the house and made her way down the avenue. Jack had it paved a few years ago and she was glad the noisy gravel was gone. She didn't need Helen at the window, making notes for her meeting with Monica.

She released the latch on the side gate and slipped through, closing it gently behind her. Closed, the tall main gates looked delicate and magical, their wrought-iron fingers wrapping around one another as if beckoning. Fairy-tale gates for a fairy-tale house. In opening, however, they revealed all their lumbering mechanical ordinariness and clanged like Armageddon.

She was heavy-footed this morning. Unsettled by Helen's arrival, by the embarrassing dead weight of what used to be closeness. It would have been easier had they been merely classmates, their lives overlapping in this class or that. Exchanging a surface-friendly word in the nightclub toilet – *I love your shoes!* Or *Great dress, I wish I had the legs for it!* – as they redid their mascara on a night out. Or an occasional polite two minutes on their lives as they shuffled awkwardly in the line to offer condolences at a local funeral. No. That last would never happen. Helen didn't come home for funerals.

She had stayed the bare length of her own mother's burial, and there was neither sight nor light of her at Annie's mother's funeral. Not that it mattered, she hadn't thought about Helen for years by then.

Overhead, the sky was lightening, taking worries away with it. In the nearby town, people would be sitting at kitchen tables and standing by windows, cups or spoons or cigarettes in hand, welcoming the sign that the long night was retreating and leaving them alive in its wake. She breathed in. Let the cold air and oxygen do their work. *Green breath in. Black breath out.*

Annie walked on the road itself, about a foot out from the verge. It was safe enough at this hour and she wore a highlighter-yellow jacket that covered her from neck to knees. Laura had given it to her; it came with one of her various community roles, she said.

'Won't you need it?' Annie had asked, but Laura shook her head.

'I have so many I'd have to live a thousand years to wear them all out. They're all obliged to give me one, but sure they're all the same. If I come home with another hi-vis anything, my mother will give me the door. Take it and wear it when you're walking the roads at dawn like a banshee. Said with love,' she added hastily.

The road was straight and dark and the wind pushed the trees inwards so that they bent towards her like adults asking a child a question. What answer would she give them? It was a habit of hers to arrange her worries as she walked, parsing them and leaving them for the trees to absorb.

She sometimes wondered if she shouldn't see a therapist rather than talking to the trees. She was even considering it properly before the first lockdown, when a year had passed since her mother's death and it still felt like no time at all. When she continued to wake in the mornings every bit as raw and undone as that first day without her. Whether she went to work or stayed home, she was tired, so tired, her jaw creaking like a graveyard gate and her vision full of ants or floaters or stars and she couldn't tell which and didn't much care. When all that got her through was the prospect of a hot shower and the water beating down on her neck and shoulders and she would have cried at how small her life was, if she had had the energy.

But time passed and she did nothing about it. When Jack had his stroke, Annie used to sit in the hospital car park waiting to be allowed in to visit, watching as the nurses and doctors walked out of the Covid wards after their shifts like they were falling on their feet. She looked at them and remembered the Irish phrase for surprise or shock, *Thit mé beagnach as mo sheasamh,* I nearly fell out of my standing, and was ever an expression more cannily, desperately accurate than in relation to those exhausted workers with their arms out to hold on to the world? What right had she to therapy, compared to these people holding the hands of the terrified and the dying? Hers was a simple grief. Nothing unfinished, nothing much unsaid in the end. Nothing more than ordinary sorrow, shattering only because it was hers. She could make do with her trees. Her bare, essential, honest trees.

The sky to the east was the pale grey-black of a well-loved jumper. There would shortly be a pink tint along the horizon, reminding Annie of the magic markers she had as a child, the combination of black and pink incongruous until the first time she saw a sunrise and thought: *oh!*

The density of the trees gave the road a shadowy, keep-out air even at the height of summer. It had felt like another world the first time her mother drove her to Helen's house. Annie had looked at the imposing gates and, inside them, the imposing house, and shaken her head. 'She said Glebe Cottage. This can't be it.'

Her mother had just smiled the smile she used at Christmas when they had to visit Granny Ivy, whose words were kind but whose voice was mean. 'Some people like to give big houses little names,' she said.

She waited while Annie got out of the car to press the buzzer, then got back in while the gates began their magical beckoning. Annie held her breath as they drove up towards the house – up the avenue, as she learned to call it – feeling like Cinderella. Eventually, when they were deemed old enough, Helen gave her the code for the little walk-in gate and it was never less than a thrill to walk right up to the house amid the keep-out trees and simply let herself in as if she belonged.

As an adult, Annie knew that it took more than a code to belong. She might have the gate code in her head, the front door keys in her handbag, her name on the security company's alert list, she might have spent the past ten months telling herself that the house welcomed her, held her, absorbed her, but then Helen walked in the door and the house shifted. It recognised her. It sounded silly, she knew, but what else would explain the ease with which Helen and the house navigated one another? The water running obligingly warm, the radio finding the station unerringly, the crisping up of the very air itself as if standing in delighted attention.

When Annie first moved in, she spent time, at first unconsciously, then consciously, cataloguing the changes in the house since she was a teenager. On the surface, little was different. The overall impression was still one of wooden floors polished to honey by decades of slippers, of richly coloured rugs downstairs and thick carpet upstairs, of good, old furniture that had to be sought out rather than stumbled across, of heavy fabrics chosen with care by Jack and Lily for their quality and longevity. Nothing about the house suggested the cheap flash-in-the-pan style that necessitated regular trend-driven updates. The house was classy, as Jack and Lily were classy. Well-structured and individual.

Yet, as Annie became accustomed to being there and settled into her own rhythms and routines, she discovered little threads of quiet change here and there. The bone-handled cutlery out of the box and in the drawer for everyday use. The American shower-and-a-half alongside the big free-standing bath, with an accompanying heated towel rail. The series of lamps that once scattered the living room replaced with recessed lighting. The downstairs loo extended into a wet room attached to the room Jack made his own after Lily died. All Jack's decisions, Jack's changes. Yet Annie resented their encroachment on her memories of the space and strained sometimes to see the old beneath the new. A double vision that gave her a headache. Which was no more than she deserved for trying to live in two times at once.

At some point, she would have to return to her mother's house – her own house – and she was at the mercy of Helen's whim in that regard. When she did, would she spend her days trying to live in two places at once? Wishing for bilocation, like poor haunted Padre Pio? Claiming that although her body remained in the shades-of-beige of her own childhood home, with all its appeal of bland yogurt, her spirit remained at Glebe Cottage. Wasn't there a saying that you never truly left the house you grew up in? If that was true, it seemed Annie had done her growing up in Helen's house.

But that was both self-pitying and untrue. The truth was she hadn't been grown-up at all until the Friday evening she came home from college and her mother sat across the table from her (*I found a lump*) and Annie unpacked her bag later that night, crying silently into the week's worth of dirty laundry before washing it all away.

It was strange how the road and the light and the quiet brought the past in close, making a Halloween of every day. She blessed herself and said a quick prayer of apology to her mother, who was nobody's plain yogurt and should be remembered as … what? Annie tried to remember what had delighted her mother and could think only of that story she kept telling when her memory started to come loose. About the time in the 1970s when the banks all went on strike and nobody had access to cash or cheques and instead people bartered for food and fuel and services, or made up their own currency and passed it around among themselves. 'Wouldn't that beat Banagher?'', she said, marvelling as though someone else had done the telling.

What made her mother happy? She was always satisfied when the gravy for a roast chicken turned out well. Gravy, then. Her mother was the gravy.

Seven a.m. by her watch and she turned and began to retrace her steps. Jack was happy to stay in bed listening to the radio, but leaving him for longer than an hour felt unfair and she couldn't depend on Helen to know how to help him.

She slipped in the side gate and back onto the grass alongside the drive. The front lawn was losing what Laura had called the 'laurel hedge mentality' the day last summer when Jack asked what she would do with the place if she had free rein. That had made him laugh and hold out his two arms in expansive surrender to Laura's vision. Jack healthy and well and standing in his kingdom. It could break a person's heart.

There was no point forcing anything, Laura told them that day. Just let everything go its own way until the time was right.

THE UNIVERSAL STOOD NO CHANCE AGAINST THE PERSONAL

When Annie went into Jack's room, he was sitting up in bed with his eyes half-open for all the world, like the doll she got from Santy one Christmas.

'Dark enough this morning,' she said, crossing back to the door and rolling the light switch to bring it up from night-time low. 'There we are. We can see ourselves again. And aren't we plenty to look at?' she continued, knowing it would make him smile. 'Well, one of us isn't quite there yet, but we'll do something about that shortly. Let's get you up and started on the physio and we can see about making you presentable then after that. How does that sound?'

She put on the radio for the morning news while they did Jack's physio. It helped with the frustration if he had something else to focus on. The radio levelled them, let them work together in the same act of listening, instead of her directing him.

Since Christmas, the news was bleaker than bleak and Annie wondered if it was doing Jack more harm than good to listen to it, but whenever she put on a music station instead, he shook his head and pointed at the radio. Lately, there was a growing sense of optimism, what with talk of vaccines and schools reopening and the suddenness of longer evenings. The certainty of the grand old stretch, as steadfast as ever. But it would take more than a few extra minutes of daylight to undo that awful one-two punch of the pre-Christmas joy of restrictions lifting, followed by the darkest January in living memory.

Annie and Jack lifted and stretched and listened to reports of assaults and murders, shaking their heads that for some people this was the so-called normal to which they returned.

After his physio, Jack needed a few minutes to recover. Annie had got in the habit of opening his wardrobe door and plucking out shirts, trousers and jumpers, holding them up for his yay or nay while he caught his breath.

'Who are you feeling like today? City slicker?' Annie laid a pale blue shirt against a dark navy jumper. 'No? Fair enough.' She brought out a heavy cream shirt and dark green knitted cardigan and held them up, 'Country squire?' Jack nodded his approval. 'Good choice. It's near perishing out there today. They're due to get snow up the country so we'll have all the cold but none of the fun. We might need to crank up the thermostat, make that old boiler earn its stripes.'

Jack's body already lacked the solidity he had a couple of months earlier. Before the stroke, he walked daily, anxious always that the muscle naturally wasting with age would turn to fat. That would never happen now; he had lost weight since the stroke, his appetite vanished along with his speech, as though his mouth were on all-out strike. All within normal limits, Annie and Dr Shields agreed, but its commonplace nature made it no less heartbreaking. The universal stood no chance against the personal.

It would get worse. Things always did. Age consumed people, in a monstrous sacrifice to relentless time. Annie's mother, towards the end, was the merest wisp of a woman, then a breath, then nothing. The cancer hollowed her out first, it was true, but it was in cahoots with a far more insidious thief. While the chemotherapy and radiotherapy might have robbed her mother of much of her energy and independence, it was dementia that stole her away little by little and then entirely and all at once.

Routine was their saviour. When life was small, routine

meant choice and control. So they walked every day for as long as her mother was able. Slow walks sometimes. Three times a day sometimes, if her mother was agitated and couldn't hold on to the idea that she had been out already. Annie built a scaffold of routine around her mother and secured her within it for as long as possible. Gradually, the planks and the uprights and the bracings fell away until her mother slipped between them completely and floated free. Fanciful nonsense, Annie knew, but what good was there in imagining her mother split in two, a mostly healthy body dragging a decaying brain? Nothing lay down that road that would have helped either of them to navigate the sad drudgery of reality.

She warmed shea butter in her palms and began to rub it into Jack's feet.

On childhood Friday nights, her mother used to come home from work, humming with exhaustion. While she changed into her pyjamas, Annie would fill the bright blue foot spa with warm water and peppermint gel, thrilling in anticipation of the relief it would bring her mother's poor aching feet. 'Oh, now,' her mother would say, easing her feet into the water and closing her eyes as Annie turned the dial from one to two to three.

'Oh, now,' she said out loud, and Jack looked down at her. 'Okay,' she said, as if that was what she had meant all along.

While the stroke had softened Jack's body, it hardened his brain, it seemed to Annie. The connections that were once so nimble, so capable of engaging and entertaining and enhancing, suddenly rigid and flattened.

'We need to start a new book today,' she said, as she smoothed shaving foam over his cheeks and drew the razor gently along the skin.

When they first became friends, Jack had told her that Lily never liked the feel of bristles and he used to get up and shave before getting back into bed for a cuddle. He shaved for his Lily, he said, even after she was gone. 'You romantics ruin things for all the other men,' Annie had laughed and Jack tapped the side of his nose, 'Au contraire. We simply set the right standard.'

They had bumped into one another in the graveyard, their family plots a short distance apart. Her mother was in the ground a few days and everything had that raw ragged look. The mound of earth was already starting to sink, edging her mother closer to the day when she would vanish as if she never was. Annie visited every few days, packing and petting the earth in a bid to keep it high and fresh.

Jack tipped his hat towards her and she raised her hand in reply, then turned back to yanking out the weeds that clung to her father's gravestone. A minute or two later, she felt a shadow fall over her.

'Pauline was a fine woman,' Jack said. 'I'm sorry for your loss, Annie.'

He looked so familiar, even without the tweed blazer that was Dr Danny Furlong's trademark. He had retired, she remembered. He wore his own clothes now.

'Thank you,' she said, and when he offered her his hand to help her to her feet, she accepted.

After that, they said hello when they noticed one another in the graveyard. If it wasn't exactly true to say Annie timed her visits to coincide with Jack's, then it would be no lie to say she looked for him when she was there. At home, she was on her own, and at work, an exchange of general grievances was all the idle chatter there was time for. After her mother died, Annie had taken agency work at a nursing home nearby. It was the easiest decision – no decision at all, really – and postponed further unsettling and upending. If anyone thought it was a strange choice for her to make after giving up everything to keep her mother out of the place, then Annie herself would be first in line to agree. There were days she wondered what it had all been for, when her mother had no final moment of awareness, no quiet peace in finding herself at home at the end. It was possible, Annie conceded to herself, that she simply wanted to be able to say her mother died at home. That it was Annie herself who saw it as a badge of love, when her mother might have been happy reliving her past anywhere at all.

Annie liked to talk to the nursing home residents, but after two warnings for the slow rate at which she was getting through one and on to the next, she had to content herself with a few remarks while she whisked them in and out of beds and chairs and showers.

'It's like working on a supermarket checkout,' she told Jack one sunny Sunday morning.

They were sharing his flask of tea and her scones on one of the flip-down benches that dotted the old stone walls and, oh, it was relief to know that no matter how bad the week, she could measure the distance to their Sunday morning chat.

Now, with Jack dressed and shaved, she stood back a few steps and looked at him appraisingly. 'I suppose you'll do,' she said, and he flapped his hand at her. Intentionally. The way he always had.

Over breakfast, Annie read out a list of books from the notes on her phone so that they could choose their next read.

'I know you enjoyed the last thriller and I said it was too soon for another one,' she said, wiping some stray Ready Brek from his chin. 'But I'm inclined to agree with you now. The prospect of spring always feels nicely murdery. Something about new beginnings maybe. How about something classic in the Agatha Christie line?' She tilted the bowl to get the last scrape. 'You heard the forecast as well as I did: one or two more cold snaps and then we're out into the chilly sunshine and walking down the avenue to have a look at the creeper dressing up for us. Perfect weather for a little light bloodlust.'

She was aware – all the time aware, every bit of her aware – that Helen was awake, moving around upstairs, showering, returning to her room. When she heard her footsteps on the stairs, she stopped talking, unbearably self-conscious. Helen would no doubt think it was all a performance for her benefit. Helen never had loneliness that lingered like damp in the walls. Helen had never been trapped and spinning inside her own head, waiting for a word from someone else to stop the washing-machine cycle of her thoughts. Lucky, lucky Helen.

It annoyed Annie to have to interrogate the chat that characterised so much of her friendship with Jack. No, on second thought, it needled her to think that she was worrying about Helen rather than Jack.

She smiled at Jack. 'There's Helen now. We can see if she has a good book recommendation for us. I'll clear these things away and leave you two to chat. I won't be far, if you need me.'

Helen spent the morning in the living room with Jack, leaving Annie free to change the sheets and give Jack's rooms a good once-over. Not her favourite part of the job, it was true, but Annie could hardly claim to look after Jack's health and then let him lying in grubby sheets and dust-pocked air.

While she worked, she tried to hear Helen's voice, some proof that she was making an effort, that they were connecting. Their relationship was their business, of course, but Jack's spirits were a core part of his health, were they not? Jack down in the dumps was Jack less likely to be cooperative about things like physio and showers and letting her load the wheelchair into the boot of the car to take him to the library and then into Susan's for a carefully thickened smoothie.

It was a source of itchy unease that Helen continued to think Annie had only moved into Glebe Cottage after Jack's stroke. Before that, she knew, he had mentioned in texts and calls that Annie popped in every few days to play poker or teach him how to cook something, but stopped short of telling Helen the whole story.

She hadn't pushed him to tell Helen anything. She told herself it was his house, his business, but in truth she was afraid that she would come across as having taken advantage somehow. The truth was both better and worse. That in the early days of that first long fear-filled lockdown, they had each confessed their dread and loneliness – Jack, who saw nobody every day, and Annie, who, as an agency worker, was looked at with suspicion and accused of bringing Covid into the nursing home. It made sense for Annie to stop working at the nursing home altogether and go back to helping Jack, this time from within the same house. To work a couple of hours a day doing the shopping and cooking and filling his prescriptions. The rest of the time, to simply keep one another company. With neither rent nor mortgage to pay, and with no outgoings other than food and utilities, the drop in income was perfectly manageable on a temporary basis.

She made sure to go for a walk on Sunday evenings when Helen and Jack had their regular FaceTime call, staying out for an hour to give him the space and time with his daughter. One Sunday, she left without a jacket and had to return after twenty minutes. Without meaning to, she glanced in the living room window and saw Jack sitting with his iPad on his lap, the call already over.

She had nothing to be ashamed of, Annie told herself, refolding the angora blanket at the end of Jack's bed. Not then and not now. What Jack told Helen was between them and she had no call to be stuck in the middle. It wasn't as though herself and Helen were still friends, or had kept in even the most cursory contact. Annie's responsibility was to Jack.

And yet.

Yet.

NOT BELIEVING DOESN'T MAKE IT LESS TRUE

Annie was doing an online food shop on her phone when Helen came into the kitchen. 'He's asleep. I think I might head out for a little while.'

Did Helen realise that she hadn't called him *Dad*, or even *Jack*, since she arrived, Annie wondered. Only *he* or *him*. Maybe that was habit; Jack had always been the only male in this house.

'Alright,' Annie said. 'I'm doing the food order for the week if you need anything?'

Helen's return flight was provisionally Monday, she had said, without offering any further information on what might render it definite, or change it, or what her plans were for the duration of her visit. Whether she was in or out for meals. Whether her husband and children would join her at some stage.

'I think I'm alright for everything, thanks.'

The implication was that Annie could worry about stocking the kitchen for the three of them. If Helen wanted to treat her like staff, let her. Two could play that game.

'I do a standard food shop and also one for my own personal items. They're paid separately, which I'm happy to verify online, if you like. The two orders are delivered together so as not to take up a second delivery slot,' Annie said. 'They were as rare as hen's teeth during Covid.' *Hen's teeth?* Was she one hundred years old? And *items*? As though she were unable to say the word *tampons* to the woman who had once been the girl who showed her how to use them.

Annie watched the blush creep up Helen's neck. As teenagers, she and Laura used to try to make Helen blush. They rarely succeeded, and she wished Laura were here to enjoy this victory.

'I thought I might take the Audi and go to the supermarket myself this morning,' Helen said. She paused. 'After I've met Monica.'

Point to Helen. Annie had to admire her for dropping her boss's name so casually. Likely she hadn't been going to say anything at all and here Annie had handed her the perfect opportunity.

That put me in my place, she felt like saying. But what purpose would it serve? Jack was more important, and letting Helen be Helen was the price she had to pay for continuing to care for him.

'Great,' she said. 'Jack's car keys are by the front door. Is there anything you'd like to know before you go?'

'I'm sure Monica will fill me in,' Helen said.

She closed every door between them on the way out with the extreme care of adult anger.

Helen of old would have slammed it, then opened it again purely to give it a second slam. Did she and Conor fight loudly, Annie wondered. Or had she grown out of it altogether? Conditioned by motherhood, maybe. A baby sleeping fitfully in a room nearby proving enough to stifle her drama.

Annie got to her feet and went through to the living room. Jack was still asleep. She adjusted the towel between his head and the wing of the chair, not wanting him to wake with a crick in his neck.

It made her feel greasy and manipulative, as though she was performing warmth towards Jack simply in response to the coldness between herself and Helen. As if she was trying to prove a point. Jack deserved better. And Helen was his daughter. She had every right to be here, to be worried, to be involved. How many times had Annie wished that Helen would take more of an interest, give more than a cursory video call with her children, during which she herself flitted in and out of the background, offering a prompt here and there? *Did you tell Papi Jack about ...?*

Annie went back to the laundry room for the ironing board and brought it through into the living room. Ironing helped her temper. It wasn't something she ever bothered with herself, but the thought of Jack in anything other than a perfectly pressed shirt was unimaginable. That was the thing with this job, it was hard to say where it began and ended. No, that wasn't quite correct: Helen was to say where it began and ended and would be home shortly to do so. Nothing much Annie could do about that, but in the meantime she could keep her hands busy so that her thoughts had somewhere else to go.

When they were sixteen, Helen had a boyfriend – the secret boyfriend, she and Laura called him, as the two people in their world aware of his existence. He was at university, a twenty-two-year-old, which was somehow less shocking then than it might be today. Or maybe not. What did Annie know about boyfriends anymore?

She spat on the iron – the sizzle conjuring her mother beside her for a moment – and took the first of Jack's shirts from the basket.

The secret boyfriend had invited her to a party, Helen told them, and while that would ordinarily be next to impossible, as luck would have it, it was the night of the Irish television awards, which meant her parents would be in Dublin, her father simpering and preening alongside other minor celebrities, while her mother hung on his arm and his every word.

Poor Jack. Annie looked across the room to where he sat in his chair, slack-jawed and vulnerable. During one of their lockdown whiskey Sunday afternoons, he had confided that those nights were, for many years, the thing he looked forward to most. Confessed with a wry little laugh. A jut of the jaw that suggested he recognised his own foolishness. Perhaps

Helen was right about the preening, but so what if he was? What harm did it do?

Anyway, Jack and Lily were to be in Dublin on the night in question, and the girls were to stay with Helen, having promised that they would under no circumstances throw a party. An easy promise to make as Helen's plans for them lay elsewhere.

'We're all invited,' Helen told them. 'The more the merrier. College boys for everyone!'

They were not all invited, as it turned out, but by the time they had walked from the bus stop to the house where the party was to be held, the reality of unaccustomed heels over distances greater than the entrance hall of Glebe Cottage made them more inclined to stay a while anyway. Helen's boyfriend kept her tucked into a corner of the kitchen, sitting her on the worktop and licking trails from her neck to her ears. Like an overzealous cat, Annie thought, as she held her drink and tried to keep an eye on things without looking like she was keeping an eye on things. Worse than being a sixteen-year-old at a grown-up party was being a sixteen-year-old Peeping Tom at a party.

Laura drifted off, leaving Annie standing alone in the doorway. She tried to cultivate an air of mystery, but suspected she was more Easter Island than sphinx-like. Was it for this she had lied to her mother? So she could stand awkwardly among these boy-men, with no more appeal than the thick lugs that crashed their way through the school corridors. The bravado bullshit was exactly the same, but with added alcohol and poorly understood ideas of who they might be and their confidence about what they might add to her life. Well, fuck that. She had no intention of being trapped in this little town by some boy. Not with the whole world to see.

Twenty of the longest minutes of her life later, Laura reappeared, arm in arm with an older girl in bare feet and with a crystal on a piece of leather around her neck.

'Having fun?' Laura asked Annie.

Annie shrugged, but before she had time to reply, the older girl put her head on one side. 'Hands,' she pronounced.

'Do you think?' Laura said. She narrowed her eyes and looked at Annie's hands, one on the paper cup, the other at her side.

'Hands what?' Annie asked.

'I was explaining to Laura that emotions have a physical manifestation,' the girl explained.

Of course you were, Annie thought. Like it's perfectly normal and not at all rude to analyse the bodies of people you've just met.

'You store your emotions in your hands,' the girl said.

'Right,' Annie said. She was damned if she was going to pretend it was some kind of insight to see that the cup was squeezed a bit tightly in her hand. To read a less-than-thrilling half-hour at a party full of strangers as something that had universal relevance to her life.

'You don't agree.'

Saying it was reductive would likely drag out this charade and Annie couldn't be bothered explaining herself to a girl who thought going barefoot was appropriate anywhere other than the beach. 'You don't know me.'

The girl shrugged. 'Not believing doesn't make it less true.'

Later that night, making their way home with their shoes in their hands, Annie thought again about the barefoot girl. And when they had to stop – again – for Helen to vomit, she turned from where she stood holding back Helen's hair to Laura keeping watch on the edge of the road and said, 'Helen must store her emotions in her stomach.'

'There won't be much left to feel,' Laura observed, and the two of them laughed, while Helen hiccupped and cried and spilled vodka and promises into the ditch.

Turned out the barefoot party girl was right, Annie thought, snapping Jack's pale green shirt out of the basket and smoothing it onto the ironing board. The merest hint of stress and, sure as eggs, Annie would be found working it out through her hands.

It was afternoon before Helen returned. Annie and Jack had taken a slow tour of the garden, completed the crossword and eaten their lunch, and were sitting in the living room browsing audiobook recommendations, Annie interpreting Jack's hand flaps based on what she knew of his taste up to this point.

'That gives us a shortlist of six,' she told him, raising her voice a little as if it might slow her heart, racing since she heard the clank of the gates heralding Helen's return. 'I'll check to see which ones are available.' She looked at Jack, nodding in his chair. 'We'll leave it in the fickle hands of fate. Well …' She corrected herself. 'Not so much the fickle hands of fate as the reliable hands of the library app.'

Helen bypassed the living room and went directly to the kitchen, where the sound of cupboard doors opening and closing suggested she had gone shopping as planned and was figuring out where everything went. Or – Annie remembered her earlier thought – maybe she was slamming the door of the same press repeatedly. She would stay where she was, she decided. If Helen was looking for attention, she could look elsewhere. Annie wasn't going to go rushing in all agog to know what Monica had said. She had her pride.

NOTHING MUCH CHANGES, DOES IT?

Annie's pride was no match for her curiosity. Within five minutes she had risen from her chair and gone to find Helen.

'Jack's having a rest,' Annie said, in a bid to legitimise her presence in the kitchen. Helen nodded and continued looking out the window into the garden. Annie crossed to the dresser and switched on the baby monitor. From there she could see the bottle of wine, unopened, in Helen's hand.

'My mother loved this garden,' Helen said. 'I used to think she loved it more than she loved me.'

'The garden was easier to manage,' Annie said drily, forgetting that wasn't the sort of thing she was allowed to say any more.

Helen's laugh was sudden and short. 'I'm trying to decide if it's a good idea to have a glass of wine.'

Annie said nothing. It wasn't a question, or at least not one that invited a casual answer. Would the looming conversation – for looming it was, that much was clear – be easier to get through if Helen had a drink inside her?

'A small glass,' Helen said, and took the fancy corkscrew from the drawer where it had always been.

Annie loved that corkscrew. Some things were worth spending money on, she thought every time she used it.

Helen poured herself a glass and waggled the bottle at Annie, who shook her head. 'I'd better not,' she said, glancing towards the baby monitor.

'Isn't he lucky he has you?' Helen said carefully. She took a sip of wine and for a second Annie feared the tight line of her lips might take a bite out of the glass.

'I'm working, not judging,' Annie said. It was a lie, of course. What was life for if not judging other people and finding them wanting or finding ourselves wanting? What else drove anyone towards the next thing, if not the desire to do better – to be better – than the next person?

'I got plenty of judgement from Monica,' Helen said, hooking her ankle around the chair opposite and pulling it towards her so she could put her feet up on it.

Annie was surprised to hear Monica had been anything less than supportive, but Helen was always at her most sensitive when she was feeling defensive.

'Don't mind Monica,' Annie said, leaning against the worktop and facing the dresser so that she had a clear view of the monitor. Jack was in his chair, neck at a good angle, eyes closed, chest – she watched for a moment – chest rising and falling. 'She forgets sometimes that not everybody wants it straight between the eyes.'

Helen raised her eyebrows as if Annie were deluded, then reached for the wine to top up the glass.

Annie put on the grill to heat, slicing cheese while she waited for the kettle to boil. Then she toasted two slices of bread on one side, buttered them, loaded them with cheese and put them back under the grill to melt. By the time she had the teabag squeezed out and milk added to the cup, the cheese was bubbling nicely.

'Here.' She put the plate in front of Helen. 'Daytime wine needs toasted cheese to soak it up.'

She didn't say she had been remembering their wilder days, Helen's sensitive stomach. Helen probably didn't remember it anyway. Doubtless her memories of one single teenage party were long overtaken and pushed out by other, better parties, with catered food and cultured company.

Helen pushed her finger into the melted cheese, making a

little runnel, or a little ridge, depending on how you looked at it. 'Here's you with your ironing and me with my dodgy stomach. Nothing much changes, does it?'

But the low-level hum of the baby monitor on the dresser behind them gave the lie to her words and she sighed and pushed the plate away.

'Will you tell me what it was like?' she said. 'I wasn't here, so tell me all of it. Please.'

Afterwards, Annie wondered if it was that *please* that made her truthful. Or the fact that it was the first direct question Helen had asked her, the first hint that she didn't have it all figured out. Or the slapped look on Helen's face. Annie could never bear that look. Or because there was a risk that Helen might not ask again.

Whatever the reason, she told her everything. Almost everything.

Meeting Jack in the graveyard, their gradual friendship, the slightly ragged appearance that, when pressed, saw him confess that the cleaning and cooking had got a bit beyond him. She sketched out the state of the house the first time she visited, omitting the joy she felt at the front door that was swiftly overtaken by horror at the thick layer of dust and grime on everything, as if the place was long abandoned. Forcing cheer to overcome Jack's evident shame. His fumbling explanation that the cleaner had left and he had yet to get around to finding someone he trusted. His insistence on registering with the agency so that Annie's offer of help would be above board and without reproach.

As she spoke, she was aware that she was stealing all the warmth and life from her and Jack's friendship, putting them on the plane of acquaintances, some sort of community society, perhaps, that met on neutral ground for prescribed periods of time to discuss agreed topics. What else was she to do? She and Jack might have come to feel like family to one another, but not to Helen, and to insist on their closeness would be pointless, if not outright hurtful.

She did not tell Helen that Jack was lonely. That she herself was lonely. That in the midst of another long day of listening to other people talk, they each found themselves trying to make little moments in the day for their own voices.

She did not tell Helen that to her younger self it would have seemed a monumental failure to have Jack as her best friend. To say the words aloud would be to cringe for them all. But who else had come to know the details of her day like Jack? Who else had phoned her because they were wondering if a navy jumper over a blue shirt would make them look like someone on a neighbourhood watch committee? Who else had read the bloody book instead of citing their busy lives as if that was some great badge of honour, when they were well able to find time to gossip? Who else had suggested they make Friday night takeaways a thing, purely because they remembered that Friday evenings filled her with dread?

Instead, she told Helen that she and Jack had a shared interest in politics. That they buddy read together, their tastes different in some respects and similar in others. Enough to keep things interesting. Jack preferred the audiobooks and got huge enjoyment out of Annie's mispronunciations of characters' names, while Annie crowed over the details he missed by not being able to flip back a few pages and reread something that didn't quite land the first time round.

Helen listened and nodded and drank her wine. 'You could be talking about any randomer,' she said, almost conversationally, when Annie stopped talking. 'Isn't that funny? Whatever I knew of him is gone.'

A stroke did not make a stranger of a person, Annie wanted to say. Not in the way dementia did. Dementia like a prowler circling her mother, causing her to shrink back against the walls of herself, holding her breath in case she gave herself away. Dementia with its moods, destructive as a toddler, not caring what it threw out. A stranger's name precisely as disposable as a daughter's. Dementia like woodworm, eating away at a person from the inside, while outside everything looked perfectly fine. A stroke was none of those things.

How quick we are to make strangers of those we love, she thought. How much effort is sacrificed to the self-deceit that we ourselves will never grow old, will never be in need of understanding.

'You know I used to call him Danny when I was angry with him,' Helen said.

Annie nodded. She remembered. How clever they had thought it then, Helen's coded suggestion that Jack-the-man was the veneer.

'He walked in on me once when I was bleaching my lip,' Helen went on. 'I had the powder on the little plastic disc, you know?'

Annie nodded. She knew. Every woman knew.

'He thought it was cocaine. I almost let him believe it, he seemed to care so much. *Actually, Danny, I think you'll find it's bleach,* I said instead. I think the words "man of the world" might have been used.' She looked at Annie and shrugged. 'How did he get from there to' – she gestured towards the baby monitor – 'here.'

Annie described finding Jack after the stroke, careful to skim over the question of what she was doing there and why. Again, she told Helen that the ambulance would have taken too long, that he seemed stable, steady enough on his feet that she could help him to the car and get him to the hospital herself. She did not mention the ice in her hands and in her throat. The statistics that ran rings around her mind while she waited for those big, slow gates to open. FAST, the stroke awareness acronym said. Face. Arms. Speech. Time. FAST. As if one look at him wasn't already enough to know the answer. Two million brain cells dying every minute while she revved the engine gently instead of crashing through the gates. The garbled speech that tore at her while she kept her voice cheerful and her hands at ten and two instead of clawing at her face or tearing the steering wheel from its column. *Not again,* raged the voice in her head. *I can't do this again.*

'I'm glad you were here,' Helen said, when Annie finally finished speaking, although Annie knew she really meant she was glad anyone was here. 'Can I ask about the decision for you to move in here?' Helen asked. 'Not that I'm questioning it, of course …'

Of course.

'… but can I ask why that solution instead of a care home? I'm curious.'

Monica had not done her dirty work for her, Annie realised. It was a shame that she hadn't formulated an opening sentence while she was ironing. She could have gifted herself at least that much.

'Actually,' she said, a punctuating, know-it-all actually that was the worst of all possible starts, 'I stayed with Jack during the first lockdown. With the over-seventies having to cocoon at home, I was here nearly every day dropping off food and having a bit of a chat through the window. In the end, it made more sense than both of us living alone.' Stop there, she told herself. You don't need to explain any more than that. Jack was in the whole of his health and it was his decision as much as yours.

'I see,' Helen said. 'So you are no longer living at your mother's house?'

'Not just at the moment,' Annie said. 'It's still my home, obviously. This situation with Jack was intended to be temporary. Then he had the stroke and it seemed clear he wanted to be in his own home so it made sense for me to stay and help out until …'

'Until …?' Helen prompted.

Annie shrugged. The very concept of 'until', already mutable, had changed beyond all recognition in recent months. Helen shouldn't need that explained to her.

'I see.'

Helen would see whatever she wanted to see, Annie knew.

There was nothing to apologise for, nothing to explain. She was answerable to nobody but herself and – possibly – Jack. But Helen's face had the look.

'When I first moved in, I used to go into town to collect Jack's prescriptions and everyone I met had that exact expression.' Annie jerked her head towards Helen.

'What do you mean? What expression?'

'The one that said they were filing me alongside those women in cheap magazine articles. You know: younger woman moves in with older man with designs on taking him for all he has.'

She was grateful again for Jack's insistence that everything would be done through the agency. For respectability, he said. And so she would have her stamps. *You'll thank me when you're drawing your pension,* he said. *You can come to visit me in the graveyard and tell me I was right all along.*

'Don't be ridiculous. It never crossed my mind,' Helen said, while her thumb ran and ran and ran along the edge of her index fingernail.

'Jack is my friend,' Annie said. 'We're friends. No euphemisms.'

With any luck, Helen wouldn't see this as an opportunity to ask about Annie's current (arid) romantic situation. If asked, she could give a potted history of boyfriends. Perhaps a humorous summary of Mike breaking her heart.

Mike. His name a tiny thorn she could never quite loosen. Mike who wanted her to move to Dublin with him once her mother was in remission. Mike who agreed to put off their plans when her mother fell and broke her hip. They waited, and while they waited, they made the house fall-proof to the extent possible – grab rails in the bathroom, handrails in the kitchen, non-slip flooring throughout, an armchair so high that her mother need only slide her bottom into it without hardly bending her knees at all, a guard rail on the bed – and all the while they continued their plans, at a rate that her mother laughingly claimed made her head spin.

She was putting her key in the front door after a long day flat-hunting in Dublin when she heard the phone in the hall ringing. It would be for her mother – nobody under the age of fifty used the landline any more – but she hurried to answer it rather than risk her mother tripping over in a rush.

'Annie, thank God,' the voice on the other end said. 'It's alright, we found her, she's alright.'

It took some time to piece together the details. The neighbour that saw her mother on the road in her slippers. The waitress in the café who brought her mother her tea and watched her stir the jam into it. The loss of her coat somewhere and then, mortifyingly, her skirt, left behind in the café toilets. At least the waitress had the presence of mind to go after her and bring her back in, telling her that her friend would be along shortly and she should wait for her here, where it was warm. Bribed with more tea, biscuits, the gift of her own skirt, which she draped on the back of the chair opposite, sitting in her blouse and tights for a friend who wasn't coming. It was months before Annie could close her eyes without that image rising to meet her.

Some parts remained a mystery, like the gap in time where she somehow made it from their house into the town centre, presumably having taken a lift from someone. A stranger, maybe. Annie's heart chilled. *Even older women* … but she had to stop herself there. They dripped in one by one, all the tiny details that made up her mother's strange day. The evidence that the little slips with car keys in the bread bin and slippers in the supermarket, the names of people or things sliding away from her, the occasional blips they had assumed to be lingering chemo brain, had even taken to laughingly calling her 'senior moments', were something more. By the time they got the test results, they were no longer surprising. Early-onset Alzheimer's, rapid deterioration, then long periods of plateau, then another plunge.

With her brothers' lives set up far away, they could offer little more than platitudes and silences and vague promises of getting home often. The reality was that she was all her mother had. What other choice was there?

A clean break would be best, Mike said, and Annie nodded firmly and nearly thrust her hands through the lining of her pockets.

'I suppose I should be grateful he wasn't on his own,' Helen said.

I suppose.

She must have heard how it sounded as well because she added, 'I mean, thank you. For getting him to hospital after the stroke. Really. Thank you.'

'After my mother died,' Annie began, before she had quite decided she was going to, 'I had a rough few months. I don't know if you know, but she was sick with one thing and another for quite a long time, so when she died, I … found it quite difficult for a while.'

Helen nodded. 'The way people often get sick at the start of their holidays, as if their bodies are finally letting their guard down.' She flushed. 'Oh God. I didn't mean that to sound like your mother dying was some kind of holiday—'

Annie waved away her apology. 'I know what you mean. You're right, it was like that. At first I had no energy to do anything and then when I managed to drag myself up and out, I found I was angry all the time.'

'I'm sorry,' Helen said. 'That sounds—'

'People are very nice, but they just want you to be over it. They want you to be safe to be around. They don't want to feel bad about what they're doing or not doing, or for wanting to focus on their own stuff.' She sighed. 'All of which is to say that Jack was very good to me without making it obvious he was being very good to me. He saw me, I suppose you'd say, and it was such a relief.' She looked at Helen and smiled. 'If you're quietly freaking out about where this is going, don't worry. No euphemisms, remember? What I'm trying to say is that Jack helped me and so when he asked for my help, I was more than happy to give it.'

'But all that,' Helen took a sip of wine, 'that friendship, all that was before the stroke. I mean, now he's—'

Annie shook her head in warning. 'Jack is still Jack. He's still in there. You just have to look a little harder to find him.'

'How?' Helen's voice was steady, but her hand holding the glass shook slightly. 'How do I do that?'

'You pick something to have faith in. A favourite moment to hold on to. Not a reel of things, don't overstretch. One good one will do.' She thought of Friday nights and the peppermint smell of the foot spa, her mother's sigh of pleasure, two cups of tea and *The Late Late Show* theme tune. 'When my mother was sick and what was in front of me was too hard to look at or to deal with, I looked at that one moment in my mind's eye instead. The same memory every time.' She looked at Helen. 'Everyone talks about the importance of memories after a person dies, but sometimes they're every bit as necessary while the person is here with us.'

'Do you have a memory of Jack?'

Annie smiled and stood. 'Everyone has a memory of Jack. Speaking of the man himself, I'd better go and check on him.'

When she reached the living room, Jack was awake, listing a little to one side, the towel propping his head slipped to the floor.

'Sorry,' Annie said. 'Myself and Helen were chatting in the kitchen.'

He flapped his hand at her.

'Exactly,' she said. 'All we're short is Laura and it would be like old times.'

THE FIRST REAL THING

Laura glanced at the clock on the dashboard and tried to remember whether or not she had adjusted it when wintertime started. She pulled out her phone. Dead battery. Shit. She had promised Coraline she would be home in time for TV and snuggles on the couch. But time had flown by while she was pottering around in the community garden and she had promised Geraldine she would drop into Second Life and give her a hand with the stocktake. Not that it really mattered if they had five men's XS shirts, or fifteen. But Geraldine was set on doing it today. And she had been complaining about being tired lately. Shit, shit. She turned the key in the ignition and the car's engine coughed once, twice – shit, shit, shit – then started.

'Sorry, Cor darling,' she muttered, pulling out without indicating and raising her hand in apology to the car behind her. 'You'll understand when you're older.'

Laura pulled up at home two hours later. Glancing up, she could see that the light was off in Coraline's room.

'I thought you were going to be home by teatime,' her mother said, appearing in the hall as Laura closed the front door gently and clicked the lock.

'Hello to you, too. Is she gone up already?'

'Is she gone up already,' Kitty repeated, shaking her head. 'Hasn't she had the same bedtime for a year or more?'

'I'll go up and give her a kiss goodnight,' Laura said, turning to go up the stairs.

'You'll do no such thing. I have her settled but she might not be asleep yet and I don't want you disturbing her. Look in on her before you go to bed, that'll do instead.'

Laura nodded and began to take off her coat.

'I'll put the kettle on. I don't suppose you've eaten,' Kitty called over her shoulder as she went into the kitchen.

'Not yet, no.' Laura sat on the bottom step of the stairs to take her shoes off, wondering for the briefest minute if she could sneak up in her socks to check on her daughter. Blow a kiss from the bedroom door. It wasn't worth her mother's wrath, she knew. She depended on her mother to mind Coraline in the afternoons. Not to mention the fact that they lived in her house. Without her goodwill – a far nicer word than obligation – who knew where Laura and her girl would be?

'What kept you?' her mother asked, putting a cling-film-covered plate into the microwave and pressing more buttons than seemed necessary.

'I finished up the stocktake for Geraldine so she could go home. She was looking a bit washed out.'

'Has she seen the doctor?'

'She says she's a bit tired. Nothing a tonic won't fix.'

'A gin and tonic, more like,' Kitty said.

The microwave pinged and Laura opened the door to take out the plate.

'You're supposed to let it sit a full minute so it can finish cooking.'

'It's only reheating. If I let it sit there, it'll go cold again.'

'Suit yourself,' Kitty said. 'I only cooked it.'

Living in a household of women made for a fair bit of snippiness. Even before Coraline was born, when it was just the two of them, and before that again, when it was the two of them and Granny Lo, who moved in to help out when Laura was a baby and lived with them for eight years until she died.

Granny Lo had never got over losing her beloved son, Laura's father, and was sadness from the crown of her wispy hair to the wool of her tights. A thin frame of sorrow draped in sighs and layers of black linen and wool. Granny Lo called Laura 'heartling', which meant sweetheart, she said, and which she used to call her darling Philip. Everything was couched in terms of Philip: the first time she held him, the last time she spoke to him, the time this, the time that. Death, Laura grew up believing, was a kind of accounting, with two columns: *ever* and *never.*

Laura looked at her mother, bent over a crossword at the other side of the table. Pretending she wasn't sitting there solely so that Laura wouldn't have to eat alone.

'I'll try and get back earlier tomorrow and cook. I'll do a curry or something, so we can get two days out of it.'

'It's to be cold again tomorrow,' Kitty said. 'A curry would be grand.'

'Did I tell you Helen is back?'

'No! When did she land?'

'Yesterday, I think.'

'How are herself and Annie getting on?'

Laura shrugged. 'No idea. I'll give Annie a text later on and see.'

'She'll have poor Jack in a fancy nursing home in no time,' Kitty said. 'You can sing it.'

Her mother always had a soft spot for Jack. As long as Laura could remember, there had to be absolute quiet in the living room while his soap was on. Jack Fitzgibbon: their local celebrity, with the shiny family and big house.

Her mother loved the look of Glebe Cottage. Loved hearing about the parties Jack and Lily threw during the holidays. Loved dropping Laura over there and asking what it was like inside. Edging for an invite, Laura used to think, and close her eyes against the mortification of the idea. As if her mother, with her fondness for bacon and cabbage, her furry slippers and nylon dressing gown, would ever fit in such a place. When she oohed and aahed over the Christmas Day soap special, Laura stabbed the turkey on the plate in her lap and commented that Jack had complained about having to film it during the Indian summer in September, actually. 'If you look, you can see the sunblock marks on the tops of his ears.'

She looked at Coraline sometimes, trying to imagine her daughter discovering a similar seam of cruelty, an *actually* running through her like a stick of seaside rock. It would never happen, she thought. Cor was already a better person than she was.

'Jack doesn't need a nursing home,' Laura said. 'He's doing okay at home, Annie says.'

'Annie would know,' Kitty agreed, then added, as she always did, 'That girl is the next best thing to a saint.'

'She'll be a saint spending her time peeling and coring avocados for Helen's brunch,' Laura said, raising her eyebrows at her mother, who, inexplicably, crossed herself.

That was enough bitterness, she told herself. Hadn't she just this minute resolved to do better? To be kinder than she had to be?

'How did Cor get on in school today?' she asked. 'No more trouble with the teacher?'

Her mother had taken vocal exception to every teacher Coraline had had in her four years of school. It was charming – if disorienting – seeing her take up for her granddaughter in a way she never had for her own daughter. If Laura had come home with stories of being unfairly picked on by a teacher, her mother would have assumed she had done something to incur the teacher's anger. A teacher herself, she passed Laura's schooldays assuming that strict-but-fair was her colleagues' watchword. Yet the merest hint of a quiver in Coraline's voice saw her haring down to the school with the speed of a cat hearing a tin of sardines opening.

She nodded occasionally as her mother recounted Coraline's day, her eyes soft as she talked about her small granddaughter. The detail was unimportant beside the image of her mother and her daughter walking home from school hand in hand, talking it all out, Coraline occasionally skipping and having to be reminded not to drag on GranKit's bad shoulder. She got up and kissed the top of her mother's head. 'I'm going up to have a shower. Leave the dishes, I'll do them after.'

Laura dressed quickly, shivering in the cold air of the bedroom. No doubt Helen had the thermostat in Glebe Cottage turned up to twenty-two or twenty-three degrees, cost and environment be damned. She glanced at her partly charged phone, but her message to Annie *Well????* showed as unread. She hadn't seen it. Taking care of Jack was a busy job. It wasn't as though it meant Annie and Helen were laughing together into a bottle of wine, sharing all the old jokes and memories without her. Was that the familiar flutter of worry at being left out? Jesus! She was a grown woman, for goodness' sake. A mother. A single mother, at that.

No, a *lone* mother, with all its connotations of outlaw self-sufficiency. Of riding into town with her hair flying behind her and Cor tucked in front of her in the saddle. As if it was a horse she rode, rather than a man-child who was bested by a thin bit of rubber.

Stop. She didn't need to do this. She had let Enda go with love, she reminded herself. Things could simply be what they were.

She looked at herself in the mirror as she towel-dried her hair. She could hold her own if she met Helen again, she thought. Good skin and thick hair went a long way in your forties. She wouldn't be half-afraid of magnetic Helen Fitzgibbon now.

They had stood out to her immediately: Helen Fitzgibbon and Annie Fleming. She would watch from a corner as they whispered and giggled and clutched at one another in what looked for all the world like their own force field. As the sole student who had come from her primary school – and, worse, the daughter of the strict Irish teacher – Laura felt like something of a social pariah, stuck with the mousy girls who were themselves desperate for a friend. She needed to sit with someone for lunch, didn't she, even if all they could find to talk about was school itself.

But Helen and Annie were another story altogether. If they were in school now – in Coraline's class, say – they would have a portmanteau. Hannie, perhaps. Or Helennie. Given and spoken with part-bitterness, part-envy.

Laura's absorption by them was as sudden and complete as her separateness had been.

One ordinary Wednesday morning – a double-maths morning – Sister Breeda, the principal, came into their class and told them that Annie wouldn't be in school that day, or indeed for the rest of the week. Her father had died, Sister Breeda said, and they were to pray the sorrowful mysteries of the rosary for Annie and her mother and brothers. While they closed their eyes and offered up the rote words, Laura watched the door through a crack in her eyelids, waiting for the beaded curtains of her eyelashes to reveal Helen, late and without Annie. Later, she would learn that Annie had spent the day at Helen's house while her mother made funeral arrangements.

When Friday afternoon rolled around, the fact of Helen's ongoing absence alongside Annie's was no longer remarkable but had passed into the realm of the so-what, alongside the short-lived news of Hannah's new baby brother and the disappearance – 'moonlight flit', was the expression going around – of Mrs Murphy's husband, Patch, with Therese, who had moved in next door to the Murphys a year ago.

In the slug-slow minutes before the bell rang to let them home, Sister Breeda came into their room again, the nudges shivering from one girl to the next as they waited to see where she would stop. The nun glided alongside Laura and asked her to stay behind after the bell. While she whispered with the teacher in the few remaining minutes, Laura glowed with shame at being singled out.

Anyone inclined to dawdle was quickly dispatched by Sister Breeda, who looked up and down the hall before closing the door and going to stand beside the teacher's desk. Laura wondered whether to stay where she was or to stand or to approach the desk, but fear froze her to her seat and she did nothing.

'As you know, Annie Fleming's father was buried yesterday,' the nun began.

Laura nodded. There had been some lunchtime speculation earlier in the week about whether their class would attend the Mass, but the general consensus was that a father wasn't important enough for that. It wasn't like a brother or sister, the likes of which prompted a guard of honour outside the church, which, together with the hour-long service, gave everything the excited feel of a half-day. Or a mother, which prompted community concern over cups of tea about whether or not the leftover parent could manage.

'Annie is going to come back to school next week and I wanted to ask you to keep a special eye out for her and make sure she is … coping,' Sister Breeda said, nodding slowly as if agreeing to a request Laura herself had made.

'But Helen will be with her,' Laura blurted.

It wasn't at all what she had wanted to say, which was that Annie barely knew she was alive, and so any supposed comfort she, Laura, could offer would surely be rejected out of hand.

Sister Breeda frowned.

Laura had noticed that teachers often frowned when talking to Helen and, now, it appeared the same held true when talking about Helen.

'Helen lacks your … experience in this area,' the nun said eventually.

She stood and held the door open while Laura gathered her bag and coat and thought of things to say to get herself out of this unwanted job. Chief among them being that she had been a baby – *a raw baby,* her mother said whenever it came up – when her father died and so it was absence she had to deal with rather than death, and that absence was just how things were and invited strong feelings only when Laura asked if they could go to Spain on holidays and her mother sighed and said they had to make do on one salary so they were lucky they could go to the mobile home in Kerry. At such times, Laura felt an oozy hatred for her father. For going and getting himself killed instead of staying around to ease things for his wife and child. But those were private thoughts, certainly not ones she was about to share with Annie Fleming.

The weekend flew by, the knot in Laura's stomach twisting tighter each time she thought of casual-yet-helpful things she could say to Annie. It wouldn't be so bad if Annie was on her own, but imagine having to go up and talk to Annie while shiny Helen Fitzgibbon was standing beside her! Listening. Taking it all in. Maybe imitating Laura afterwards behind her back. Or for other people. It didn't bear thinking about and yet it was all she could think about.

'You know when someone dies,' she began, on Sunday evening, when she and her mother stood by the sink together doing the dishes. 'What kinds of things can you say to make them feel less sad?'

Her mother turned on the hot tap and rinsed the suds off the dinner plate before placing it on the draining board for Laura to pick up and dry. Usually, Laura resented having to dry the dishes, because drying meant having to clear the table and bring everything to the sink for her mother to wash. Then wipe down the table. Then do the actual drying. Then put everything away and clean down the draining board and the worktops. So, really, her mother did one job next to Laura's three, or even four. She had learned not to say that out loud, as her mother would sigh and start listing all of the other things she did, like the food shopping and cooking the food, in addition to her actual job. She always said it like that, her *actual job,* as if looking after Laura and their house were not a real part of her life, but something she got stuck with because someone else wasn't pulling their weight.

But today Laura didn't mind having to do the extra things. With her hands moving, her stomach felt better, as if the rhythm of her movements was rocking it gently.

'Sister Breeda asked me to look out for Annie Fleming,' she said, hoping it would prompt her mother to answer.

'It depends on the circumstances,' her mother said eventually, rinsing another plate. 'Mark Fleming died of a heart attack, so at least it was quick and painless. I'm sure they find that a comfort.' Her voice was crisp and she walked away from the sink, leaving the saucepans unwashed.

Laura's heart sank. It always made her mother sad to think of her father dying the way he had. The explosion, the fire, the panic, maybe, or the fear. It was impossible to tell exactly how it had happened and her mother hated to be reminded of how bad it might have been. Laura didn't like to think about it either, but it didn't upset her in the way it upset her mother. As if it had happened really recently. Perhaps, she thought guiltily, because she didn't know her father, so she couldn't imagine what his fear or panic or worry might have looked like. Sometimes, when the water was running for her Saturday evening bath, she stood in front of the bathroom mirror and made the kinds of faces she thought he might have made. As the bath filled and the small room filled with steam, she would pretend it was the smoke from the burning ship, changing her expression as the steam spread from the outside edges of the mirror to obscure her face entirely. It didn't make her feel closer to him, but only confirmed her suspicions that she was, as some of the girls claimed, a bit weird.

She tried to think of other things that might help, besides the fact that Annie Fleming's father had died quickly. Sister Breeda had mentioned her experience, but the joke was that Annie didn't know what it was like to have her father die. All she knew how to do was live with a mother whose husband had died. Which seemed to be a lot of worrying about money. And respectability. And privacy. Her mother was very against the idea of telling people their business. She kept thick net curtains on all the windows – front and back – so that even if people looked in, they wouldn't find out anything. Annie didn't know what she was worried about. The house was always clean and tidy, with plenty of food in the fridge, albeit all healthy stuff, no matter how many times Annie pleaded for frozen waffles or pizza or instant mash potato.

None of which would be the slightest use to Annie Fleming when she arrived back in their classroom on Monday morning.

As it happened, Annie was there before her, sitting at Laura's desk, in the seat usually occupied by Mary O'Leary, who was displaced and glowering beside the space that would shortly house Helen Fitzgibbon.

'Hi,' she said, dropping her bag and sitting down.

'I was told to sit here,' Annie said without looking at her. 'In case you think I wanted to.'

'I didn't ask either,' Laura said, stung. 'It's not like I'm trying to start some kind of dead dad club.'

A sharp movement in her eyeline and she turned to see Annie suddenly bent in to the desk, her shoulders shaking.

I'll be suspended, was all Laura could think. Day one – minute one, practically – of her special job from Sister Breeda and she had Annie in tears already. She looked in panic to see if anybody else had noticed, but the few people sitting down were talking to one another, or, in Mary O'Leary's case, gouging her name into the wood of the desk.

Annie snorted and Laura realised she was laughing, not crying. Was that better? Wasn't there some hysteria thing where the two things were the same? Should she slap Annie like she saw people do on TV?

'That's the first real thing anyone's said to me in days,' she said.

'What's so funny?' Helen had come to stand beside the desk. Beside Annie, really. Staking a claim.

Don't tell her, Laura begged in the quiet part of her mind. She won't understand.

But Annie told her.

'Funny,' Helen said. 'A dead dad club.' She looked at Laura for a long moment, as if trying to recognise her. 'We're doing homework at mine after school,' she said eventually. 'Want to come?' And the relief of her question, the warmth of her approval, felt blessed, like finding a fiver in the bottom of your bag when you had forgotten your bus pass at home.

Laura hung her towel on the radiator and looked at her phone screen. The message to Annie still showed as unread.

Friendships didn't have to last forever, she reminded herself. All those years away she hardly thought of Helen Fitzgibbon or Annie Fleming at all. Friends could serve their purpose and move out of each other's lives.

She pretended she didn't hear her own echoing thought: *Just as long as Helen has moved out of Annie's life too.*

I CAN SMELL TOAST FROM HERE

In the dim predawn, Laura watched her daughter sleeping flung out like a puppy. Laura could pick her up and carry her out to the car and she wouldn't wake. Sometimes she gave her an extra spoon of mashed potato, more gravy, fattening her like the wicked witch in 'Hansel and Gretel', thinking and not-thinking that it might make her harder to steal away.

'Shove over,' Laura whispered, nudging a sleepy Coraline until there was enough space to climb in beside her.

The heat radiated off her daughter. It was her normal state, although it had taken years of middle-of-the-night runs to the out-of-hours doctor before Laura allowed herself to accept that fact and relax. On the rare occasions that Coraline stayed with Enda, he was liable even now to phone in a panic about *how hot is too hot?*

'She runs warm,' Laura said soothingly each time. 'Maybe check she hasn't brought a blanket in under the quilt with her.'

Every time, she reassured him it was fine.

If anything, she liked his worry. Because it meant he was taking his parenting responsibilities seriously. Because she could see a reflection of his goodness in his care for their daughter. Yes, all that. But also because she liked to know that he was worrying. That he had to worry. That his cashmere socks and glass of wine and quiet living room were spoiled by the reality of having to make space for someone else. Having to acknowledge that someone else – their needs, their breath, their body – were as necessary, as real, as his own.

She would never un-wish her daughter. Never. Not on days when she looked around this tiny box bedroom with its divan bed and shelves in place of a wardrobe and knew she would eventually have to offer Coraline the bigger bedroom. Not even on days when the world was heavy and effortful and the rain bent sideways trying to drown them all and she thought with longing of her rucksack in the attic, half-fantasising about dislodging the family of mice living in the side pocket and taking off. She could work anywhere, do anything. Without the endless search for external validation, a person's needs were few. But if her needs were few, Coraline's were many yet, and Laura would honour that until such time as her daughter could make her own way. In the meantime, the best she could do was to give Coraline room to grow.

'What are you doing, Mammy?' Coraline asked, turning in a spiral of pointy elbows and knees to look at Laura.

'I'm thinking about how much I love you,' Laura answered. 'Even when you're like a tiny torture device in the bed.'

'Is it Saturday?'

'No, my love. Two minutes and then we have to get up for school, alright?'

'It's going to snow today.'

'I don't think so, my darling.' Laura wondered if she had the energy to explain that snow in Donegal didn't necessarily mean snow in Cork, and decided she didn't. Let the day itself do that work for her.

'Can we stay here at home if it snows?'

'It won't.'

'But if it does.'

Did people ever outgrow their hopes of snow? 'If it does, then yes, we can stay home.'

'And have school-from-home with GranKit, like in lockdown?'

'Yes.'

'And then culture hour?'

It was what they had called the hour after lunch when

everyone was too tired and irritable to do anything but watch TV. 'Absolutely.'

'Alright then,' Coraline agreed. 'Is today a garden day or a Second Life day?'

Laura pretended to think. 'Both, I think. The shop first and then over to the community garden. I might try and see Annie as well.'

'And Jack. And Jack's garden.'

Laura's heart lifted at the thought of that beautiful garden. It was there she first realised that plants had whole lives of their own – diseases, recovery, pairings both good and bad. She would be sure to call, she decided. She wanted to check on the patch of chamomile lawn she had planted in a bid to convince Jack to do the whole thing. *Mint, maybe, for cocktails*, he had said, and it took her a second to cop that he was teasing her. That was before the stroke, of course. A chamomile lawn might be all the more welcome now, she supposed. Soothing and evergreen.

'Can I come and see my daffodils?'

'It's too early yet for your daffodils, my love.'

'Soon?'

'Soon,' she agreed.

She gave in to the request for one song before they got up, drowsing while Coraline dragged the arse out of 'Old MacDonald'. No way that farm had alligators snap-snapping here and snap-snapping there.

One of the reasons she worked like she did was so that she could be there for Coraline in the mornings. Afternoons were different. Children were more robust in the afternoon. Mornings, they were only half-alive, caught in the feral world between waking and dreaming. Gentle hands in the morning meant a better day for everyone.

When the pandemic unemployment payment ended, she could go back to working at the bar, seven p.m. to midnight, Wednesday to Sunday. That would have her here at home for dinner every day and she could still volunteer three mornings a week at Second Life after dropping Cor at school. But that meant her gardens would suffer. It would likely come down to a choice between keeping on with the community garden or the garden at Glebe Cottage, and that was hardly a fair fight, even without the fifty-euro note Jack used to leave on the passenger seat of her Clio, or her free rein with his account at the garden centre.

While Coraline brushed her teeth, Laura looked at her own reflection in the mirror and considered cutting a fringe. It was the perpetual question: would she look better with more face or less? She pulled her hair up into a ponytail and fanned the ends over her eyes. Her mother had refused to let her have a fringe as a child, claiming they made children look bold. Perhaps that was what Laura still wanted. To look bold. To be bold. Wasn't that what haircuts were for?

'What are you doing?' Coraline asked her, the words muffled against her toothbrush.

'Admiring myself,' Laura said, as she always did. 'Aren't I lovely? Come on, slowcoach. I can smell toast from here.'

They said that smelling toast was a sign of having a stroke, didn't they? Whoever they were that made the kinds of pronouncements that shaped the days and the fears of ordinary people. As she followed her daughter down the stairs and into the kitchen, she wondered if Jack had smelled toast that time he had the stroke and if the smell had confused him or made him happy.

A TINY TWO FINGERS TO EXPECTATION

At the school gate, Laura tugged the ear flaps of Coraline's hat so that they met in the middle under her chin, giving her the chipmunk cheeks that made them both laugh.

'If it gets too cold with the windows open, make sure you put on your extra fleece,' she told her. 'And leave your hat on.'

'I'm not even next to the window,' Coraline protested.

'I know. Sucks to be Evie. But leave your hat on anyway, okay?'

'Okay.'

Laura allowed herself one quick glance back at her daughter before moving out of the way of the next drop-and-run parent. In some respects, the prohibition on loitering or chatting simplified the school run, but in other ways it added another layer of sadness on top of the world their children were being handed. Give it another year and Cor would no longer remember that her mother was once allowed to hold her hand right into the classroom.

'We'll have snow yet,' someone said to her as they passed and she nodded, unable to summon the energy to decipher whose bit of face was under the hat and the glasses and the cloth mask. A nation of burglars, they looked like. Stealing the future to pay for the past.

Overhead, the sky held grimly to the palest blue. No sign of the telltale yellowy-grey that typically presaged snow. Maybe the forecast had got it right for once and the cold weather front would glance off the north-west and vanish out into the Atlantic. Sitting in the car with the blower on, waiting for it to warm up, she thought of a tour guide on the Aran Islands telling her that the islands rarely got snow. That things had to be desperate altogether on the mainland before the soft western rain would agree to harden and the sodden ground to freeze. Listening to him, Laura was glad she didn't live there – what good was life without seasons? She spent a month on a beach in Greece once and the endless sunny monotony did more damage to her liver than any number of break-ups.

At Second Life, Geraldine spent the morning guarding the weather. Shuttling over and back to the window and opening the door to peer out at the sky and make another noise of dismay. No sign of tiredness, Laura noted, but a lot of people thrived on the idea of a nice small crisis. Every time the news came on the radio, she shushed the silence and turned the dial to deafening.

By eleven thirty, they had entertained the sum total of two customers, only one of whom bought anything – a Garth Brooks CD and the fucker had the nerve to try and haggle.

'Sure who else would want it?' he said.

No doubt he thought he was being charming. Laura thanked him and took the euro. At least he didn't tell her to smile.

At the door, he turned back. 'Smile,' he said. 'It might never happen.'

Had she ever wished for anything quite as deeply as she wished his CD would get stuck in the player in his Land Rover, condemning him to *If Tomorrow Never Comes* for all eternity? Laura didn't think so. Gas and air the day Coraline was born, maybe, but it wasn't a certainty. She could have been grinning like a chihuahua under her mask for all he knew.

Geraldine was huddled by the radiator refreshing her weather app, an incongruous Scrooge in her fingerless gloves and an iPhone in her hand. 'I hate this weather,' she said. 'They think that the snow will come south as far as Tipperary.'

'Far enough away so,' Laura said.

'I'd rather have it than be waiting for it,' Geraldine said.

Laura wanted to say they didn't have to be waiting for it either. They could simply get on with their day as if the forecast didn't apply to them, *because it didn't*.

'I'm telling you, if I had the money, I'd be stretched out beside a pool for the rest of my natural,' Geraldine said.

Here it came again: the story of how Geraldine had the six numbers in the Lotto one Saturday night, except she hadn't actually played them that week.

'The same six numbers, week in and week out,' she was saying. 'Imagine.'

If Laura was in the mood, she would engage with the whole thing. Ask why she hadn't played that day (she had to run her mother up to the hospital that afternoon – indigestion and not a heart attack at all, thank God – and the wait was so long it was past the cut-off by the time she made it to the supermarket) or how long they had been her numbers (eleven years, no word of a lie) or the first place she would go if she won (Disney was the original answer, but now that her children were older, she thought New York, maybe, or Australia) or whether she kept doing the same numbers in the hope that lightning might strike twice (she did, faith, and here she would bless herself and kiss her crossed fingers with her eyes cast to heaven) or the reason behind her choice of numbers (5, 14, 29 – her children's birthdays – 11, 31, 41 – no reason other than they felt right). Such engagement was a kindness; Laura already knew the answers. They all knew the answers. They all knew the numbers, for God's sake, the whole town was like an episode of *Lost*.

'Tell me, do you ever blame your mother for missing out on the Lotto that time?' Laura asked. It was a kindness to let Geraldine close the story on her own goodness.

Geraldine clapped her hand to her heart and shook her head, her eyes wide. 'I do not! If it had been a heart attack I'd never have forgiven myself.'

Eventually, after yet another weather check at the door of the shop, Geraldine decided to close early.

'There'll be nobody out browsing shoes and blouses in this cold.'

'You're the boss,' Laura said.

Before cashing out, Geraldine wrote a little sign that she sellotaped to the inside of the door. *Closed today*, it said. *Please hold on to your donations for another day – and stay warm!* She pointed to the row of snowmen she had added for good measure. 'Manifest!' she said.

Christ.

Laura surveyed the shop floor and tidied the few bits that had been displaced in the three hours since opening. If she won the Lotto, she would travel the world. Herself and Coraline living small and thinking big. Wild and free and unschooled.

But that would mean leaving her mother home alone.

Laura sometimes wondered what might have happened if her father had been killed a year earlier and she herself was never conceived or born. Whether her mother would have gone on to meet and marry someone else. Whether her dreams would have been different. But her mother never entertained discussions of what might have been.

Laura sighed. The time for that freestyling kind of life had come and gone. No responsibilities also meant a no-stakes, lesser kind of love.

If she won the Lotto, she would make a handsome non-Christmas payment into the carbon-offsetting programme, then crank the thermostat to twenty-two degrees and fill the bath to the brim and lie there topping up the hot water until the skin of her fingers looked like vacuum-sealed salmon.

Laura locked the shop door and hurried down the footpath. The street was empty, lending the town an air of unreality. She thought of all her years in New York, when she had not once looked down the street and found it empty. Yes, but here she could get on an early train without a man staring at her while clearly – *clearly!* – stroking himself through the pockets of his tracksuit. Perhaps no matter where she was, she was destined to look around herself and think: am I really here?

The windscreen of the car had refrozen, so Laura put the blower on high again and tried not to think about the dirty little particles dancing from her exhaust pipe to some child's lungs. When this car gave up, she would have to seriously weigh up the cost of replacing it with another. Go electric, the ads said, but where did people think the electricity was coming from? As if there were teams of volunteer mice in the walls of every home, heroically pedalling their way to cups of tea and dishwasher cycles and overnight car charging. She sighed. God grant her the serenity of someone living in the twenty-first century but with the ignorance of the twentieth.

Which reminded her: she took off her gloves and texted her mother.

Any word from school?

Her mother believed in immediate answers. It was polite, she said, but Laura suspected she assumed that people were sitting around waiting for her response.

typing …

NO. PHONED SEC. EARLIER. NOT FINISHIN EARLY.
typing …

REFRESHD APP AND STILL NO.

Laura clicked her tongue against her teeth. She should have thought to do that herself. She looked at the clock on the dashboard. *13.15*. She could nip up for Cor herself, save her mother the trip. Although … she looked at her phone. *12.15*. Too early yet.

The car was taking forever to heat up and the ice showed no sign of budging. She felt around under the passenger seat in case there was a stray bottle of water that might help out, but came up empty-handed. She pulled her hat and gloves back on and ran across the road to the café. Its window glowed bright and foggy with oven heat, like something out of Goldilocks, but the nine little tables were all empty. Susan was behind the counter, making up sandwiches to deliver to the factory.

'You open to the public or too busy feeding Big Pharma?' Laura asked, taking off her gloves again and rooting in her pocket for the fiver she had shoved in there earlier.

'They keep us alive, I keep them alive,' Susan replied, as she always did. 'Early lunch?'

'Geraldine closed up,' Laura said. 'Anyone with sense is at home.'

'It's Baltic,' Susan agreed, reaching for a plate and closing the door of the fridge with a swing of her hip.

'I swam in the Baltic once,' Laura said. 'It really wasn't that cold.'

'Is that right?' Susan said, but she was polite rather than interested. 'Here or takeaway?'

'Here, if that's okay. It was summer, of course.'

'What was?'

'The Baltic. Doesn't matter. I was half talking to myself.'

Nobody was ever truly interested in someone else's tired old travel stories from when they were young and footloose and fancy-free. It was different in your twenties when every conversation featured a travel-tip swap of some kind: a tiny little hostel outside J-Bay that wasn't in the guidebooks, or the only boat company crossing to Ometepe Island that hadn't ever sunk, or how to refuse *airag* in someone's yurt in Mongolia without causing offence. That time had passed. The small window of reckless, feckless joy closing so gently that she hadn't even heard it until it was too late, leaving her indoors, trapped in a spiral of recommendations for orthodontists and last-minute bouncy castle hire and where to get sensitive-skin-friendly school shirts.

'Here you go. Almond milk latte and a pecan plait. All the nuts.'

'Better hope I don't have an allergy,' Laura said.

'Don't even joke about it. You'd close me down,' Susan

said, and started packing sandwiches onto a stainless steel tray for delivery.

Laura took her mug and plate to a table in the window. It was worth the faint chill from the glass to watch the sky change colour, cycling through possible moods like a drunk on a night out. This was what she had left the deadening corporate world for. The quiet of her own thoughts instead of the clamour of people talking for the sake of it. The ability to take half an hour out for a coffee and to watch the world go by instead of trading her freedom for an online calendar that was an exercise in busy one-upmanship. A tiny two fingers to expectation. A life with air and space. A greener life. This was what it was all about.

It was one of the things she and Annie had reconnected over, when their paths crossed a couple of months after Laura moved home. She was working a few shifts a week in the florists', trying to convince herself that she could save enough to get a place of her own before the baby arrived, and Annie came in every two or three days for fresh flowers for her mother. When she didn't appear one day, Laura called to the house on a whim with a little bunch of tulips. Annie's eyes were red-rimmed, her face blotchy. 'My sister-in-law is here,' she whispered. 'John said she would help, but she's just sitting there letting me make her cups of tea and talking about how it's great to get a break from the children.'

'Come for a walk.'

'I shouldn't. My mother—'

'Can your sister-in-law manage to sit in a room with your mother and stop her walking out the front door?'

Annie nodded.

'Then get your coat and come on.'

They had fallen back into friendship with surprising ease. This time, they were simply two lives in phase, and grateful for the comfort of living alongside one another.

There were very few people either could have texted at six in the morning or three in the afternoon to go for a walk and

– with some frequency in those days of hormonal overload and a return under her mother's roof on Laura's part, and carer's frustration on Annie's – a no-strings vent.

Walking had always been their thing, even as teenagers. Whenever Helen wasn't there – when she was sick or sulking or away for the weekend – Laura and Annie walked. Not to anywhere in particular, or with any particular design, but walking simply for the sake of walking. They didn't talk about death or dying or parents, except indirectly, couched in the language of striped skies or blazing furze or rutting animals.

Once they had come close to a direct conversation. It was during the Christmas holidays, the first since Annie's father had died, and Annie had phoned Laura's house that morning to ask if she wanted to meet up.

'Meet up to do what?' her mother asked.

Laura shrugged. 'Go for a walk or something.'

'Are you smoking?'

'Of course not.'

'Because if you are, you needn't think you'll be coming home here to me,' her mother warned, and Laura nodded. 'I know.'

She met Annie at the gable end of her house.

'Is your Mam working today?' Laura asked, and Annie nodded. 'She was off Christmas Eve and Christmas Day but she had to go in today.'

'Bet she's happier with something to do,' Laura said.

'The boys are both at friends' houses,' Annie said. 'The house is so quiet I'm afraid to move around.' She stopped. 'That sounds stupid.'

Laura knew. 'Houses can be weird like that. I don't mean ghosts or whatever ... more that memories take up a lot of space. There's more air out here,' she said, and Annie bumped her shoulder gratefully.

When Helen returned, they slipped easily back into their

usual rhythm, spending most of their evenings and weekends at her house. Glebe Cottage afforded them the greatest freedom. Even on days when she didn't have a migraine, Mrs Fitz seemed to spend the afternoon and early evening resting, coming down when it was time to start dinner. It was a bit like having a poltergeist in the house. Or a really quiet baby.

On midweek winter days, they lit the fire and listened to music. When it got warm enough in spring, they took a rug out to the garden. In summer, when days were long and warm and there was no school, they sat with their feet in the little silver-green river that ran the bottom of the garden and talked for hours about nothing in particular.

The house came to feel like theirs. On Friday evenings, there was a frisson in the air, as though the house itself were waiting for Jack to descend from Dublin. Helen and Lily prepared for his arrival, while Annie and Laura waited to be told to leave.

'Everything has to be …' Helen kissed her fingertips, 'for the star. It isn't enough that he's living in a hotel the rest of the week.'

Laura felt guilty for being impressed. To be a full-time actor seemed unimaginably glamorous compared to the farmers and dentists and salesmen that otherwise filled the male shapes in their lives, but Helen insisted it was nothing. Less than nothing, to hear her dismissive tone.

Helen rarely came to Laura's house. The time her parents went away for a two-night party, she stayed at Annie's house. Laura was briefly put out at the idea of the two of them having a sleepover and considered inviting them both to stay at hers, but the thought of her mother around her friends – around Helen – was impossible. Her mother sitting at the table and having dinner with them as though that was totally normal. No little plates of this and that left in the fridge, but huge kill-me-now plates of turkey and ham or something equally mortifying, with apple tart and cream afterwards, as if they would eat it, or anything like it. Laura nearly died at the thought of it. Better by far to let Helen and Annie have their weekend without her. She tried not to mind when her mother asked why she wasn't invited too and then answered her own question by saying maybe they wanted it to be just the two of them. As though Laura was someone they endured. Someone they needed a break from.

It wasn't true, she knew. Maybe in the beginning Helen wanted Laura there because she was out of her depth with Annie's loss, but they had become a proper three. She defended Laura when people teased her about her mother working in the school. 'Oh, are you still stuck on that old story?' she would say, or 'Grow up, would you?' or 'Do you have a thing for older women, is that it?' before rolling her eyes and drawing Laura away. She wouldn't do that unless she was really her friend, would she?

Laura blew into the foam on her latte and wondered what Helen and Annie were talking about right now. Hard to imagine it would be all cosy catch-ups, when the reality was that Helen's arrival meant that things were in a state of flux for Annie. Or the prospect of flux, at least. For all Laura knew, her mother was absolutely right and plans were already in train for Jack to be moved to a nursing home, leaving Annie at another crossroads. And there was nothing Annie hated more than unexpected change. Not that she would ever admit it. After Jack's stroke, Laura had had to take her up the Boggeragh Mountains – county bounds be damned – and walk the legs off her before she would admit the depth of her worry.

Outside the window, a group of tiny birds flitted from one side of the street to the other. Was it play or purpose? With birds there seemed no difference. Maybe that was the secret to their contentment.

Laura drained her mug and stood. Who was to say they were more content than anyone else?

HOW MUCH WAS HIDDEN IN
THAT ONE WORD

Her father was already in his chair by the window when Helen came downstairs, itchy-eyed and irritable after yesterday's daytime drinking.

He was freshly shaved, his hair neatly brushed. Dapper, even, in slacks, crisp shirt and jumper. Dark green Moroccan babouches on his feet. His babs, he called them. Her mother used to give him a pair every Christmas, in shades of pale grey and green and, once, a duck-egg blue that met with disfavour and was swiftly replaced by a 'far less gauche' terracotta pair.

Those slippers were the house's signal that the weekend had safely arrived. Her father would come home on a Friday evening and slip his feet into his babs with a groan of gratitude. The same sound of appreciation he awarded her mother's pre-dinner Martini and Helen's plate of crudités, placed alongside his elbow as the voice of Willie Nelson filled the room. '*Finally*,' he would say, raising his glass to the two of them.

Pick one memory, Annie had said. Well. That was one, wasn't it?

She looked at his head leaning against the wing of the chair for support, the newspaper ignored in his lap – what was it even doing there, for God's sake, it wasn't as if he could pick it up, let alone read it – and thought that they had only ever lived alongside one another. Never together. Not really.

How improbable that a person could live out a whole life,

with all its plans and furies, and still end with just enough awareness to know all they had lost.

She found Annie in the kitchen. 'Is that all he does all day since he got home? Sit in that chair and wait to go back to bed?'

Annie didn't turn but continued to scrape leftover porridge into the food bin. 'I can see how it might look like that. Why don't you make yourself some breakfast while I get Jack settled with his morning radio show and then I'll talk you through his day?'

It's not your kitchen, Helen thought. It was *her* kitchen. It had always been her kitchen. The least lonely room in this ridiculous house. The place where she could sit on shadowy winter evenings and talk to Annie or Laura on the phone until bedtime, or on long summer mornings where she read for hours to distract herself until Annie and Laura were free to meet up after lunch. Where she could pretend her mother had simply gone to meet a friend or gone upstairs with a basket of laundry or gone to change her blouse before her ordinary father came home from an ordinary local job in time for dinner, the way other fathers did.

By the time the kettle boiled and the microwave had spun her porridge in a careful, warming circle, she was calm enough to recognise that her anger was nebulous rather than Annie-shaped. She made a pot of tea and placed two mugs on the table. That would have to do by way of apology.

'Jack wakes a little after six and puts on the radio,' Annie started. 'There's a button on the side panel of his bed that he can trip with the back of his hand. He gets up at seven once the news bulletin is over. Once he's dressed and organised ...'

How much was hidden in that one word. *Organised*. What losses it held. Independence and dignity and personhood. What thefts.

'... we do half an hour of physio. I can show you what to do, if you like? Or Donal the physio can show you when he comes on Friday. Jack complains, of course, but having the news on in the background distracts him enough that he gets through and it really works wonders to keep his muscle tone. After the physio, a little bit of the right music gets him in form for the day.'

'What's the right music?' Helen asked. It was hard to imagine her father – her famously non-dancing father – motivated by music to move his body.

'We've developed a few playlists. Some oldies, some classical.' She smiled almost to herself. 'He likes story songs although he won't admit it.'

Story songs? Like folk songs, or more the middle-of-the-road, late-night-radio sentimental stuff? There was no need to ask Annie; she could look at the playlists herself later. She imagined them listed by days of the week to ensure some variety. Or perhaps they were more whimsical. *Jack's Jams,* maybe. Or *Jack's Joys!* Or some other system that encoded some private joke between the two of them. *AJ 90s* or *Jaffa.*

'I shave him every second day,' Annie was saying. 'He doesn't like the feeling of bristles, but we kept having a bit of a run-in over who got to control the razor, so every second day is our compromise.'

We. Our.

Helen moved the teapot an inch to the right. There were such awful stories of cruelty and neglect. Old people pinched and slapped, their ribs cracked and their needs mocked. Their life savings taken from them under the guise of caring. She should be grateful for Annie's diligence.

On it went, the recitation of her father's carbon-copy days. His radio programmes. His meals and snacks at regular intervals – 'little and often', Annie said, as though it was news – so that his intestines were never asked to do too much at once.

Helen thought of Réiltín, who as a baby had such severe reflux she had to eat tiny amounts every two hours. Every hour when she was going through a growth spurt.

'Is there a food diary?' she asked, remembering the notebooks filled with her writing, neat on good days, lurching off the lines on bad days, itemising every feed, every sleep, every nappy.

Annie shook her head. 'His weight is more or less holding, so there's no need.'

The *yet* hovered unspoken.

His rests after each light meal. Annie didn't call them naps, Helen noticed. Had Annie co-opted her mother's careful vocabulary? Maybe *rest* was deemed a more adult-appropriate word. Although, if it were Helen herself, *rest* would have uncomfortable connotations of the impending, more permanent nap.

His medical routines. The nurse who called once a week. Helen watched Annie closely for a flicker of jealousy at mentioning someone qualified, but could discern none.

'What about his social life?' she asked, when Annie had taken them right through to dinner time. *The rest you already know,* she said, and Helen searched for the barb in the suggestion that her arrival last night had meant nothing special to her father.

'Some friends call from time to time for twenty minutes or so. Any longer tires him out. His old work colleagues asked to come, but I discouraged them.' She shrugged. 'Pandemic restrictions can be useful.'

It was the right call to keep Jack's work crowd at bay. He would hate them knowing he had gone from Dr Danny Furlong to this. Or worse, gossiping about it at gallery openings and boozy lunches and awards shows. A shame, they would call it, with the kind of vicious glee she had seen her father himself apply to other fallen godlings.

'How is he coping in himself?' How she hated the creeping Irishness of that suffixed 'in himself'.

'It varies. Sometimes he is very alert, listens to the radio, rolls his eyes in the right places. Other days he gets impatient and wants it switched off. I wouldn't characterise it as anger exactly. Certain things frustrate him. Losing his speech is a particular bugbear of his. For someone so chatty, of course it would be. Other days he's quieter. Lost in himself. He doesn't seem upset though, which is good, and that particular mood never lasts long.'

Frustrated or not terribly present. Still the same man, clearly. The man whose casual disregard was what set her running in the first place, if not the reason she had stayed away so long.

If she lived nearby, could she have taken on this role herself? Impossible with work and the children. Unlikely, too, given the way she and her father had left things after her mother's funeral. Not a cooling so much as a reddening. A firing-up of past wrongs. (*Jesus Christ, Helen, can you hear yourself?*) A stoking of points of pain and pride that needed distance to safely accommodate.

'It's best to keep it simple. Chat to him when he seems engaged. Tell him what's going on in the world. If you need to ask him something, ask one question at a time, preferably with a yes-or-no reply.' Annie smiled. 'Keep it loose. Be open. That's all it is, really.'

Helen nodded. *Be open.* Funny to hear the words from Annie's mouth, when she used to be the most closed of the three of them. Always afraid that life would pass her by. Terrified of getting stuck here. So afraid of falling pregnant to some local boy that she left secondary school a determinedly unapologetic virgin. *Nobody from here is getting it,* she used to say, to Helen and Laura's howls of laughter.

'I need to go out after lunch,' Annie said. 'Jack's prescriptions are due to be refilled and the arch supports for his outdoor shoes could do with replacing. Will you be okay to stay with him for an hour, or should I pop him into bed?'

Helen would have been tempted to opt for the latter, if it weren't for the shame of acknowledging that she was afraid to mind her own father alone. 'That's fine,' she said, then repeated it, more firmly. 'We'll be fine.'

'I know,' Annie said.

Something in her voice, some note of condescension, made

Helen want to ruffle that patient, unreal exterior. 'Did your mother have a stroke as well?'

Annie said nothing for a minute, just looked somewhere beyond Helen's shoulder. 'She had dementia, which is a different road entirely.'

Where was she gone in her head? How much they no longer knew about each other. This woman who was once the girl who knew everything. The first to know when Helen started her period. Her first heartbreak. Her fear of being in this house alone.

Annie got to her feet. 'I'll get going so.'

Despite having said it was fine – *we'll be fine* – Helen felt a flicker of loneliness as she watched Annie's car drive towards the gates, pause while they opened, then turn left for town. She was being ridiculous. This was her father, for goodness' sake. Not some stranger she couldn't pick out of a line-up.

Besides, he was napping. Resting.

While she waited for him to wake, she checked her to-do list and sent a quick text to each of the children, reminding Rex he had a project due at the end of the week, Ruan he needed to take five euro to school for odd socks day – and also to wear the odd socks – and Réiltín to enjoy the gallery visit as part of her art class. To Conor she sent a little nudge to make sure that Réiltín ate her dinner with them instead of sloping down after everyone else had finished. It was important to know what she ate. To know that she ate. *Annie's gone into town, so I'm parent-sitting,* she added, then deleted it, unsure if she was looking for praise or reassurance.

She put her phone away, but felt a bit creepy sitting in the second wing-back chair watching her father sleep. Instead, she moved to the old green sofa. The feel of the velvet against her ankle held a world of memories. This had always been her seat, while her parents sat facing each other. Their little world of two, with Helen a corner thought. Her anger – her jealousy – was long dormant, but never fully extinguished. All she had to do was flick her wrists and out it would come. Like lightning. Or – she thought of Rex and Ruan – Spider-Man. An almost invisible filament holding her in place.

The rest of the room had changed little since her mother died. If Helen were to do one of those spot-the-difference puzzles, her mother's absent vases of heavy-scented French lavender – one on the mantlepiece and another on the table – would be the sole Xs. This morning, the room smelled fresh and woody. Sandalwood, maybe, with a hint of lemongrass. Masculine tones. She wondered if they were chosen by Annie, or if her father had sniffed and selected diffusers from some upcycled dresser in a garden centre.

Otherwise, the room was as bright and airy as ever, with the big picture window looking out over the drive on one side, and the French windows giving on to the garden on the other. The walls were the same old-linen colour, the heavy dark green and gold brocade curtains still held their neat tasselled waists, the thick rugs on the floor were barely thinned by the extra years of feet in shoes and socks and slippers and babs. People had always remarked on the room's warmth. Its friendliness. *A real living room,* her mother called it, whenever anyone complimented her décor. As if she lived in its comforts night and day, rather than saving it for when her father was home.

Conor didn't avoid her spaces when she was away, instead teasing her that he sat in her chair and worked at her desk and slept on her side of the bed. Her friends thought it was sweet.

She sighed. This bloody house! Its size and silence were never good for her.

When her father woke, it was with a jerk, the towel under his head slipping to the floor. Helen picked it up and refolded it.

'Now. What do you fancy doing today?' she asked. Too loud and too bright. With any luck he hadn't noticed.

He wasn't due the pureed fruit and yogurt for an hour

or more. Annie had said he sometimes liked to watch a bit of television, but surely the prospect of improvement in his condition depended on engaging in some activity? She couldn't do the physio or the – her brain shied away from the term and its connotations – *personal care,* but she could certainly hold his arm while he did a lap of the garden. Granted, it was wintertime, but he had gone out yesterday and it could hardly be all that much colder today. It would do him good to keep moving. *Jack is still Jack,* Annie had said. Even if it was hard to shake the feeling he was an actor playing a nursing home resident.

Helen moved to the window and tried to gauge how long it might take them to walk to the stream that ran the full length of the bottom of the garden. On her own, a couple of minutes – it was less than two hundred metres, she used to run it in thirty seconds – but with her father, she thought it might take a bit longer. Anything up to ten minutes, even.

There was no hint of rain in the pale sky, so they would be under no pressure to move quickly. They had all the time in the world.

'I thought we might take a walk down to the stream. How does that sound? See if the fish are out and about.'

He smiled as she brought him his wellies from the back door. Smiled as she slipped off his babs and pulled on his wellies, trying to ignore the intrusive memories of the children when they were little and helpless. Smiled as she stood in front of him, squared her feet and her shoulders, and took his hands to help him to stand, the way she had seen Annie do it.

He got to his feet easily enough and let her tuck his arm in hers and begin to lead him across the room. Halfway across, Helen realised she should have got their coats before starting off. She looked around. A houseful of handrails and none where she needed it. Was he sufficiently steady to sit on a chair at the dining table? It would be ten seconds, tops. She pulled one out with her foot, settled him into it.

'I'll get our coats and be back in a tick,' she said, then wheeled away towards the hall.

She put his scarf and coat on, tucking the scarf inside the neck of the coat, then put on her own. If she were on an aeroplane, they would admonish her. Well, this wasn't a plane or an emergency or oxygen mask or, indeed, a dependent. It was, at worst, a situation of dependency. Words mattered, even if no one else heard them. Especially when no one else heard them.

'Here we go,' she said and opened the French windows to the garden.

Close up, her mother's garden looked forlorn. The grass was longer than it should have been and the trees and shrubs were overdue their winter pruning. Whoever was looking after the place was cutting corners. Annie might not realise it, but Helen did. She had grown up watching this garden. A spot-the-difference out here would have more Xs than plants.

'I wonder when the gardener is due back in,' she said to her father. He mightn't be able to reply, but that didn't mean they had to walk in excruciating silence. 'I must remember to have a word with them next time about tidying up some of these ragged edges.' She gestured with her free arm, the other being engaged in keeping her father steady.

Had her mother lived, would she have been here in Helen's place, walking her father around the garden, talking to him of this and that? Helen thought not. Much as she worshipped her husband, her mother was not good with illness or weakness. Far more likely that she would have parked him in a chair to watch while she pottered around doing her winter maintenance. Or that she would have declared herself 'overwhelmed' and gone to rest. As a child, Helen had thought the word meant tired, so routinely did a nap trail the announcement.

'You're not to worry about me missing work,' she told her father.

It likely wouldn't have occurred to him even had he been in the whole of his health. 'With no holidays this past year, I have plenty of annual leave owing. I was able to work online throughout the lockdowns. Lucky, really.'

She thought of the boys, their eyes small and red from days spent living online. School, then friends, then relaxation, all mediated through a nine-inch screen. And Réiltín. Holed up in her room, more and more of her sucked into that other world. Her real, tangible life vanishing by inches.

Lucky, yes. But not for everyone.

'I know you understand I couldn't come when you were in hospital.'

His hand moved on her arm, either reassuring pat or involuntary tremor.

'I phoned every day. I'm sure the nurses told you that. And of course you had Annie.'

Annie who had found him after the stroke. Providential, Helen had thought when she heard. But of course Annie was already living here then. If her finding Jack had turned out to be a little less lucky on Annie's part, it was perhaps also a little less grateful on Helen's.

Was it some kind of subliminal awareness that something was being kept from her that had stopped Helen from reaching out to Annie after the stroke the way she would have done with someone more distant? Someone who didn't come with the baggage of once-familiar? If she felt it, Annie did, too. That much was clear from the very first text. *Jack appears to have had a stroke and is in hospital for tests. I've given the staff your number and they will phone as soon as they know more.* If Annie had phoned herself, would that have been enough to melt whatever coldness had solidified between them? Or if not quite a thaw, then a willingness to engage in warmer conversation at least? But she had been equally happy to hide behind texts, she reminded herself. To delay coming back here for as long as possible.

'I thought we might get out for a few hours one of the days. Inject a bit of fun into things!' Helen realised she had managed to sound both critical and a bit desperate. 'What do you say? I thought a nice garden centre, maybe? Bit of a walkabout and then the café?'

When he stopped and clutched her arm, she thought for a second that he was pleased at the idea. His face, however, was all alarm.

'What is it?'

He shook his head and gurgled, his words glue in his throat. *Like trying to carry water in a colander,* she remembered.

'Is it the wind? Are you too cold? Is there something you need? Something you've forgotten?'

The rising smell made his distress suddenly, mortifyingly clear.

'How about we go back indoors?' she said, steering him carefully in a wide half-circle so that they were facing the house.

If the walk towards the end of the garden had seemed slow, the walk back to the house was glacial. Helen wasn't sure if she should acknowledge what had happened or if that would make things worse. Nor could she begin to imagine what might happen when they got back inside. Was this something he sorted out for himself? His hand tremored under hers. Surely not. Should she try to help? It seemed unthinkable, but so too did the idea of letting him sit in misery until Annie came back. Even a poor clean-up job would be better than accusations of neglect or unfeeling. She could hardly pretend not to have noticed.

Something to distract them might work. She cast around for memories she could share. There was the time her parents were having a loud dinner party and she couldn't sleep, so she stomped downstairs and exploded into the dining room shrieking about *ravening whores*, an expression she had overheard her mother use before anyone arrived. Christ. It was enough to make her blush even now. 'Hordes,' her father said simply, shooing her back upstairs to bed. 'Ravening hordes.' Too embarrassing.

Jack shuffled along beside her, every step releasing a fresh waft of shame. All that pureed fucking fruit.

'I thought it might be nice to video call the children later. Say a quick hello. I'm sure they'd love to see you.'

With horror, she realised that her brain had absorbed this particular situation and drawn her a direct line to the nappy changes and toilet-training accidents that had featured so prominently in her life for a time. She glanced at her father to see if he had discerned her logic, but he was grimly focused on his feet.

'To be honest, they don't talk to me much when I call.' That sounded excessively self-pitying. 'They prefer to text. I tell myself it's a generational thing to see the world differently.'

They prefer to text. For the first time she wondered if they, too, were avoiding direct contact. Hadn't she just realised that was what herself and Annie did? Letting texts create the illusion of a functional relationship? Jesus H. Christ. Was she literally training her children away from her?

In the embarrassed quiet, she heard a car on the road outside, then the rattle and scrape of the electronic gates opening. Oh, the relief! Like the cool of moisturiser on burned skin.

'That must be Annie, back from town. I hope she doesn't mind we went out without her,' she said. She squeezed her father's arm, drawing herself closer to him. 'Never mind. We can all go together next time. That garden centre trip we talked about might be nice.'

HOW WOULD I KNOW IF NO ONE TOLD ME?

While Annie whisked Jack off into his study –his bedroom, Helen corrected herself – Helen chopped a yellow pepper, a courgette and a red onion, drizzled them with a little olive oil and honey, and popped them into the oven to roast. She and the puree were in it together now.

When that was done, she defrosted two fruit scones for herself and Annie – her father wouldn't eat anything like that, surely? Could a scone be pureed? – placing them companionably on a large plate in the centre of the table, with a smaller plate for each of them. Together with the teapot in its knitted yellow cosy with pink flower pompom – her mother would be turning in her grave – it made quite the country kitchen tableau. Very Cézanne.

'Lovely, thanks,' Annie said, taking a scone.

'I like the tea cosy,' Helen said.

'Cheerful, isn't it?'

Was she being deliberately evasive? Maybe she was holding a grudge about the state of things when she returned. Helen cleared her throat. 'Does that happen to him often? Accidents like that, I mean?'

'It happens. It's nothing to be embarrassed about, but you know Jack. Always so fastidious.'

Helen thought of her mother sending her father's shirts out to the laundry. At the time, she assumed that her mother was too grand or too lazy or too sad to do them herself. It had never occurred to her that it might have been her father's preference. His fastidiousness, as Annie called it. She thought of her mother holding up each returned shirt in the light of the French windows, checking the collars and cuffs to make sure they had done a good job. *If you want a job done right, do it yourself,* Helen would think. But that phrase belonged to Annie's mother, not Helen's.

'While we were out for our walk, I noticed the garden is looking a little bedraggled.' She was really on fire with her word choices, Helen thought. Between 'accidents' and 'bedraggled', she could have been a Victorian lady. 'I thought I must ask you who takes care of it.' *I thought I simply must ask …* Christ.

Annie looked at her strangely and, for one horrible second, she thought it might be Annie herself. Out there with a strimmer in the fading light or on her chapped hands and knees picking weeds after a full day of taking care of Helen's father, feeding him and minding him and wiping his backside, and here was Helen picking holes in her commitment, like a crow with an apple.

'Laura does it.'

'Laura … Our Laura? Laura O'Brien?'

Annie nodded. 'She was giving Jack advice on it and then she came over to help out last summer and Jack asked if she'd make it a regular thing. I assumed you knew.'

'How would I know if no one told me?' Helen heard the tightness in her voice and swallowed some tea to loosen it. 'When did Laura start a gardening business?' She aimed for an interested tone and thought she hit it. More or less.

It was a reasonable question. As far as Helen was aware, Laura had gone travelling after school and was never heard from again.

Except that wasn't true obviously. If Helen didn't know what Laura was doing, it wasn't because Laura had vanished, but because Helen didn't care to know. She had been too consumed with shedding the shame of failing her school leaving exams and engineering a new life for herself at boarding school. A new life that included a large, shallow pool of friends, all happy to chat for hours without ever really talking.

'She worked in finance in New York for years, then wanted something completely different when she came home.' Annie smiled. 'She always loved Lily's garden.'

Lily's garden. Since when had her mother stopped being Mrs. Fitz? But the mention of Laura and New York and finance all in the same breath was too much to withstand. Laura with that sort of intensity? Unimaginable. 'I suppose she wanted to come because of Covid.'

'No, she's back a decade or so.'

So Laura and Annie were both back here. Together. Friendly. Friends. The two of them.

'Burnout, was it? That brought her home, I mean?'

'You'd have to ask her,' Annie said.

Was she protecting Laura's secrets or did she not know either? *You'd have to ask her.* Maybe she would. If her mother's beloved garden was being used as free therapy, she had a right to know.

'She might want to come and have a look at it. It seems like things might have grown a little too far.' Helen aimed for jokey but it didn't land.

Annie shook her head. 'There's a whole community-wide rewilding project at the moment. During the first lockdown, there was a community support WhatsApp group we were all on. It was supposed to be about food delivery slots and making sure we didn't all walk in the same place at the same time, but things went a bit rogue. You know the way. People wanted more wildlife in their gardens, something to mind or for children to look at. And of course you couldn't get a puppy for love nor money. Anyway, Laura made a few suggestions and it snowballed and next thing everyone was obsessed with counting bees and ladybirds and nearly had the Biodiversity Ireland website crashed with the weight of citizen science.'

Her smile suggested a fond, private memory. As if Helen knew nothing of this. As if WhatsApp groups and neighbourliness and bee-friendly planting and native species and no-mow were unique to this little corner of Ireland.

'Jack loved it. He used to say Lily would have got such a kick out of him finally seeing the power of a garden. He spent hours online researching and updating the group and deciding whether to try this or that. Choosing native wildflower seeds and that kind of thing. *Letting nature tell us what she needs,* he called it.'

That certainly sounded like him, managing to be both pompous and engaging. Helen could picture him, eyebrows furrowed, never losing an opportunity for a pronouncement.

'When does Laura come in to do the garden?' Helen asked.

'It varies. A few hours every week usually. Less in winter when things need to be left alone. I can ask her to call in the next day or two, if you like?'

Lily's garden. Laura always loved Lily's garden. Laura's garden.

'Please do.'

While Annie washed and dried her plate and mug, Helen picked scone crumbs off the table with her thumb and told herself she was entitled to be annoyed.

Annie's phone buzzed. 'Laura says she'll come around tomorrow.'

'Great!' Too hearty, Helen thought. She wasn't auditioning as a children's television presenter.

'She's looking forward to seeing you, she says.'

'Likewise!'

Get it all out of your system, she told herself. Then maybe you'll act like a real live human being tomorrow.

In the doldrums of the late afternoon, the three of them sat in the living room. Annie read aloud from the day's newspaper, stopping after a while to offer it to Helen to take a turn. Annie,

Helen noticed, had avoided the more violent headlines and so she followed suit, with the result that the atmosphere of cosiness was undisturbed by murder and rape and climate change, giving a strong impression that political shenanigans and dognapping were the worst of humanity's excesses.

Annie insisted on cooking again and when her father woke, Helen decided to make good on her promise to make a video call to the children.

'Let's see who we have. What do you think? Will we try Rex first? Or Ruan? I should have made them share a phone and then we wouldn't have to dither.'

The politics of who to contact first were always complex. No matter who it was, she might be seen as having chosen. Rex was the more sensitive of the two and so her default impulse was to phone him first. But did that not mean she was somehow assuming that Ruan felt things less just because he expressed them less? Wasn't that how teenagers ended up in the worst kinds of despair? Not to mention the fact that she might be enabling Rex's squeaky wheel tendencies – a charge Conor occasionally laid at her feet. Whenever the boys – or they themselves – were irritable with one another. 'You need to let them fight it out between them,' he would say, in that slow, careful tone that suggested infinite patience was needed to explain the world to her.

'We'll phone Conor,' she said. He was, after all, the neutral option.

But there was no answer, which left her back at square one. She dialled Rex and held the phone out so that they could both watch it ring out. Then Ruan. She began to feel silly, with her phone at arm's length and her children ignoring her.

While the phone rang, she realised she didn't want – she *really* didn't want – to perform being a good parent for her father. Who himself had been oblivious to such pressure, only occasionally asking a question that showed he remembered a previous conversation – a school project, a comment about a friend, a show she liked. And she had been so pleased, so fucking *grateful* that it took her years of adulthood to realise he was practising basic party techniques to make her feel important.

'Should we try Réiltín?' she said, and made a show of looking at her watch. 'It's coming up to six o'clock there, so they're probably having their tea. Knowing Ré, she'll have the phone on the table beside her plate. She wouldn't get away with that if I was at home,' she added, and had to stop herself nudging her father like a character in a bad sitcom.

But Réiltín didn't answer either and Helen had to work hard to stop the little curl of fear that reached around her ribcage towards her heart.

'Ré was a long shot, to be honest,' she told her father. 'She's had a tough year and seems to be blaming me for most of it. Largely because I'm there, I suspect.' Easier to think that than to interrogate whether it was, in fact, something she had done.

The finger of fear was scraping, scraping, and she kept talking.

'You didn't worry about me much when I was growing up, did you? I remember you saying that when you introduced me at parties. That you didn't have to worry about me.'

Her father tried to lift his hand towards hers, but Helen pretended not to see it. She enjoyed the freedom of that little cruelty.

'Was it because you weren't at home much that you didn't worry? It's hard to muster concern when you don't know what's going on, I suppose.'

Scrape, scrape, scrape went the finger.

'Of course, that doesn't explain why Mum didn't worry either. I feel I can tell you – I can tell you, can't I? After all these years and all that water under all those bridges – that I would have quite liked someone to worry about me. That sometimes it was hard not to feel I wasn't worth worrying about.'

She was breathing quickly. Her father had stopped trying to get his hand to hers and was instead shaking his head.

'You were proud – both of you – that I wasn't a bother. But, you see, the thing is that not bothering anyone means that no one is bothered. Not when you're alone or lonely or you cram all of your emotions into a tiny little box and push it far far far in under your ribs so that it's hard to get at. A little Pandora's box full of inadequacy and fear and all the horrible things you believe about yourself. All packed in there, like sardines in brine.'

She stopped herself before she said more. Before she let herself down by adding that if that box was jolted, briny water might rise out and drown her.

TELLING IT STRAIGHT

'How much does he actually understand?' Helen asked Annie over dinner. Grilled salmon this time, with baby potatoes and green vegetables. Tasty right now, but the smell of fish would linger in the kitchen overnight and give her the dry heaves in the morning. *The gawks,* they used to call it. *The smell of Lynx Africa gives me the gawks.*

'Everything,' Annie said easily.

Helen was surprised at her certainty. 'I suppose you've seen it all before.'

'Yes and no. There are often similarities, but ultimately stroke reaction is as individual as anything else.' Annie speared a piece of roast broccoli with her fork. 'Knowing Jack beforehand makes a difference, too. I have a baseline for him.'

Was that a dig? Helen knew Jack beforehand, too, after all, and was nonetheless mystified at how – she stamped quickly on the 'if' that came to mind – his brain worked any more.

'I mean I know what he was like in the months immediately before the stroke,' Annie corrected herself, spearing another piece of broccoli.

'Yes. Covid changed us all.' Helen's smile was so tight she could have hung a line of washing from it. 'It was difficult not to be able to get home to him after the stroke.'

It was plausible, if not exactly true. It wasn't that she hadn't thought of him while they moved their lives online, walked the same prescribed square every day, tried to coexist in a small space with the minimum of interpersonal damage. It was that he was simply one of so many things to worry about and it was all entirely out of her hands. Annie's casual company, casually mentioned, had seemed almost heaven-sent.

Annie looked at her. That straight-at-her look that had called teenage Helen on her bullshit so many times.

'Families are complicated,' Annie said. 'You probably heard I came home years ago to mind my mother when she fell ill.'

Helen had heard. According to her own mother at the time, Annie dropped out of her nursing course with a year left to go and martyred her twenties and thirties playing nursemaid at home. All said in that particular *such friends* tone she used for Annie. No recognition of Annie's ever having wanted to leave. No understanding that a grown woman might want to develop a whole new relationship with her parents. Any ideas Helen had of coming home after university shattered like the peanut brittle they used to make in home economics class. Back before peanuts were quite so deadly.

'Mum was unwell for a long time before she died,' Annie said, as if she could read Helen's mind. 'She was finally in remission and finding her feet when the Alzheimer's began to take hold. It seemed ridiculous to pay someone else to care for her when I was perfectly well able – if not yet fully qualified – to do it myself.' She took a sip of water. 'She would have done it for me.'

What made Annie so sure of that, Helen wondered. Who could be that confident in the depth of another's feelings, that certain that love or duty or patience would see off all the nasty undersides? She had long decided it was a fiction people engaged in – usually after death – to absolve themselves somehow, or to align the wishes of the deceased conveniently with their own, when the truth was that few people knew what anyone wanted even when they were alive and hale and hearty enough to tell them directly. The notion that being ill or dead conferred some transparent emotional communion was self-serving and silly.

'Or at least there's nothing to lose in thinking she would have.' Annie shrugged. 'Anyway. Her grave is next to your mum's and Jack and I used to see each other there at weekends and chat a bit about this and that. The weather. Local bits and pieces. How much he missed work. He told me how you were doing, about the children. I didn't pry,' Annie added. 'In case you think—'

'No, no. We were always a bit of an out-of-sight-out-of-mind kind of family, so it's nice to hear that he talked about us.'

'Oh he did.' Annie's nod was earnest.

Was it a little too earnest? Was she protesting too much? Turning a passing comment or two into regular updates about Helen and her children? But why would she? To get Helen onside? Or to distract her?

She listened while Annie explained again how her father had begun to find the house a little too much. Cooking a little too difficult. As she talked, she spread her hands wide, as if her pale pink palms were testifying her blamelessness.

'I would have thought you were overqualified for running errands and keeping him company,' Helen said.

'As I mentioned, we had become friends,' Annie said.

Again that direct look. Like she was saying it before Helen could.

Clearly something kept Annie here, instead of going back to finish her nursing training. *We,* Annie said, often, when talking about her life now. Annie who had always loved this house more than anyone.

Nonsense. Annie had a home of her own.

Yes. But: Helen thought of Annie's boxy little child's-drawing house, with its beige carpet and orangey pine furniture. There were houses and there were *houses*.

'You're asking yourself why I didn't go back and finish my course,' Annie said.

Her laughter at Helen's rising flush fell short of snide.

'You and everyone else, believe me. The plan was always

to slot back in after Mum died, but the system has changed altogether. It's a degree course these days, which means three years of university and having Mum's house means I'm not eligible for a grant so I'm working and saving.'

That all sounded very commendable in theory but it could hardly be true to say that her earlier vocational training – not to mention years of working as a carer – wouldn't garner some level of exemption. Maybe Annie didn't know how the system worked? Helen opened her mouth to ask, then closed it again. That kind of information was readily available. Usually, what people didn't know was what they didn't want to know.

'Jack being Jack, he wanted to be sure that I didn't lose out on a formal employment record, so I dropped a shift at the nursing home and started coming in a few hours a week to help out. He had clipped the gate post with the car a couple of times, so I drove him where he needed to go, did a bit around the house, you know. He was reluctant to ask anyone else to help.'

Helen listened carefully for signs of a guilt trip. *You know,* that might have been one. Or that *anyone else.* But on balance she thought Annie was telling it straight.

'He was born stubborn,' she agreed and caught Annie's grateful smile.

'By the time Covid arrived and the first lockdown was announced, I was calling in most days for a couple of hours. We discussed what might be the best thing to do …'

We. Helen heard it, let it go.

'… but after a few weeks of dropping his shopping to the door and waving through the window, we agreed it was silly for us both to be sitting in empty houses. Him needing help and both of us needing company. So I moved in here. My official hours were increased, but still part-time. Please don't think the agency suddenly started saying I was full-time or anything.' She shrugged slightly. 'I cut his hair, his nails. That sort of thing. The things that were awkward for him to do himself. The rest of the time was … normal. Crosswords.

Cooking. Gardening. I wasn't very good at that but Jack would bring out a chair and FaceTime Laura. Sitting there with his coffee, the pair of them getting such a kick out of telling me what to do.' She smiled. 'The weather was great here at the time.'

Helen remembered. She had checked it, guiltily, on Wednesdays and Sundays before texting to say she hoped he was having a good week (Wednesdays) or had had a good weekend (Sundays) and was staying safe. At the time, it was as much as she felt capable of. Her bubble of worry was at capacity with herself, the kids and Conor. Stretching it all the way to Ireland and her father risked structural damage to an already-thinning ability to cope.

'We were just getting to grips with the second lockdown when he had the stroke,' Annie said. 'Luckily I had just got back from a walk so I was able to get him straight over to the hospital. The rest you know.'

Helen looked at Jack, snoring lightly in his chair. *The rest you know.* But she didn't. She didn't know anything. Not why Annie had continued to live here through the summer and into the autumn, when things were largely back to normal. Not how long her father could live like that. Not how long Annie would stay – could stay – considering she seemed to be saving for college. She didn't even know if she would be on her flight home on Monday.

It would be the easiest thing in the world to panic.

'What happens from here?'

'He could continue as he is for quite a while. Lots of people do. The main risk is another stroke, which could leave him far more compromised or bring a very sudden deterioration or kill him outright.'

Helen liked her lack of euphemism. 'It's hard to imagine this is as good as it's going to get for him.'

'This is good,' Annie insisted. 'It mightn't look it to you, and I'm not denying there are frustrations for him, but he is comfortable and entertained and as lively as possible. There are lots of things he enjoys.' She paused. 'I don't know what your plans are, whether you feel he should be in a nursing home or something, but I feel quite strongly that he is happiest here and that things are manageable.' She looked at Helen. 'I'm not trying to tell you what to do. I feel I owe it to Jack to tell you what I think.'

Helen thought of her father and Annie in the garden, Annie pulling weeds while her father directed from a chair. She thought of Annie the morning of the stroke, just back from a walk, her endorphins gobbled up by her father's alarmingly fallen face and sloppy arm.

'I appreciate the advice,' she said. 'As I'm sure you appreciate I have some things I need to think over.'

'Of course.'

It wasn't until she was in the kitchen, elbow-deep in sudsy dinner dishes, that Helen wondered if she had somehow given the impression that she herself was considering staying and taking on her father's care.

THE LITTLE FLAME OF SELF-PITY
DIDN'T TAKE MUCH FANNING

Helen took her time drying the dishes and putting them back in the cupboards. She could hear Annie's voice in the living room encouraging Jack through his evening exercise – four sets of careful rotation of wrists and ankles in his chair, followed by several creeping laps around the living room. It was unbearable to watch. Besides, they likely wanted their privacy.

Instead, she used the time to move the garish primary-coloured plates and bowls to the back of the press and pull forward her mother's dove-grey Wedgwood with the discreet silver trim, where it was nearer to hand.

There. Much better.

Despite her dawdling, when she went into the living room, her father had a lap or two left to do. It was, Annie said, too cold for him to walk outside in the evenings.

'We're holding out for spring, aren't we, Jack?' Annie said. 'Everything brighter and greener. We just have to let time do its thing. Laura has us on a promise of daffodils. A riot of them, she swore we'd have.'

'*When all at once, I saw a cloud, a host of golden daffodils,*' Helen said. 'That'll be you shortly.'

Annie smiled and steered Jack towards the double doors to walk the width of the entrance hall.

Why was it that her words so often seemed patronising rather than cheery? She meant it the same way Annie had.

Both of them essentially saying *we want you to see the spring.* Yet something in her tone or – more likely – in Helen herself had coated the words in a sticky layer of gloom. She couldn't win.

'There you go, Jack,' Annie said, when Jack was settled in his chair. 'Not too shabby for one evening, although we might try and add another lap tomorrow. See if we can't get Donal's weekend off to a good start when he checks in on Friday. Donal is Jack's physio,' she explained to Helen. 'As good a man as you'll find, but not what you'd call jolly, is he, Jack? We have a bit of a competition going to see can we get him to crack a smile.' She smiled and rubbed Jack's shoulder. 'Well done tonight, old timer. I have a bit of paperwork to catch up on in the kitchen. Shout if you need me.'

Her smile at Helen as she passed was so similar to the one she had given Jack that Helen nearly held out her hand for a pat, too.

As teenagers, their smiles had been reserved for adults and teachers. The edges of mouths tugged upwards reluctantly or ingratiatingly or otherwise purposefully, as circumstances and self-preservation required. Occasionally – very occasionally and very hard-won – smiles were for boys. Usually fleeting, breaking through the veneer of shruggy disaffection that hallmarked the nineties. Among themselves, for Helen, Annie and Laura, it was gales of laughter or companionable silence. All or nothing.

'I've nearly forgotten how to look forward to spring,' Helen said to Jack. 'January and February are two of my busiest months, I hardly have time to notice the flowers coming in.'

She was going for chatty and relaxed, the way Annie had, but it didn't quite come off, instead sounding as though she was bitching about her busy life to a man whose plan for the coming weeks featured ankle rotations and – if he was lucky – an extra lap of his hallway on his own two feet.

She had lost the knack of talking about her life without complaining. In their twenties, everyone was well able to entertain roomfuls of friends with stories of commuting hell, house shares and workplace hijinks. The same stories in their forties generated unease rather than hilarity. Or, sometimes, the kind of exhaustion one-upmanship that passed for common ground in the friendships of middle-aged women with young children and elderly parents. Nothing in life was as serious as middle-age.

'You always loved the springtime,' she tried again. 'I remember you used to come home on a Friday evening and walk around the garden in the dusk with Mum.' Helen would bring her dolls into the living room and line them up inside the glass doors, a sad little parade of faces looking out and waiting for her parents to return from whatever grown-up land of laughter and shared jokes they were touring without her. 'Then when the evenings got longer, you would both sit out there with a glass of wine. You used to say there was nothing finer.' She smiled. 'We'll have to bring back that tradition.'

Her father flapped his hand and noised. In agreement or to make the point that wine was no longer an option. No matter. It was enough to remember and to show willing.

'You know I used to open the sliding door so I could hear what you were telling Mum. Usually it was stuff about the script, about what was next for Dr Danny Furlong. You used to get so cross when the storylines were more about your patients than about your character. I remember the evening you came home and told Mum they were extending filming to a permanent hospital location. I heard the bottle pop and the champagne fizz up and out. I had never seen anything so glamorous in real life.'

Her father was smiling.

'I drove you mad as a teenager pointing out they were fooling no one having a GP working in a hospital and nobody seeming to know or care how he suddenly switched track.' Helen laughed. 'I was partly doing it to annoy you, of course, but when you're spending your days listening to teachers going on about the Leaving Cert and career path this and that, Dr Danny and his magic transferable skills felt like the weirdest blind spot in the nation's cultural consciousness.'

She leaned in towards him.

'For a while in my twenties, I used to tell people my dad was a doctor. It didn't really feel like a lie.'

He dipped his head the way he used to at award shows when they called his name among the nominees and the camera cut to him in the audience.

Looking back, it was hard to reconcile her teenage embarrassment with the actual circumstances of her life. Yet how she had envied Annie and Laura with their houses empty of fathers! Dead people couldn't mortify you. Oh, sure, they couldn't give you pocket money or drive you places either, but those things paled before the sheen of shame on school mornings when her father's onscreen Lothario character had been involved in yet another comically bad clinch with a young actress and she had to walk into school through a tunnel of boys moaning theatrically and rubbing their hands up and down their own backs as if caressed by an invisible lover. It wasn't that she wished pain or suffering on him; it was that she wanted him already long dead, so that her own embarrassment might never have begun. She thought of Réiltín's mortified face whenever she tried to find out anything about her life. The fact that it was normal didn't make it any less ugly.

'Look at you, bright as a button.' Annie came into the room with a towel over her shoulder.

'We were talking about Dr Danny Furlong,' Helen said, suddenly proud of her efforts to cheer her father.

'No wonder you're smiling, Jack,' Annie said. 'Nothing you like better than being talked about, you attention-seeking old feck.' She turned to Helen. 'During the first lockdown, I used to hear him chatting away as Dr Danny Furlong to people who weren't there. I was afraid you were losing your marbles, wasn't I, Jack? When I eventually asked you, what did you say to me, do you remember? You said we were all going stir-crazy with lockdown. Oh, you let me hanging there for a good few minutes wondering what to do with that answer.'

Helen waited for the reveal. Evidently she, too, was supposed to feel the worry of that wondering.

'Turned out he was afraid the lockdown would rot his brain and so he had set himself to reciting as many of the scenes and scripts as he could remember from over the years. You had an impressive array, hadn't you, Jack? If he'd been allowed to keep the scripts, we'd have had ourselves quite the playhouse.'

Her father was honking noisily, delighted with Annie's attention. And there was Helen thinking she had given him some great gift of his past. More fool her.

Annie was brisk and efficient in her movements, talking away all the while. 'Time for your shower. And I might remind you that I'm armed with knowledge of all your ticklish spots.' She had him up and out of the chair in the time it took Helen to uncross her own legs and stand.

She watched their slow progress across the hall. It was strange to watch Annie going brazenly into what used to be her father's study, when they had spent nearly every teenage weekend tiptoeing past or listening with an ear pressed to the wood before scampering into the living room to see if her mother had left the bottles of spirits unmarked in the drinks cabinet.

'He won't care anyway,' Helen would say, but Annie always insisted on checking first. 'Just because you're afraid of getting caught.' Helen was scornful. 'You're such a suck-up.' Annie would shrug in response, as if Helen had it all wrong but she couldn't be bothered explaining it to her.

Should she go in there? Follow Annie and her father? Start running water or snapping on shower caps or warming pyjamas or whatever as if she had every right to be there?

But did she, though? A person could only enter that room by invite or by virtue of necessity, and she had neither.

The little flame of self-pity didn't take much fanning. She wasn't trained for this. She was overly emotionally invested. A child shouldn't have any dealings with their parents' genitalia. That way lay madness. And more therapy.

Out of nowhere, a memory. Herself and Annie and Laura, walking along the perimeter of the school grounds one lunchtime, then stopping for a sneaky smoke. On the other side of the wall, a man was draped across a motorbike, staring at them. Good(ish) girls that they were, they didn't stare back, but lit their one precious cigarette, passing it back and forth, each conscious not to hold it too long in case the smell lingered. They had religion after lunch and you couldn't be certain Sister Finbarr wouldn't call you up to the front to read one of her moral-drenched *Reader's Digest* stories. They were chatting about something, Helen supposed. Weren't they always? Which was why the grunting took a little while to sink in.

Laura was the first to understand, to giggle. 'Gross,' she said, turning her back.

'What?' Annie asked, then, 'Oh,' and she blushed a hard red to the roots of her hair.

As they walked away, Helen, already standing with her back to the man, had to rotate through three sides of a square in order to see him. One hand on the saddle of the bike – for balance, her brain registered – and the other massaging a fleshy pink bag that reminded her of the chicken drumsticks her mother laid out on oven trays and brushed with butter in the hours before they were due to have visitors. In looking away, her eyes locked with his, and he let out a low moan, his mouth opening as though gasping and his eyes rolling back in his head. She stumbled to catch up with her friends.

'Had a good look, perv?' Laura said cheerfully, linking her arm through Helen's and making it impossible to tell them what she had witnessed.

Helen waited for Annie to shower her father and get him into his pyjamas and into bed before knocking on the door.

'Is it okay if I come in to say goodnight?' She hated the false cheer in her voice.

Her father was sitting up in his hospital bed with the guard rail up and a fancy-looking remote control under his palm. All the furniture in the room was flush with the walls, leaving a wide empty square of floorboards in the centre where his desk used to be. Where was that lovely rust-coloured Aubusson rug he used to have? Relegated to the charity shop or to the attic, along with all the other trip hazards. The sole cheery sight in the room was a series of three large triangles painted into the corner by the window. In shades of green and grey and purple, with a white cone on top, it took her a moment to realise it was a mountain range. Clever. The boys would like something similar for their room.

She walked across to the bed to kiss her father goodnight, trying not to flinch at the overpowering smell of baby powder. Triggering, Réiltín would call it.

This was what people had to look forward to. They lived their whole lives as best they could and if they were lucky they got to the end with a portion of their faculties remaining and someone moderately kind to wipe their arse for them. There had to be a better system. She remembered saying – screaming, if she were to be truthful – the same thing during each of her labours, sharp and difficult as they were.

Her babies. Her children. She would rather die than have them do this for her.

But of course she wasn't the one doing it for her father, was she? It was Annie who was doing it. Annie who had always envied Helen her father.

'Hopefully you'll get to talk to the children tomorrow,' Annie said from the en suite, where she was on her hands and knees mopping up excess water from the non-slip vinyl flooring. 'Jack is very proud of them, aren't you, Jack?'

Did she really need to be on her hands and knees? Wasn't it all a little bit deliberate, putting herself in a subservient position while asking a power-play question? How did she even know they had tried to talk to them today anyway? It wasn't as if Jack could have told her, which meant she must have been spying from the kitchen.

And what, exactly, did Jack even know about them, to make him so proud? What could he possibly know about Réiltín, locked into her room and her silences, or Rex, with his imagined slights, and Ruan, who would happily give away a kidney if a stranger on the street asked him.

Her irritation followed her into the living room, where she banged cushions off the backs of sofas in a bid to avoid thumping Annie herself. She was furious at her own uselessness, she told herself. Thud went the cushion.

But that was the sanitised version and she would never sleep tonight with that lie strangling her. She was useless because this wasn't what she wanted to do – if it was, she would be doing it, for fuck's sake. Rather, she was furious at being made to feel bad about it.

By the time Annie came in, the question felt like it was already outside Helen, a being in its own right.

'Why are you still here with Jack? What's in it for you?'

'Why not Jack?' Annie's voice was low and – Helen was surprised to hear it – equally furious. 'Why not care for a friend instead of a stranger? Not everything has to be cut-and-dried, Helen. Not everyone's life is in neat little boxes of work and home and here and there and past and present. Why not spend as much time as I can with someone I care about? Why not spend my time with someone who values me? Why the fuck not? At least Jack still knows who I am.'

She swept out and up the stairs, leaving Helen standing in stunned silence.

NO VISIBLE DISTRESS

Annie knew she shouldn't have lost her temper. Rule number one of the job: keep your cool with the relatives. No matter what they said. No matter that they rearrange the kitchen as if they had every right in the world to have everything their own way forever.

But this wasn't any old relative, it was Helen Fitzgibbon, for Christ's sake. Pushing every button she knew of and inventing a few more and then pushing them, too. Frankly, it was a miracle she hadn't slapped Helen's face for her.

She wasn't some sad, lonely loser whose best friend was a seventy-something whose arse she wiped. She knew it as surely as she knew her own name and yet she let Helen, with her smug houseful of her own people, undermine that certainty.

It didn't matter. Annie shouldn't have raised her voice.

Yet she had and no doubt she could be expecting a phone call from Monica in the morning to tell her that she was very sorry but Helen had opted for another service or another solution or another life. Jack would see out his days face-to-the-wall in some nursing home somewhere simply because Annie couldn't control her temper.

Her sleep was exactly as disturbed and cranky as she deserved. It was a relief to rise in the dark and slip downstairs and out into the wind that bit away every thought of anything but itself. Her boots crunched on the frost in the verges and it was hard to believe that anything could survive it.

Only a few short months ago, the road had been a green tunnel, the trees on either side stretching their branches up and out to one another, the tips trying to reach one another across the man-made divide. On those days, she resented the road for what it said about humans and their need to impose and elevate themselves. A taking for granted that saw them in their current predicament. Their illusion of control melting like snowflakes on wet ground. A green breath in and a black breath out, indeed.

But on mornings like today, she wouldn't walk if the road wasn't there to reassure her. She loved nature, yes, but more when it was easily accessible to her. A hypocrite, then, Annie Fleming.

She tramped on, crushing the frost with her boots – the gleeful, malevolent child part of her imagining it was Helen's fingers – walking and walking and walking the rage out of herself.

At the back door, she breathed and tried to let it go. She imagined walking out the door the following morning and finding a pile of her moods and irritations waiting for her. Slipping into her pockets.

People had to live in the world they were in, there was no good pretending otherwise, and right now her world included the prospect of an apology to Helen in the hopes she hadn't emailed Monica already.

Annie got Jack up, did his physio, dressed him, gave him his breakfast, alternately spooning and wiping, all the while her mind turning over what she might say to Helen.

'I'm poor company this morning,' she said to Jack, by way of apology. 'I slept badly and even the cold outside didn't clear the thick head I woke with.'

He was quiet in himself too and she wondered if he had overheard her fight with Helen. If he was disappointed in her. In them.

She settled him for his rest and went to find Helen in the kitchen.

'I apologise,' she said immediately. The only way to do it was to do it fast. 'For raising my voice and for swearing. It was unprofessional to say the least, and I apologise.'

That was enough. Sincere without being obsequious. She didn't want to over-explain. She was in the wrong, yes, but there was no need to lie down on the ground to be walked on.

'Thank you.'

For a moment, it seemed like Helen might leave it at that. The bitch.

Then Helen added, 'I didn't mean to cause offence. You hear so many stories of unscrupulous … I don't mean to imply I thought that about you, but simply to explain that I was perhaps a little paranoid, especially given the distance.'

Oh, she worked with language alright. The careful way she waved that particular elderly abuse brush near enough to Annie that the drops would be sure to splash on her before pulling it away.

'It might be advisable for you to go through some of Jack's paperwork this morning,' Annie said. 'For peace of mind, as you say. Everything is in the bureau in the living room, it's all clearly labelled and dated. You'll see that Jack's accounts are solely in his own name. If you have concerns, I'm sure Mark Kane, his solicitor, will be happy to assist you. Mark is fully apprised of all particulars.'

She turned on her heel and went back to the living room, where she had to sit on her hands to stop them shaking. If Jack woke, they could flitter and flap at each other, she thought. A pair of them in it. Shimmying like a couple of demented dancers.

When Jack woke, he seemed quieter still. Annie gave him a few minutes to wake up, chatting cheerfully about Helen and Laura getting to meet up later that morning. 'Getting the band back together,' she said airily. 'Not that we could carry a note between the three of us.'

She put his newspaper on his lap and the pencil with its big rubber grip in his hand, the same as she always did. He could no longer write, but it calmed his hand to have something to hold. There was a rustle and the paper slid to the floor. Annie replaced the newspaper and watched as it slid and fell again. She pulled the phone from her pocket and dialled the medical centre.

'I've phoned Dr Shields to come and check on Jack,' she told Helen. It was when she heard her voice wobble that she realised the depth of her dread.

'Is something wrong?' Helen's shoulders shot up towards her ears. 'He seems the same to me.'

'He's quieter than normal. I don't like it.' Annie saw Helen's face. The tiny raise of her eyebrow. 'I'm not messing, Helen, or pulling some kind of power move. I wouldn't waste the doctor's time like that.'

'I never thought you were,' Helen said.

'Dr Shields is coming shortly,' Annie told Jack. 'It's not quite Friday yet, you're right, but she's going to pop in anyway. Give you a bit of a once-over. Kick the tyres.'

Not a lie. Not quite the truth either.

While they waited, Helen asked Annie for the names of the community care team, taking out a small leather-covered notebook to jot down the names.

'I think that's everyone, Jack, isn't it?' Annie said. She held up her hand where he could see it, and counted them off on her fingers. 'Donal for physio, Astrid for occupational therapy, Meena the public health nurse,' Annie said. 'Astrid is doing virtual calls at the moment, but I'm sure we'll be back in person again soon.'

When the doorbell rang, Helen went to answer it, returning a few minutes later with Dr Shields.

'Hi Jack. Hi Annie,' she said from the doorway. 'How is everyone doing? You're in clover I'd say, Jack, with Helen home to dance attendance on you, too. Blessed art thou among women. When weren't you, I suppose, isn't that it?' She replaced her mask and gloves with a fresh set from her bag and rubbed a sanitising wipe over her blood pressure cuff and stethoscope. She crossed to where Jack sat. 'Now, let's have a little look and listen, will we?' She smiled at Jack. 'Sure you know the drill as well as I do myself.'

Annie joined Helen at the window to give Dr Shields room to work.

'I'm going to ask Annie a couple of questions about you, Jack. I'm not trying to be rude, it's just that it's easier for her to answer. If there's anything you don't agree with, you let her know and she'll set me straight.'

Annie watched her careful hands, her face that gave nothing away.

'No change in his speech?' Dr Shields asked Annie, who shook her head. 'The hemiplegia?' Annie shook her head again. 'Not noticeably colder or breathless? No visible distress?'

No. No. No. *Visible distress*. How Annie hated that distinction and all it implied. She glanced at Helen, who was watching the doctor closely. That was her right, Annie reminded herself. There was no call for sneery internal surprise at Helen's interest.

'Everything okay?' Helen asked, leaning forward.

Annie looked at Dr Shields, who was slowly moving her index finger backwards and forwards for Jack to follow with his eyes.

'I'll just …' She didn't finish, but went and fetched a tiny light from her bag, which she shone in Jack's eyes. First one, then the other, then the first again.

'Have either of you noticed anything different in his vision?' she asked the women.

'No,' Helen said.

Annie thought back, then shook her head. 'He's made eye contact as normal since I got him up this morning,' she said. 'You dropped your newspaper a couple of times earlier, Jack, didn't you, but it seemed more of a coordination issue. He woke up from his rest about an hour ago.' She looked at Helen for confirmation. 'An hour or thereabouts, would you say?'

Helen made a little gesture that might have been agreement or might equally have suggested that Annie herself needed to be checked out. *For fuck's sake, Helen.* Annie was sorry she'd tried to include her at all.

'Do you think …?' Annie asked, and Dr Shields shook her head.

'Jack, I'll neither baby you nor alarm you,' the doctor said. 'I think it might be a good idea to nip over to the hospital. I'm not happy with the vision in your right eye and I want to rule out another small stroke. It could be a thing of nothing, but I haven't the equipment here to make sure, so I think you'd be better served by the hospital team, for peace of mind. Is that alright?'

Jack's hands began to dance in his lap and Annie took them in hers. 'I know you don't like going, Jack, but it's the right thing.'

'Are you sure?' Helen said.

Dr Shields smiled cheerfully. 'I'm not sure at all and with any luck I'll be proved entirely overprotective of our lad here. His peripheral vision has reduced, that's all, and I'd like the hospital team to tell us why.'

'Will he go as an inpatient?' Annie asked.

'I imagine they'll keep him overnight for observation,' Dr Shields said. 'Might be no harm to get a few of his things together while I give the ambulance and the hospital a call to expect him.'

She turned to Jack. 'It'll be like last time, Jack. I imagine they will admit you to the stroke unit so you'll be well away from the Covid ward and all of that. I'll see if they'll let someone' – she glanced at Annie and then at Helen – 'stay while you're getting settled.'

Annie hoped things weren't about to get awkward.

Helen frowned. 'As he's incapacitated, I imagine that, legally speaking, he is entitled to have me there.'

Annie told herself she was glad for Jack that Helen had stepped up so quickly. Although she suspected it might have been simply an ingrained response to an implied infringement of rights. That was Helen's job, after all. Not to mention her personality.

'The rules have been slow to change here,' Annie explained to Helen. 'There's national recommendations to allow visiting on compassionate grounds, but individual hospitals seem to interpret them differently.'

Helen raised her eyebrows and took out her phone. To google the latest advice, Annie assumed.

'I'll pack your few bits, Jack,' Annie said. 'Your good pyjamas and dressing gown. You found it cold on the ward the last time, remember, so I'll put in those thick woollen socks and the slippers we hadn't got around to exchanging. They won't be too big with the thick socks. Let me see, what else? Your phone and charger, of course. Will I download one of the audiobooks we were picking from? You can start from there and I can start from here and we'll be straight on to chapter two tomorrow when you get home, what do you think?'

She was aware that she was talking too quickly but couldn't seem to slow herself. He hated the hospital the last time. Hated the food, the relentless poking, the squeaks and the smells and the constant light. He wouldn't be comfortable there no matter what books or socks he had, but she had to try. Helen would be the one at his bedside and so this was all Annie could do for him.

While she was packing, Helen came to find her.

'The hospital information is a little unclear,' she said. 'I'm going to go in the ambulance with him and see if I can brazen it out when I get there.'

Backseat driving, the nurses called it. Or hurling from

the ditch, if they were from certain counties. When an adult child arrived out of nowhere with their demands and their comparisons to other standards, other systems. 'I'd say gently-gently might be your best bet,' Annie said, going into the bathroom to collect Jack's toothbrush and facecloth. Would someone brush his teeth for him after every meal? He hated the feel of furry teeth. 'They won't take kindly to being told what's what, no matter what your phone says.' She walked past Helen and out to the little console table in the hall, rooting around until she found Post-it notes, Sellotape, a thick black marker.

'They'll understand. We can't care for him the way he is.'

We haven't been caring for him at all, Annie wanted to say, but didn't. *Please brush Jack's teeth after each meal,* she wrote, then stuck the Post-it to the front of his washbag. She thought for a second, then added a smiley face before taping the whole thing securely to the fabric and placing it on the top of his overnight bag. Inside the lip of the bag, his name tag was perfectly legible, but she inked it neatly onto the tag of his pyjamas and onto the soles of the too-big slippers. Helen watched as she picked up Jack's phone, checked that the Find My Phone function was switched on and paired with her own, and put it in his bag with the portable charging pad. On second thought, she took the phone back out and taped another Post-it to the phone case, *Please keep me where Jack can reach me.* A smiley heart added this time, and back it went into the bag.

'Is it easier to deal with hospitals when you know the score? When you have the inside track, so to speak,' Helen asked suddenly.

Annie thought about her mother. The incidents, accidents, events, illnesses. The nights she slept – or didn't – on chairs beside trolleys on A & E corridors. The minimal information from harried staff. 'No,' she said. 'Who you are outside doesn't matter a damn. Once you're inside the hospital door, you have no jurisdiction. It's like watching someone else's child throw a tantrum – you can have opinions, but that's your limit.'

Helen nodded.

'They'll know everything from Dr Shields,' Annie said. 'If they refuse to let you in, ask to speak to Louise or Emer and explain that you're concerned about his level of communication. Tell them he has been struggling to eat—'

'You never told me that.'

'It's not exactly true. But if you tell them that he takes a long time to eat, then they might be more likely to let you stay so that you can do that bit of it. They're rushed off their feet and sometimes that sort of thing makes a difference.'

'It should hardly—'

Annie held up her hand. 'I know it shouldn't, Helen. Believe me, I know, but the reality is that it does. You can campaign all you like later on, but we have to work within it for now. If that doesn't work, ask if you can come back this evening, or at mealtimes. They might have some discretion, especially considering you had a negative PCR test a couple of days ago.'

'What if none of that works?'

Annie sighed. 'Then phone me and I'll come and bring you home.'

'Maybe it should be you that goes,' Helen said suddenly. 'Being his carer and everything, they would know that you can do all of those things.'

'It wouldn't matter,' Annie said. 'You're his family and you're here, so if anyone will be allowed in, it's you.'

Helen looked like she might say something, so Annie hurried on.

'It'll be family or no one, so please play nice and make sure you get in.'

'I'll get a bag together myself so, in case I'm there a while.'

'Louise or Emer,' Helen said to Annie, as she slid in the two small bags and climbed into the back of the ambulance after Jack.

Annie nodded and watched them down the avenue and out on to the road. She waited until Dr Shields had turned out on to the road behind them before going into the hall and pushing the button to close the gates.

The house was quiet after the commotion of stretchers and Velcro and the cheery chat designed to reassure and check whether or not Jack could follow instructions. He did the best he could and she had to stop herself from explaining what he was saying in reply. From explaining him.

It was only the second time she had been alone in the house. The other being Jack's stroke. *His first stroke*. Dr Shields knew her business and if she suspected another stroke this time, then odds were she was right.

While she waited for the kettle to boil – tea being the surest reflex – she reran the morning in her head, looking for anything unusual in Jack's speech or movement. Was there something in his behaviour she had missed? She made the tea and stood looking out at the birch bark cherry trees, stark and beautiful.

His right peripheral vision, Dr Shields had said. He was fine getting up. She would swear to that. Had he seemed startled when she walked into the living room and spoke before arriving in front of him? She didn't think so. Breakfast and lunch were normal, with the usual low-level issues with slackness on one side of his mouth. There was nothing different. She would have noticed if there was.

But there was something different: he was quiet. Too quiet. And she had noticed. Not right away, though, because she was distracted. Thinking about Helen. Angry with Helen. She was tired, too. Exhausted, even. 'You and everyone else, Annie,' she said into the empty kitchen. Who did she think she was, complaining when she had a job and a roof over her head and another roof if she chose to use it? She thought of Jack's face, his eyes closed against the lift of the stretcher into the back of the ambulance.

She poured the tea down the sink and went upstairs for no reason other than the ridiculous hope that the guilt and self-pity might stay behind in the kitchen.

She stopped on the central landing and turned to the left, towards what used to be Helen's parents' room. What Helen used to call 'the lair', with typical teenage melodrama. It was true Helen's mother spent a lot of time in the grip of a migraine or recovering from one – although rarely at weekends, Annie had noticed.

'That Lily Fitz is a delicate flower,' Annie had overheard her mother tell someone once, in that tone she used sometimes. She never used that tone around Helen, instead asking kindly how her mother was feeling.

Annie pushed open the bedroom door. It wasn't that the room was off limits to her – she dusted and hoovered it once a month – it was more that no part of her life overlapped with it.

Helen had brought her up here one afternoon, tiptoeing and putting her finger to her lips in cartoon-character exaggeration. She pushed open the door and pointed to the bed. Annie hadn't wanted to look. It felt wrong, somehow, like peeping on someone in the shower. But Helen beckoned again and pushed the door wider. Through the afternoon gloom, Annie could see Helen's mother lying on the bed with her hands clasped across her stomach. She could have been a corpse in a coffin, Annie thought, were it not for the floral eye mask and the bright yellow foam of her earplugs. Helen crossed to the bed and straightened the blanket so that it covered her mother's hands.

Afterwards, she grabbed Annie's arm, searching for complicity. 'She's ridiculous,' she said. 'I mean, really.'

Annie looked at her hand and thought of Helen tucking her mother in. 'My mother wears an eye mask and earplugs, too,' she said. 'She finds it hard to sleep without them.'

It was a lie. Annie's mother came home from work and, without fail, declared that she could sleep in a puddle of water, so exhausted was she. And indeed Annie sometimes found her asleep at the kitchen table, her dinner half-eaten, or in the bath, her fingers and toes shrivelled and frightening in cold water. A flash forward – of which Annie was mercifully ignorant at the time – to the raspy little half-woman-half-witch lingering in the bed, her memory as cleanly wiped as a baby's backside, looking at Annie with about as much affection as she would give a stranger or a dishcloth.

Annie had gone to Mrs Fitz's funeral, playing tag with a neighbour to come and sit with her own mother, with the result that she arrived late and missed paying her respects and had to stand at the back among the old men with their throat-clearing and their handkerchiefs balled in their pockets. She didn't see Helen or Jack, but queued at the lectern to sign the condolences book so they would know she had been. Assuming anyone read those things.

She had gone home to her own mother and wished with a savage, bitter tiredness for her to grab on to Lily Fitzgibbon's coat-tails – her shroud tails – and follow her into the ground. To see their mothers alive together was to marvel at God's range or, perhaps, to admit that no one entity could have dreamt up two such different specimens of womanhood. But this once, *just this once,* she cried inside her own head, they might share a purpose.

'Enough,' Annie said, clapping her hands in the empty room. 'Christ almighty. Enough.'

THREE FOR A GIRL

She should clean Jack's bedroom while she had the chance, Annie thought. Give it the kind of thorough deep-clean that was impossible in the little gaps in the everyday, where life was lived at a maintenance level. She hadn't pulled out the bed and hoovered behind it since the day it was delivered.

But Jack wouldn't be home tonight and a person could clean after dark as easily as in daytime. She would go for a walk instead. Take advantage of a rare hour to look around her in the afternoon light.

She hesitated in the hallway after putting on her coat. It would be appallingly sentimental to wrap herself in Jack's scarf, she knew, but there was nobody there to comment, so she went ahead and took it from its peg in the utility room and wound it around her neck, enjoying the comforting peppery smell of Tom Ford Noir.

She patted her pockets, double-checking she had her phone in case Helen rang, and locked the front door behind her.

The air was crisp and cold, her breath creating a stage entrance for her all the way down the avenue and out the side gate. She turned right, away from town, simply because she had gone left earlier. She would walk for thirty minutes, then turn around and come back.

The winter sun was high in the sky, the light winking bright, striping the road so that she could both see and not see. She thought of Jack losing his peripheral vision and what it might mean. Likely nothing, was the somewhat sad reality. It wasn't as though he drove any more, or read, or did anything that required significant hand-eye coordination. His hands had already given up their part of that equation, so perhaps his eyes following suit was not as devastating an outcome as it might have been twelve months ago. Annie held her gloved hands to her eyes, blocking all but the shaft of light and the road directly ahead. Like being a horse with blinkers. One of those poor buggers that takes tourists around the lakes of Killarney, with one bag under its nose and another under its arse. How awful the human race was, as a whole.

She dropped her hands and walked on, careful to cross the road to walk on the widest part of the bend. It wasn't something they taught children properly, that you walked on the right only when the road was straight; for bends, you walked on the outside edge. If a car were to come from behind her, would the driver see her, given the sun? She imagined it hitting her. The driver would claim – entirely legitimately – that they were blinded by the sun. The whole court – judge, jury, court registrar, legal teams, reporters and all – would be brought here to the side of the road for a reconstruction and asked to imagine what it would have been like. Some of them would shake their heads at the impossible task faced by the driver. Others would imagine what it was like to be Annie, and shiver.

She shivered herself at her own ridiculousness and stepped far into the ditch to check her phone for a call from Helen. Nothing. She could phone her, she supposed, but it was unlikely there were test results yet. She would wait until she got home and text then. A text seemed less pushy. More in keeping with the distance between them.

Three magpies rose from the body of the dead rabbit they were investigating, two flying left and one right, winking in and out of the light, appearing and disappearing.

'Three for a girl,' her mother used to say on the rare Sundays when her father and her brothers didn't have a match or training and they were all out for a spin on some quiet country road, their navy Datsun Sunny lifting and scattering magpies as they passed. Michael and John would twist themselves out windows to see if they could find another. 'Four for a boy! Four for a boy!' they would shout triumphantly and her mother would put her hand back through the gap to squeeze Annie's knee. 'We have enough boys.' And Annie would be delighted and guilty all at the same time.

She should phone her brothers. Instead of always claiming busyness or a constant round of appointments for Jack. Or blaming the pandemic, universal fall guy for every unpleasant task. A bit like perimenopause, or teething.

During that first long lockdown, she spoke to them over Zoom on alternate weeks. They were dividing up the task of talking to her, she knew. This tag-teaming was not an arrangement that happened by accident. She didn't mind. If she was honest, her parents' habit of grouping them together – *the boys* – had followed them all into adulthood.

There was little to say to either of them beyond the shop-worn sentences about the strangeness of it all, the quiet, that day's numbers. If Michael had been drinking, he might say he was glad Mam was dead before all this carry-on started. At least she got to have a funeral. Annie made non-committal noises, uncertain whether he was bringing up their mother's death as a means of introducing the topic of the house. With John, there was no doubt. The house loomed large over every conversation, or, more accurately, the money the house implied.

She imagined them sometimes, phoning each other when they had beer on board to talk about the house. About Annie and the house and when she would sell it and the fact that she should sell it, it was the right and proper thing to do seeing as she had lived there rent-free all her life. Were they to have nothing, was that it? She could hear these conversations as clearly as if they were happening on the screen in front of her. Instead, the screen would invariably flicker and freeze, whichever of her brothers was tasked with her coming and going from the screen, allowing them to lay their faulty connection at the feet of technology. Every week, she had closed her laptop and gone into the living room to find Jack had already placed a glass of wine beside her chair. They would sip companionably in front of the nine o'clock news while she tried not to think how much simpler it would all be if this was her real home instead of a temporary relocation for convenience. But it wasn't and it wouldn't ever be. Her home was where she had lived with and cared for her mother, at the expense of her own life and choices. If her brothers wanted it, they would have to come and take it from her. They had homes of their own – what did they need with hers?

When Jack no longer needed her, she would move back to that house of her childhood and try to make it feel like home again. Trust that, somehow, a coat of paint, a few bright throws, and upcycled shabby chic furniture could effect a transformation. According to Instagram, that was all it took. That and the right attitude. Well. There was a first time for everything.

She checked her phone again. Nothing. She turned and began to walk home, the wind cold in her face but the sun a warm backpack between her shoulder blades. It reminded her of giving Coraline piggybacks when she was younger and they all went to the St Patrick's Day parade together.

As if summoned, Laura's car appeared around the bend, Laura herself waving madly as if their meeting was some great coincidence.

'I was on my way over to you,' Laura called through the open window. 'Want a lift or are you walking something off?'

'Jack's gone into hospital,' Annie said. 'Dr Shields thinks he had another stroke this morning.'

'Ah shite. I'm sorry.'

Laura reached over and opened the passenger door and Annie climbed in and put on her seat belt.

'What happened?' Laura asked. Her whole body turned towards Annie, in that way she had of being fully present. It would have been more comforting had the car maintained a straight line instead of veering wildly towards the ditch.

'Watch the road,' Annie said. This was why she didn't usually get into the car with Laura. Why no one did unless they had to. She learned too late, Laura always claimed. The years of living in New York had ruined her for driving.

'How bad is it?' Laura asked.

'I don't know yet. Dr Shields thought there was some vision loss. The paramedics took him in for tests.'

'I can drive you there?' Laura offered.

'Helen is with him,' Annie explained.

'Ah. Helen. Our Lady of the Mysteries. No. Our Lady of the Disappearances. How's that going?'

'Sort of okay and sort of weird. We don't really know what to do with each other.'

Laura winced. 'Polite Helen is the worst.'

Annie shook her head. 'She's fine. It's not her fault she couldn't get here sooner. Not even Helen can tell a pandemic what to do.'

'So she's cranky?' Laura pulled the car up to the gates of the house and Annie got out of the car to tap in the code, which saved her replying. Laura had mentioned once, casually, that if Annie gave her the code, she could come and go to the garden without disturbing anyone. Annie let the comment go without answering. She didn't know how to say she felt weird about handing out all-access passes when it wasn't her house.

She motioned Laura in the gates and up to the house, closing the gates behind her and following on foot. By the time she got to the front door, Laura had gone around the back to the garden. Annie went in the front door and turned off the alarm, pushing the switch on the kettle before going into the living room and through the double doors into the garden, where Laura was standing with her hands on her hips, looking around her.

'Tea?' Annie said and Laura shook her head.

'Work first, tea after.'

'Okay,' Annie said. 'I'll be inside when you're ready.'

By the time Laura came in from the garden, enough light had faded from the sky that the back sensor lights had come on. Annie had cleaned Jack's rooms – his suite, he jokingly called it – from top to bottom, standing on a stepladder to wash the cornicing with a damp cloth, stripping the bed and remaking it with clean sheets, hoovering behind each piece of furniture and, finally, mopping the floor with strong bleach. Once that was done, she opened the windows a crack and lit a honeysuckle-and-sea-salt candle. It felt strange to close the door knowing there was no one in there, but the alternative – leaving it open only to be confronted by the empty bed every time she crossed the hall – was worse.

While Laura talked about pruning and mulching and whether it might be nearly time to give the nesting boxes a once-over before the season started, Annie loaded the washing machine and mmhmmmed at what seemed to be appropriate intervals.

'Tim is going to bring over an old log. I thought we'd put it down near the river.' She looked at Annie. 'Are you listening? Jack will want an update, you know.'

'I'm listening. An old log near the river to sit on.'

'Not for sitting. For hedgehogs. And mushrooms, if we're lucky.'

Laura's face was clear and open. Mushrooms on an old log really would make her happy, Annie realised. Beside her friend, she must look a decade older. Like she could have babysat Laura instead of sitting beside her in school.

'Has Helen called?'

Annie shook her head, busying herself with the kettle so that Laura wouldn't see how much that stung. 'I texted a while back but I haven't heard anything yet.'

'That's a bit shitty,' Laura observed, and Annie was tired, suddenly, at the memory of how it had been between them. So close, their little group of three, but never entirely without the insecurity, the snide comments, and Annie forever making peace.

'I was thinking,' she said instead. 'Jack might have spent his last night here at home.'

'Don't think the worst,' Laura said. 'Not before you have to. Another stroke doesn't mean he'll die.'

'I know that.' But he hadn't reached the magic six-month marker either, when the chances of him having a stroke were about the same as they had been before the first one. Annie could never decide if that was a comforting statistic or not. Surely those were not good odds, considering that he had actually had that first stroke. But she found it hard to articulate her argument and so when the community care team held it out to her – in the absence of anything more concrete – she accepted its dubious comfort. 'I meant we might have to consider nursing home care,' Annie said. 'He might need more support than he has right now.' More than one live-in carer who wasn't even family, and occasional respite, whenever those services fully reopened.

'Would Helen move home? Or take him to live with her?' Laura asked.

What is your obsession with Helen? Annie wanted to ask. *I'm talking about Jack.* But that wasn't fair. Laura's question was perfectly reasonable. Helen was his family, her choices were germane to the whole situation. 'I don't think moving country is exactly on the cards for him if he's had another stroke,' she said instead.

'I threaten my mother with the nursing home regularly,' Laura said. 'I miss your stories from there. Jack is a great man, but he's not much of a source of useful horror stories. We still talk about the woman who was FaceTiming her family and accidentally recorded her room-mate in the shower. Or the woman who kept putting pairs of her knickers into visitors' bags and accusing them of stealing.'

'It wasn't that bad,' Annie said. She should never tell Laura anything. 'Tell me, do they teach the kids at Coraline's school how to walk on a country road?' she asked, and let Laura be distracted by answering.

After Laura left, waving cheerily and calling that she would phone in the morning, Annie thought again about the reality of a nursing home for Jack. The care would be exactly that – care. All the rest of it – his audiobooks and crosswords and soaps and music shows and taking his time choosing his clothes and his daily shave – would be promised and intended but often not delivered. She had seen the reality of that for herself. No matter how strong the intention, there were only so many hours in the working day.

True, she hadn't been in the frame of mind for the place when she was there, and she could say, hand on heart, that everyone did their best. The problem was that their best was judged at the level of the worker, not the patient. The client, as they were encouraged to call them. Since money was changing hands, she supposed. 'Client' made it all sound nice and clean and transactional. The patient, as she thought of them always, with all the due care and attention that word demanded. Old and lonely could be diagnoses, too, even if the care system wasn't set up to recognise them. For all the focus on mental health among the young, the emotional needs of the elderly – that ugly, distancing word – were ignored as simply a function of age. People had a strange idea of dignity. She thought of her mother in those final months and weeks. Dressed in her own clothes, no name tapes or notes. Fed whatever titbits of food she felt like eating, no matter the time of the day or night.

After the initial diagnosis, her mother received a landslide of messages from friends and neighbours and acquaintances offering help and support and company, few of which ever materialised. The kitchen calendar filling up with those friends' names written in shaky black biro, then, underneath, in shaky red biro, the reason for their late cancellation. Ill or away or unexpected family visit. The ones that came took Annie aside and whispered about how difficult they found it, how they wanted to remember her mother the way she had been. Annie wanted to scream at their luxury. As if her mother hadn't seen them through cancers and separations and bereavements or simply their phases of being an asshole or a bad friend. When people show you who they are, believe them, she thought savagely.

Father Dolan was the one visitor who reliably kept coming. Twice a week, rain, hail or shine, there he was with his squeaky shoes and his dandruff and his sweet tooth, keeping her mother up to date with the parish news without ever expecting her to hold on to any of it. He never made it look like work either.

She would continue care work in people's own homes, once Jack no longer needed her, Annie thought. No more living-in, though. That was a one-off. For Jack. For this house. For Helen and the past and the girls they used to be.

She was draining the pasta water into a basin to pour on the few small weeds peeping up around the flagstones on the patio – she and Jack had promised Laura they would forego conventional weedkiller – when the phone rang and she nearly scalded herself in her haste to snatch it up.

'Helen.'

'He had a stroke alright. They got the test results back a little while ago. They're keeping him in and they'll run more tests tomorrow.'

'Do you want me to come and get you?'

'They're going to let me in to see him shortly for a few minutes and I'll come home then.'

'Do you need anything?' She thought of the pasta in the kitchen. She could easily make another pot. 'I'll keep dinner for you when you get back. In the meantime, tell Jack …'

But before she could think of what she wanted to tell him, Helen was gone.

IT WAS A HOMECOMING, AFTER ALL

Laura was nearly home when she had second thoughts. A quick U-turn and ten minutes later she was double-parked on the main street with her flashers on and running in the door to Susan.

'What have you that's warming and robust?'

'Veggie or for Kitty?' Susan was well versed in the meat wars in Laura's house.

'One of each, please. I want to run something over to Annie. Jack's gone back into hospital this afternoon and you know Annie, she'll have done everything except mind herself.'

'God love them,' Susan blessed herself quickly, leaving a thumbprint of relish on her smock. 'I have a leek and mustard quiche?'

'I was thinking hearty rather than damp. There's snow in the air,' she added quickly.

Susan snorted. 'Snow up the country alright. Anyway, it's your loss. The quiche is divine, even if I do say so myself. What about a chorizo and bean soup? I have spicy cauliflower as well if you fancy one for yourself?'

'Lovely. I'll take one of each and a couple of your vegan rolls.'

'I heard Helen was back, but I didn't hear she was gone vegan,' Susan said with interest.

Oh shit. Helen had been out of sight out of mind for so many years, she had forgotten to include her. Laura sighed. 'You'd better make that two cauliflower soups. And another vegan roll as well.'

That should cover whatever it was Helen ate these days. Assuming she ate anything at all. She had always been one for watching her calories. Even in the deepest winter of their schooldays, Helen would pull out two small yogurts for her lunch, the whole thing so cold she had to warm the spoon on the radiator before putting it near her mouth.

'I'll take half a dozen raspberry and white chocolate cookies as well,' she said. Helen always had a weakness for white chocolate and it was a homecoming, after all. They would give things an air of festivity.

'There you go.' Susan handed over the paper bag. 'That'll sweeten you.'

They might well need it.

Laura wound down her window to press the buzzer at the gate of Glebe Cottage. The sun was low in the sky and the wind suddenly meant business. After buzzing, she waved at the camera and closed the window quickly. Nothing happened. She wound down the window and buzzed again. Still nothing. She picked up her phone and texted Annie. *At the gate. Will you buzz me in?* She had mentioned several times to Annie that it would be handier if she had the gate code and could come and go according to the garden's needs, without depending on Annie or Jack being there to let her in. 'We're nearly always here,' was all Annie said.

She guarded the house as closely as if it were hers. Even as teenagers, Laura would see Annie trailing her fingers along the edge of the dining room table on the way to the garden, or tucking her legs up under her on the green sofa, as though to have as much of her skin as possible touching it. Laura had been in Annie's house and could understand why she liked bright, beautiful things. Even now, despite living here, Annie hadn't taken on proprietary airs, but persisted in treating the house with a strange kind of awe.

After a few minutes, her phone buzzed. *Sorry!* And the gates opened to let her through.

Annie was in a dressing gown at the door, her hair a pile of suds on her head.

'I thought you mightn't feel like cooking,' Laura said, waggling the paper bag of food.

'You're a dolly.' Annie half hugged her around the bag. 'Sorry. I was in the shower when I heard the phone. Stay for a bite? Just give me five minutes to rinse.'

Annie disappeared upstairs and Laura went through into the kitchen. She poured the soups into two small saucepans and put them on the hob to warm, then popped the rolls into the microwave. Much as she disliked the contraptions, heating a full oven would be a waste.

'Hello?'

Helen's voice. Less certain now than it used to be. Laura straightened up from the press, where she was looking for a splash guard for the microwave.

'Helen. Hello. I'm sorry, I ...' She gestured vaguely around the kitchen. *Do not say you were making yourself at home.* 'I'm sorry to hear about Jack. I thought it would help if An ... if you didn't have to cook this evening. Hospitals are tiring.' *Stop babbling.*

'I wondered whose car was outside.'

That was not a question, Laura. Do not say your name! 'Annie will be down in a minute. She was cold through after her walk so she's having a shower.'

'It's far too cold to walk,' Helen said automatically.

'You know what Annie's like. Has to walk every day or she's like a cat on a griddle.'

As soon as the words left her mouth, Laura wanted to snatch them back. Who was she to discuss Annie's mental health with Helen, who was, to all intents and purposes, a stranger to them?

'Don't tell her I said that,' she added.

Helen gave a little smile, which only made things worse. Now they were complicit in talking about Annie behind her back. Jesus. She remembered reading that the human response to danger – fight, flight, freeze – had been updated. Psychologists or sociologists or whatever-ists decided these things had added a fourth: fight, flight, freeze, *fawn*.

Bloody Helen.

'It's nice to see you, Laura. You've hardly changed at all,' Helen said.

'Plenty wrinkles on the inside,' Laura said automatically.

Helen gave a small smile. 'That smells wonderful. I didn't get a chance to eat at the hospital.'

'It's good you were able to be there with him.'

'I'm not sure I was any help,' Helen said. 'Annie would be the better person to have, but he had to make do with me.'

Still the same Helen, always comparing and waiting for someone to rush in and tell her she was great, she was the best, they were lucky to have her. If that was what she was waiting for, let her wait.

'Your family didn't come back with you?' Laura said. Should she have said 'home' instead of 'back'? It seemed the sort of thing that might cause offence to someone looking for it.

'It felt like too big a risk. The children escaped Covid so far and …' Helen shrugged. 'You never know who's going to be the statistic.'

Laura nodded. 'That's the fear, isn't it?'

'You have a daughter now, too, right?'

She'd had a daughter for quite a while, Laura wanted to say, but swallowed it. 'Coraline. She's nine. Around the same age as your boys, I think?' Knowing full well that Helen's boys were ten and eleven and her daughter was fourteen.

'Rex is eleven and Ruan is ten. It's a funny age. They get so independent and hands-off.'

'It depends on Cor's mood, I find. Maybe it's because girls are closer to us, don't you think?'

Helen looked past her. 'Oh, wow! Look at that sky!'

Oh, sure. Look! A squirrel! Laura turned back to the window to see the sky had turned the dull angry yellow of a pimple about to burst. As they watched, the first flakes started to swirl, giving the air a curdled look.

'Snow,' Laura said. 'After all.'

They stood in silence and watched as the flakes perched lightly on grass and stone, as if deciding whether or not to stay.

'Your mother always loved her garden in the snow,' Laura said.

'I remember,' Helen said.

For a second, the past shimmered between them, until the buzz of Helen's phone on the table sent the memories slipping back between the floor tiles.

'Excuse me. I need to take this,' Helen said, pulling the kitchen door closed behind her as she went out into the hall.

Helen's voice was modulated. In fact, everything about her seemed to murmur control, from her neat trousers and trainers to her pinned-back hair. If she were to turn her upside down and shake her, Laura thought, her internal organs would fall out in alphabetical order.

It was next to impossible not to eavesdrop on someone's conversation in a quiet house. Worse than sitting outside the classroom door at parent-teacher meetings and trying not to hear someone else's praise or excuses, or waiting at a bus stop beside a living room window and hearing a married couple argue with weary, vicious precision.

Laura unlocked the back door and stepped into the garden. Outside, the snow was a delicate cover that rendered the landscape strange and yet familiar, a feeling reminiscent of putting on make-up and then looking in the mirror. She didn't wear make-up any more. Sure, most claimed to have stopped animal testing, but acceptance of that statement required a trust in an industry that was literally founded on the creation of pretty artifice. Still, the feeling of being your most appealing self was hard to relinquish entirely.

Usually, she looked at the garden and saw what needed

to be done. Or, increasingly, what needed to be undone. The years of careful control and symmetry that could be unwound into something looser and more beautiful. Some wild planting. A flagstone path through a joyful, riotous lawn. Wildflower turf along the edges, and the clover left to call the bees. All the plans she and Jack had discussed for the coming spring. He had been so enthusiastic when she laid it all out. 'Lily would have loved this,' he said often. 'A whole transformation project.'

Laura couldn't imagine that Mrs Fitz, with her desire for order and quiet, would have been quite so committed. It was funny, nearly, how the living persisted in aligning the passions of the dead with their own. Her mother was the same: 'Your father would have been ...' variously proud, disappointed, surprised, depending on what it was Laura had done and – more crucially – what Kit herself thought of it. How desperate they all were for approval that they sought it even from the dead.

If Jack wanted to think that his wife would have taken pleasure in seeing her careful garden turned over to nature, let him. Who was Laura to say different?

After the stroke, Laura was careful to continue to tell him what she planned. Hoping that come the summer he could sit and enjoy the new life the garden brought. She should get mealworms, she decided. They were expensive, but they kept the robins happy. She didn't know whether or not Jack was one of those who looked at robins with their head tilts and their faintly melancholy song and saw the souls of the dead come back to visit, but even if he didn't, robins were joy enough in themselves. A rare uncomplicated joy.

The first time Laura saw this garden – the very first day she ever spoke to Helen and Annie – her immediate thought was *This is greener than anywhere*. The trees that marked the boundary on three sides were tall and broad, full-leaved as flowers in a vase, while the garden itself had – if not quite a maze – then some sort of curved spiral hedge that cut the space in two like the yin-yang symbol that half the girls in school wore on long silver chains around their necks. A bronze sundial on the left seemed to catch the sun and toss it in the windows of the house, while halfway down the right-hand side an old enamel bath seemed to have grown out of the ground, with green tendrils frothing over the sides. *A green-fingered woman clawing her way out*, Laura thought and was glad they were too old for hide-and-seek.

'Come on.' Helen led them down to the bottom of the garden, where she unfolded a blanket on the bank of the little river.

Laura sat at the edge of the blanket and accepted the biscuit Helen offered. Without the scaffolding of school and the classroom and even the other girls, she wasn't sure what was expected of her.

Annie opened her school bag and took out her history textbook.

'Are you actually doing homework?' Helen poked Annie with her foot.

'I've missed a full week,' Annie said. 'I need to at least try and catch up.'

'I missed a full week, too,' Helen said.

'Not the same,' Annie said flatly.

'How is it not the same?' Helen said. 'Same classes, same homework. Same, same, same.'

Annie glanced at Laura. Did that mean she was supposed to explain or was it silent sympathy Annie was after?

'The … um … emotion is different,' she said at last. The words came out awkwardly.

Helen looked at her, her eyes narrowed against sun or opinion. 'Of course it is,' she said.

They each took out their books and worked on their own. Every so often, Laura could feel Helen looking at her but pretended she didn't. Between the looking and the worry about what interpretation of parental loss she might be asked to provide next, she didn't get a jot of work done.

When she got home later that evening and looked at her notes, all she saw was random sentences copied out of random books, the words sailing high up off the lines and bouncing back down as if written on a moving vehicle. That was the feeling Helen inspired, the impression that the ground beneath you was moving and you had better watch where you put your feet.

She didn't expect the invite to be extended again. Whatever purpose she served for Annie on that first day back, she assumed was fulfilled. Yet, the following day, Annie slipped into the empty seat at Laura's desk, Helen joined them before school and at breaks, and spoke to Laura about whatever came to mind, as though her opinion on other things – music, movies, the wisdom of fake tan versus tights now that it was getting warmer – mattered as much as anyone's.

'You coming back to mine?' Helen asked, when the last bell rang and Laura was packing books into her bag.

Laura looked at Annie, then nodded.

And that was all it took.

They spent evenings together after school, went to town or to the cinema at weekends, exchanged notes and tops and books.

It was nearly always the three of them. Laura worried initially that Helen and Annie, their friendship long-established, were meeting up or talking on the phone without her. That twos would creep in. That was how Laura thought of it, as though twos were lurking, waiting to pounce the moment one of them was out sick or had a dental appointment or – in Helen's case – flew back from a mid-term trip to London too late to make it to school the following day. *A triangle is the strongest shape,* Mrs Connolly had said in maths class once, *because each side carries equal weight.*

'Sorry about that,' Helen called and Laura turned to see her standing in the doorway.

'We spent so much time out here,' Laura said.

Helen pulled the door closed and came out to stand beside

her. 'Our feet used to turn white and shrivelled from being in the river water.'

'Or so we assumed. Who knows what was in there.'

Helen gave a delicate little shudder.

The snow began to come down in earnest. It reminded Laura of being on a plane, when the runway came into view and the descent turned suddenly into a clear intent to return to ground.

'I should go,' she said. 'I need to collect Coraline before things get too bad.'

'Give Annie another minute. I heard the hairdryer while I was on the phone, so she will be down shortly.'

Helen didn't like to be alone. The knowledge came to Laura fully formed, like all her childhood memories were suddenly run through an adult filter. How had she never seen it back then? Helen had incorporated Laura into her life because she was afraid Annie would be needed more at home and thus be less available to her. Wasn't it funny how something that would have been life-changing information at one point in a life could have all the teeth taken out of it by nothing more dramatic than the slow passage of time?

She put on her coat and turned back to Helen. 'Tell Annie I'll give her a call later. If I don't see you again before you head home, take care.'

Should she say what she really wanted to say? They were all adults.

'You don't need to worry about Jack, you know,' she said. 'He's in good hands with Annie. The two of them together are something special.'

She didn't look back at Helen, simply held her hand up over her shoulder in a universal goodbye before walking quickly to her car.

The whole honest-goodbye thing became infinitely more embarrassing when Laura's car refused to start. Over and over she tried, only to hear the engine cough and die.

'Come on. Once more. Please.' She patted the steering wheel before trying again. But that wasn't the first time she had made that particular request and her car, it seemed, was all out of second or fifth or twelfth chances.

Through the thickly falling snow, she saw Annie appear at the passenger window. 'Battery again or worse?' she called.

'Your guess is as good as mine.'

'I'll drop you home.'

In Annie's car, they slid badly, once, twice, before they even reached the gate.

'The snow is freezing as fast as it lands,' Annie said, straightening the car and inching forward.

Laura looked at the tight white of her knuckles on the steering wheel. 'You don't need to drive me.'

'Thank Christ. I'd offer you the car but I don't think you should be driving in this either. Come on back inside and we'll figure something out.'

Helen came out to meet them in the hall. 'The roads are freezing hard,' Annie told her.

'I'll phone Tim from the community garden,' Laura said, 'His jeep might—'

But Helen was shaking her head. 'You don't want to drag anyone else out in this. Why don't you stay? There's plenty of room. And Coraline is with your mum, right?'

On the third try, her mother answered, a wheeze in her voice. 'Sorry, sorry. I couldn't press the button with my gloves on and I had to take one off and then you were gone—'

'Where's Coraline, Mam?'

'She's here with me. We're just in the door. I don't mind telling you, but we got a desperate skid. I had to leave the car at the bottom of the hill and we walked up. You'll have to get Tim or one of the lads to drop you home.'

'I'm out at Jack's and the road here is bad.' Laura heard the tears in her voice and swallowed. 'That's why I was phoning.'

'Cor is here with me anyway, safe and sound,' her mother said. 'Everything else can be sorted out. It's an act of God, what can you do? There'll be no school tomorrow, I'd say. Here, I'll let her tell you herself. She's up to high doh.'

Laura closed her eyes and listened to the excited chatter of her daughter. She thought of her mother's hands on the steering wheel as the car fishtailed under her. Thought of her holding Coraline's hand tight enough to quell the tremor as they navigated the icy road up the hill to the house. Thought of her climbing the stairs to put Coraline to bed. Three steps, then a pause, her hand on the banister. Three more. Reaching the top as Coraline came out of the bathroom, her face soap-shiny and her teeth bared for inspection. Asking Coraline to read to her instead of the other way around. A thousand tiny accommodations.

'Coraline is very jealous at the idea that I'm having a sleepover,' she said, returning to the living room, where Helen and Annie were pretending not to be waiting. 'And according to my mother, the snow is an Act of God.'

'Like old times,' Annie said, smiling.

'Let's open a bottle of wine,' Helen declared. 'It's not like we'll be driving anywhere before tomorrow.'

'I had my first drink in this house,' Laura said, when Annie had disappeared to the kitchen to find a bottle of wine.

'We all did,' Helen said. 'That awful brandy my parents brought back from somewhere.'

'How did we get away with it?'

'Free-range parenting. Isn't that what they call benign neglect these days?' Helen said, swirling the wine in her glass, her voice light.

'If your definition of good parenting is keeping your children away from alcohol until adulthood, life might be about to get a whole lot more upsetting,' Laura said. 'Your eldest is fourteen, isn't she?'

'Réiltín.'

'Pretty name.'

'Nightmare for living outside Ireland. But that's not a criterion in the moment, is it?'

'Coraline is no picnic either,' Laura said. 'Several relatives still call her Caroline. At this stage, she just answers to it.'

'She sounds like a good kid.'

'She is.'

Laura waited for the inevitable question about Coraline's father. Who he was, where he was, what he meant to her. That it didn't come annoyed her exactly as much as the question itself would have. The Helen of long ago would have poked and pried and demanded to know and Laura could no longer tell whether this adult Helen was simply more polite or less interested.

'Do you ever worry that there's a tipping point in that good-kid-bad-kid spectrum and you've already done whatever it is will tip it in the wrong direction and you're completely unaware?' Helen asked.

Laura thought again of Coraline, warm and snuggly and happy to walk to school hand in hand with her GranKit. 'Honestly, no.'

'Me neither,' Helen said immediately.

Their eyes met and they both started to laugh.

'So literally every mood and moment is imbued with this huge make-or-break significance?' Laura said, finally. 'How are you not exhausted?'

'It's a miracle,' Helen said.

There was a complicity in drinking in the waning light, with the snow coming down fast and intentional. Wine did the work of loosening their tongues and Laura wondered – again – if alcoholics were merely introverts, or, rather, pseudo-extroverts, whose range and tolerance had a liquid extension. One glass in and she lost the feeling that all the words between them were already used up.

People did this all the time, didn't they? At school reunions and nights away and all sorts of situations where new lives were made to fit into the shape of the old in the name of nostalgia or memory or a sort of social embarrassment.

As long as nobody said it out loud or in any way drew attention to all the water under the bridge – ice now, she thought, and suppressed a boozy giggle – they could get through a night.

WHAT WE WANT TO HEAR

Laura gathered an armful of logs before the path to the shed became too icy to use. Helen and Annie both offered to help, but in the half-hearted way that signalled their distrust of going outside in anything resembling real weather. Helen, Laura remembered, used to claim she was evolved from a dormouse and her brain didn't wake properly until after Easter. Her chocolate alarm clock, they used to call it. It was funny how intimacy worked, the small things on which it was based. Humans were conditioned to create relationships even on the slimmest of pickings. Like that old saw about getting someone to like you by asking them to do you a favour. Old but, as it turned out, surprisingly effective.

She stacked the logs in the log rack in the living room. It was starting to get properly cold, so she laid a fire in the stove, opening the grate to create a breeze to get it going. The draught through even that tiny gap made her shiver. She reached in her pocket for her phone.

Maybe turn up the thermostat for the evening, she texted her mother. *And don't forget to leave the kitchen tap running overnight so the pipes don't freeze.*

Mam is typing. Mam is typing.

WHO DO U THINK THOUGHT YOU THAT TRICK?

Mam is typing. Mam is typing. Mam is typing.

TAUGHT.

Laura snorted. Her mother would be fine. She considered the fire and piled on another two logs. Easy to be *flaithiúlach* when someone else was paying for the wood. To compensate, she closed the living room door. A person didn't grow up in Kitty O'Brien's house without learning how to conserve heat.

In the kitchen, Helen was phoning the hospital. Laura raised her hands in apology and turned to leave, but Helen beckoned her in.

Laura annoyed herself by complying. That was typical Helen. She always liked an audience for her life. Nothing happened unless it happened to Helen and in full view of other people. How many evenings had she spent sitting on the floor, while Helen talked to some boy or other on the phone, pulling the long cord of the phone from the hallway into the living room so they could all listen and laugh? When Helen got bored, she would hand the phone to Annie or Laura, who would have to do an impersonation of Helen, giggling and sighing until Helen bored of the whole enterprise and hung up.

Laura worried, always, that Helen would one day drop her as easily as she had picked her up. When Annie was over the death of her father and Laura was no longer necessary. When Laura's novelty value – such as it was – wore off. When other new people joined their class. Time wore on and it never happened, yet Laura felt herself in a perpetual state of wanting to please, in case she hastened the day when she no longer found favour.

'Go on,' her mother said, the day Helen called Laura to go shopping with her for her debs' ball dress, even though Laura already had hers. 'Answer your summons,' and Laura couldn't take offence when it was suddenly, horribly clear that her mother was entirely accurate.

All these years later and the memory still had the power to light her up like a beacon of shame. How eager she was to be the bystander in someone else's life! As an adult, of course, she learned that nobody had any power over her except what she gave them, but as a teenager she held every shred of her identity out in front of her for Helen to take what she wanted, like a bucket of Halloween sweets and she the willing gobshite standing in the doorway of her own dignity.

She raised her eyebrows at Annie, who was cradling her half-full glass of wine.

Annie shook her head. 'On hold for the ward.'

They listened while Helen waited, spoke to someone, waited, spoke again, waited again. Then, finally, she got hold of the doctor overseeing Jack's care and asked a series of strangely halting questions.

She wasn't looking for an audience at all, Laura realised. She was afraid. The years had knocked as much out of her as everyone else.

'They're observing him,' she said, hanging up. 'No matter how I tried to come around it, that was really all he would say.'

'If it was bad, they would have to tell you,' Laura said, made gentle by the idea of Helen afraid.

'Do you want to phone Dr Shields?' Annie suggested.

'Will you phone her?' Helen asked. 'She might be more likely to tell you anything there is to tell.'

Annie nodded and rose, taking her phone out of her pocket.

'Will you stay so I can hear too?' Helen asked, and Annie nodded.

Listening to Annie talk to Dr Shields, Laura needed no reminder about the depth of feeling in Annie and Jack's relationship. She had teased Annie at first, gleefully, when Annie told her they met occasionally for coffee. Annie smiled dutifully, patiently, as though Laura were a child, and Laura felt foolish and old-fashioned for reducing friendship to tired old metrics of age and gender. She worried that coming home might have turned her into a 1980s person, the sort who said 'ooh, how modern' at anything out of the ordinary. But she was worrying unnecessarily, it turned out. When she started coming to do the garden, she, too, found Jack great company. Interested and interesting, funny and charming. Poor Jack, she thought suddenly. Back in the bloody hospital he hated.

'Observation is the best we can hope for,' Annie said, when she was finished speaking on the phone. 'Sudden change is the enemy, it seems. Stable and under observation is what we want to hear.'

Laura admired her friend's composure. The way she presented the information to Helen in such a way that it appeared new to Annie herself as well, although it was surely the bread and butter of her training.

Helen nodded her thanks and reached for the bottle of wine to top up their glasses. Her hand shook slightly, Laura noticed and wondered whether to pretend she hadn't seen. This was what happened when friendships withered: you were stuck in a weird limbo between the closeness of the past and the politeness of strangers. Alcohol – and sympathy – were, as ever, the perfect rotten-wood bridge.

She covered Helen's hand with her own. Annie reached out and took the other. 'He's in the right place,' they said.

The making of those phone calls to hospital and to Dr Shields publicly seemed to break some sort of privacy wall between the women, so that when Helen's phone rang, she answered and remained at the table where they were all sitting. It was her husband, Laura gathered, as Helen explained what had happened with Jack, then reassured her husband that she wasn't alone, that Annie and Laura were with her. She didn't have to explain who they were, Laura noticed.

When Helen moved into a list of questions and instructions about which of the children was to do what and when, Laura glanced at Annie to see what she made of their sudden unasked-for invitation into this domestic intimacy, but Annie, as usual, gave nothing away. She sat with her shoulders relaxed, not moving except for the tip of one finger circling the base of her half-full wine glass. She had never been a big drinker. Even at parties they attended in school, Annie was never drunk, never out of control, never the one with her hair held back, streaming vomit and confidences. Never the one whose period was a week late. Never the one slipping into the back of the church to pin a scrap of paper to the noticeboard asking people to pray for a 'special intention'. Annie told her once that she figured out early that, at a certain point, the fun of alcohol couldn't hold a candle to the messy reality of it.

Helen had switched to a FaceTime call with her children. Réiltín, Rex and Ruan. Sweet suffering Jesus. Mind you, there were days she took a breath before introducing Coraline, but then she reminded herself that it fit with who she was when she had her daughter. Coraline meant 'from coral', evoking fragility and beauty, which, to postnatal Laura, seemed to summarise herself and her daughter perfectly. Her tiny girl with her shell-like perfection, and Laura's own shakiness and uncertainty. Was it so hard to be generous, to assume Helen wanted to connect her family in all the ways possible, including tying them to one another with the letter R? Or maybe she just wanted a reminder of the sound of home. To call out for her children in a sea of Jeans and Lucs and Marcs. Laura knew well the pride in being asked where she was from and gaining the almost universal favour associated with the answer *Ireland.*

Helen's phone call with her children was so clearly a disaster that to leave would draw neon attention to the fact they had noticed. Instead, Laura and Annie began a low chat of their own, so small they might as well have been humming at one another. It reminded Laura of seeing an ex on a night out and having, immediately, to look as though deep in intimate conversation with whoever was closest, even if she was only whisper-shouting about the price of drinks or the queue for the toilets.

It was no use. All the gentle murmuring couldn't drown out the sound of Helen asking questions and getting nothing but giggles and pulled faces in response. Or the sound of her bright, strained voice asking her daughter to *please answer, darling, when I ask about your day. I miss you all, you know.*

Jesus. It was worse than listening to people having sex, Laura thought. Surely there was something else they could do instead of sitting here like two pensioners on a bus tour.

'What about dinner?' she practically shouted at Annie, who, startled, sloshed the wine out of her glass and onto the table. It was a welcome distraction to stand, to search for a cloth, to rinse the cloth under the tap and wipe the table clean, tutting all the while at her own clumsiness, the light buzz of chiding herself drowning out – finally – Helen's unbearable brightness.

'We were starting to think about dinner,' Annie said, when Helen hung up the phone. 'What do you fancy?'

Again, Laura was struck by Annie's gentle deference and deflection. Was that the product of years of conditioning from their earlier friendship, or simply a reflection of her training and experience?

Wherever it came from was immaterial, as it didn't work. Helen burst into tears. 'I'm mortified you had to hear that.'

They didn't have to hear it, actually, Laura wanted to say. Helen could have taken the call in private. But what good was there in saying so?

'They don't need me,' Helen was saying. Her tears hadn't lasted and her voice was steady and sure. 'Nobody needs me.'

'I'm sure that's not true,' Annie said. 'They probably think you have enough to deal with here and don't want to worry you.'

Helen's laugh was bitter. 'They don't think about me at all. Ré barely looks up from her phone any more.'

'You're probably right,' Laura said. She ignored Annie's warning look and continued. 'Not because of you or anything you did. They're children. They're built to think about themselves and nothing else. If they thought of their parents as real people with actual problems, the fear would cripple them. It's as much as they can do to keep a lid on their own needs.'

'Do you think so?'

Laura nodded firmly. 'Every teenager is self-centred.

That's the whole point of those years, to get all the horribleness out so that you grow into a decent human being. It's a shame, really, that a lot of the people who put up with you during that process are often not around to reap the benefits of the gentler, kinder, more evolved adult.' She turned to Annie. 'You were the exception, of course. You were the model teen daughter.'

Annie smiled. 'I spent all my time here. My mother and I didn't see each other enough to argue.'

Too late, Laura remembered Annie in the early days after her father's death. Her thin white face. Her jeans that showed her ankles long before that was the fashion. Her lunchbox with its limp sandwich, in stark contrast to Laura's own lunch, bursting with colour and flavour and made by her mother each night when she made her own to eat in the staffroom the following day. Hers and her mother's lunch, side by side on the worktop. The two Tupperware boxes, water bottles, an apple or a pear, and two chocolate digestives wrapped in foil. The thought of that foil preserved somewhere in landfill, waiting for the end of days, was a wince amid the fondness.

'What were we even doing at Réiltín's age?' Laura said. 'I seem to remember a lot of hanging around waiting for life to get interesting.' She was relieved to see Helen smile.

'There were a lot of videos too,' Annie added.

'You're right! We used to spend entire weekends holed up in Helen's room watching whatever Xtra-vision had available. That must be unimaginable to kids today.'

'Having to wait forever while the tape rewound,' Annie remembered.

'Be kind. Rewind,' Helen said, and they all laughed.

'How many times did we rent *Robin Hood, Prince of Thieves*?' Laura asked.

'*The Bodyguard*,' Helen added. 'And *Point Break*.'

'*My Cousin Vinny*,' Annie chimed in. 'Oh, and *Sneakers*.'

'Robert Redford,' Laura said. She put on a high breathy voice. 'I love the word "passport".'

'We watched that so often we ruined the tape,' Helen remembered.

'See? Spending weekends watching a screen doesn't do any real harm.' Laura gave Helen a gentle nudge.

'We were together, though. It was social.' Helen's smile faded.

'Some of that must be social, right?' Annie asked. 'Chatting with friends even if it's in a different way than we're used to?'

'If that were true, there wouldn't have been such a fuss during lockdown about the mental health impacts of losing all their social outlets.' Helen's air quotes looked defeated.

It was hard to argue with that and neither Laura nor Annie tried.

'Poor Coraline didn't have the chance to miss a single day of school,' Laura said drily. 'My mother had her at the table keeping the school timetable. I think she kind of liked it actually. My mother, I mean, not Cor. I got away with murder – I did culture afternoons with her, which was basically us watching TV or doing the occasional virtual museum tour.'

'How lucky to have your mum there and not have to be trapped in homeschooling hell,' Helen said. 'Between work and the boys, I didn't know whether I was coming or going. Réiltín seemed as miserable as everyone else, but ...' She flushed. 'Getting her to go back is proving tricky.'

'Want me to ask my mother for her tips or tricks for school refusal?' Laura asked. 'Since she retired, she has nowhere to put her advice except on me and Cor and we're experts in nodding and ignoring her.'

'I don't know that I'd go so far as to call it refusal,' Helen said. 'That sounds a bit ... excessive.'

'How long since she's gone in?' Laura asked.

'She still goes,' Helen said, then her shoulders sagged a little. 'Just not every day.'

How many days, Laura wanted to ask, but Helen wasn't quite meeting her eye.

'I'll ask my mum to give you a call, shall I? You needn't answer if you don't want to. I won't judge.'

'Is Coraline like you?' Helen asked instead.

'She isn't like anyone,' Laura said cheerfully. 'Sometimes I think she must be like my dad, but my mother won't be drawn on it. You know what she's like.'

Annie and Helen both nodded and Laura felt an unexpected surge of gratitude for their history, their shorthand. Sure, over the years, she had told other people bits and pieces about her childhood, but these women were the only two to whom she didn't need to describe what it was like growing up with her mother's grief and rigidity. The blush that came to feel permanent as students goose-stepped around her in imitation of her mother's strictness. The eggs she had to wash off their front wall the day after Halloween. The impossibility – learned early – of inviting anyone over and the enormous relief of becoming friends with Helen, whose house was always open to them.

It was hard enough to stand out because of her single-parent home, the circumstances of her father's early death, without the added weirdness of being 'Briny's' daughter. *Get over it, would you?* Helen used to say, rolling her eyes at the culprit and drawing Laura away.

'I can't imagine Mrs O'Brien enjoying retirement,' Helen said thoughtfully.

'Oh, retirement.' Laura waved her hand airily. 'She gives grinds and works as an invigilator for the summer exams. And she's a godsend with Coraline while I'm at work.'

'Do you … garden full-time?' Helen asked.

Laura wondered if she knew that her nose wrinkled slightly at the word.

'No, I don't garden full-time,' Laura said, unable to resist wrinkling her own nose back at Helen. 'I do the garden here for Jack and the community garden in town as well.' She began to tick things off her fingers. 'Then I do two mornings a week at Second Life. The charity shop,' she added. 'Then there's two afternoons a week in the senior centre and I try to get into the hospital as part of their reading programme, but of course Covid has put paid to that for the moment.'

'My goodness. What a nightmare for tax returns!' Helen said.

Of course that would be where her mind went. Ever the conventional worker bee. 'Actually it's all voluntary,' Laura said.

She could see Helen struggling against the desire to ask and took pity on her.

'Social welfare. Before all this' – she waved her hand in the universal pre-Covid symbol – 'I worked in The Half-Pint from seven to closing, Wednesday to Sunday. When it shut, I went on the pandemic unemployment payment. It's reopened now, but the hours are irregular, so Matty and Mary can manage by themselves for the moment.'

She watched Helen try to maintain a neutral expression. *Bar work!* She could nearly see the thought bubble, cartoon-like, above her head.

The one thing she learned from the pandemic was that people were more than capable of feeding themselves drink at home. They didn't need her for that. The bar was supposed to be social, but, somehow, when she was at the community garden, there was as much socialising with the starlings and the one cheeky wren and the foxes and the crows. All so chatty and awkward. She had fierce fondness for them.

'I'm not sure I want to go back to it, to be honest. I think my time is of greater social value doing what I'm doing now.'

She listed the benefits, raising and lowering her fingers – social, mental health, economic, community, eudaemonic – while Helen nodded and asked careful questions that tried not to suggest that she, like many others, thought that Laura was crazy or entitled or somehow scamming the system. She only realised she had expected better from Helen when she noticed herself begin to get defensive.

'I can practically hear you thinking it's a small life,' she said, cutting short her enumeration of the various research studies that validated her decision.

'Not at all,' Helen said. 'It's … I mean, you lived in New York. You travelled the world.'

'Don't mention the war,' Annie said, smiling.

'What war? Were you somewhere there was a war?' Helen's face was horrified.

For a second Laura considered telling her that she had been caught up in something. In Central America, maybe, whose wars few people retained or even knew about in the first place. That she had been injured somehow – lungs, she imagined, tear gas perhaps – and was no longer able to work in the conventional way. That would be easier for Helen to understand and would mean Laura didn't have to defend her choices. The problem of course was that it wasn't true.

'Metaphorical war. Any fool can buy a plane ticket. You mentioned all the places I've been. The planes I took, the trains, the buses, the taxis. So many countries. So many photo opportunities. Hours of them. Miles of them. All in boxes in the attic at home. All the things I took for granted and in doing so made impossible for my daughter.'

'That's hardly true,' Helen said. 'We haven't removed the possibility of travel from our children. To suggest we have seems a bit extreme.'

Laura shook her head. 'It's the sole logical conclusion. If we bring our children up to believe that they can see the world in the way we did, all we're doing is recreating the exact same problem for their generation, except by then it will be too late for them to do anything.'

'Hoist by their own entitlement,' Annie observed.

It was Jack's expression. At least, he was the first person Laura had heard say it, when she had had a similar conversation with him. He was the one who suggested that her generation, far from being at fault, were merely rising to the opportunities, the globalisation, they were reared on. The fault might perhaps rest with his generation, he said, as the first to truly see how much better their children could have it, but without ever weighing the damage.

Helen wasn't convinced. 'The travel decisions of one individual are not going to make anything like the kind of difference we need,' she said. 'If anything, our children struggle to believe in the reality of other people, a struggle that will be made worse if they never see it for themselves.'

Laura winced at the reminder of her own poverty tourism. 'Give me your phone,' she said, putting out her hand to Helen.

'Why? Is it some terrible symbol, too? Beyond the obvious, I mean.'

Laura waggled her fingers and Helen put the phone into her hand. Laura scrolled through the apps, hoping her certainty proved correct. 'There it is,' she said, holding the phone up. 'You track the carbon miles of the food you buy.'

'So?'

'So you believe – at least on some level – in the power of the individual. Otherwise you wouldn't bother.'

'And that makes me a hypocrite?'

Laura smiled at her old friend. 'Even more terrifying – it makes you an optimist, which means you'll get here eventually.'

Helen said nothing for a moment. 'Removing travel would leave my clients in truly terrible situations.'

'The worse climate change gets, the worse their circumstances,' Laura said gently.

'Violence and destruction, everywhere we look,' Helen said.

'Then you're looking in the wrong places,' Annie chimed in. 'Everywhere I look I see plenty that needs fixing but it can be done. People want to do it. I want to, for a start.'

'Still channelling Pollyanna,' Helen said. 'How does that gratitude manifest itself?'

Annie just shrugged and held up her palms. 'It's a purely individual thing.'

The talk moved back to Jack and what the evening might bring. Laura let the words pass her by and thought instead about Helen's question to Annie, *How does that gratitude manifest itself?* There was an assumption in there that gratitude had form or presence or force of some sort. That fit with her experience of describing her life to people, wielding her less-is-more manifesto and talking about her deeply held belief in her choices. Looking at Helen in her beautifully tailored trousers and little knit jumper, her expensively cut hair, Laura wondered if her gratitude appeared to others as more shield than banner. If, in fact, a 'buy nothing' philosophy really only carried weight when lived by people with money. When others could see everything they were giving up.

If Helen were to stop going on holiday, people would view it as a sacrifice and approve. Whereas people looked at Laura and thought 1980s-adjacent: no nice clothes, lukewarm house, ancient car; sure she's only giving up what she can't have anyway and putting a big name on it.

Cross and twitchy suddenly, she excused herself from the table before she said something she might regret. Something about how failing to change their behaviour – or to recognise the need for that change – made them as much part of the problem as any emissions-spewing corporation.

FOUR CHANCES TO START OVER

In the bathroom mirror, Laura's cheeks were pink with wine and crossness, the grey at her temples glinting under the harsh shaving light. She thought of Helen's styled bob and unpicked her plait to see what her hair might look like chin-length. No. It would be terrible for work if she couldn't tie it back. She sighed and plaited it again. If she was lucky, the grey would line up neatly and give her an entirely two-tone plait eventually.

'That's the dream, imagine,' she told her reflection.

Back in the hallway, she could hear the sounds of saucepans and knives on chopping boards. Cosy cooking sounds. The occasional murmur of a voice. Let the two of them have their time together. They were welcome to it.

She made her way upstairs, noiseless in her socks. It felt like a transgression, which was ridiculous. She was here once a week at least. Often asked to simply pull the door closed after her if Jack and Annie left for the coffee shop or the library before she was finished. Despite that, it was years since she had been upstairs. She was usually in the utility room, hooking the hose to the tap, or in the kitchen, refilling her water bottle, or, occasionally, treating herself to a cup of echinacea and elderberry tea in the glow of the work done. Flowery hot water, her mother called it.

She pushed open the door to Helen's room and stepped inside. Time and memory produced their usual bowl-of-the-spoon trick of making the room simultaneously absolutely recognisable yet distorted. The trappings of the room were unchanged, the pale green walls, white floorboards, curtains, all exactly as they used to be. What was missing was the clutter. The black velvet chokers hanging on the sides of the dressing table mirror. The artificially sweet smell of Body Shop Dewberry. The TV/VHS combi unit perched on a chair by the window. The stack of spiral-bound refill pads that represented five years of learning. The Garfield poster asking *Is it Friday yet?* The photos Blu-Tacked to the wardrobe door: the three of them celebrating Helen's fourteenth birthday; the three of them at their fifth-year retreat; the three of them on the last day of school, their shirts covered in the black-markered well wishes of their classmates and their hair dripping from the water fight that had broken out.

All that energy was now transformed into a single pair of trousers draped over the back of the chair and an open washbag on the dressing table. Laura crossed the room to have a look. Open meant it was fair game. She hadn't heard of the brands tucked within, but the volume of adjectives pasted onto the teeny glass jars suggested money or fairy dust or gullibility. Everything was so terribly tasteful. Laura had a momentary deep regret for the girl Helen had been before life folded her into this smaller, tighter shape.

The last time she was in here was the weekend after their exam results, when they were trying hard to pretend everything was okay and they still meant to each other what they always had. A weekend full of *remember when?* and *wasn't that the time we?* Checking details they all knew. Already depending on the pull of memory to shore up their conversation.

Helen's parents were away at something or other and so they had the house to themselves, which felt at once grown-up and revealing – the fact that they could do anything, yet chose to do what they had always done. Pizza and movies on Friday night, dozing off one after the other in Helen's bed. Waking up on Saturday morning, their awkwardness echoing in the empty house around them.

Breakfast passed in enjoyable bitching about their classmates. Until Laura's stray comment about Eve failing several subjects, causing Helen to flush and Annie to say there was no need to break out the B. Laura didn't give her usual laugh at Annie's reluctance to say 'bitch', she was too busy realising that Helen, so apparently coy about the specifics of her own results, had evidently been more open with Annie. Laura told herself it didn't matter, as she opened the back door and went into the garden. Annie could spend hours mooning around stroking furniture inside the house, but the garden was by far the best part of Glebe Cottage. Out here, the quiet seemed absolute until she sat on the bank of the river and let the sounds find her. The little burbles of the water over stones, the birds overhead by turns sweet and shrill, the sound of a car in the distance. She was excited for university, for her chance to go and see the world, but she would miss this garden.

Helen and Annie arrived beside her on the riverbank, trailing blankets and magazines and, in Helen's case, her stereo and a stack of CDs.

'You pick something.' She thrust the pile at Laura and returned to the house.

Beside her, Annie was squeezing cream from the Delial bottle and rubbing it into her arms and legs. Never knowingly reckless, that was Annie. If she were to go into Annie's bedroom, she would find a packing list on the clipboard on her dressing table, several items ticked off and already visible in the open suitcase on the floor by the wardrobe. It wasn't her fault if Helen told her things.

'Are you nervous?'

Annie stopped and thought. 'Yes,' she said. 'But in a good way. Besides, what other option is there?'

Laura shrugged. 'Plenty of people are staying here to work.'

'Is that what you want to do? I thought you were excited to start college?'

'I am. It's just … you know.'

'I know.'

'What do we know?' Helen asked, dropping three bottles of water in the grass, along with a multipack of cheese-and-onion Tayto.

'Nothing,' Laura said. A mistake. She watched Helen's face darken for a second at the idea they were keeping secrets. 'I'm a bit nervous about starting college is all.'

'About the work or about making friends?' Helen asked.

Were those things she should be worried about, Laura wondered. 'Actually, it's more the idea of leaving.'

'I can't wait to get out of here,' Helen said. She reached for the suntan lotion and poured too much into the palm of her hand.

'When do you start working with your dad?' Laura asked.

'September, he said.'

'No specific date?' Annie asked.

'A TV set isn't like nursing school. People there are treated like the adults they are. Like the adults we are,' she corrected herself.

'Adults,' Annie said quietly.

Laura blew out loudly, the breath lifting her fringe. 'Fuck.'

Laura's phone buzzed. Her mother had sent a photo: Coraline on the sofa with a blanket over her legs and a cereal bowl of popcorn-and-Maltesers beside her. A smile that could split stones.

WATCHING FREE WILLY AGAIN. WE ARE FINE N TOASTY.

It wasn't a reason to well up. But she couldn't imagine not wanting to spend time with Cor. It was no wonder Helen had talked so much about freedom when it was all she was given.

She crossed to the dressing table and slid open the left-hand drawer where Helen used to keep her treasures. It was empty, increasing the sad-hotel-room vibe of the place. Why not stay in the master bedroom, when this room clearly meant nothing any more? Laura's bedroom in her mother's house had remained her own, even during her years away. If she needed to put her hands on an old photo album or love letter – how sad to think Cor might never have either, might be reduced to a phone mediating her past as well as her present – she knew exactly where to find it. It made her feel safe, even in those first scary days when she brought Coraline home from hospital, as if her potential was somehow wrapped up in all of her teenage clutter and having it close at hand meant it was still available to her.

She and Annie and Helen had all promised to write to each other, of course. Letters or, in a pinch, postcards. *Thinking of you,* every postcard said, no matter the actual words written on it.

Laura and her mother went away for two weeks every year, always to the same mobile home outside Dingle. Far enough to feel like a holiday, her mother said, but close enough that they didn't waste two days travelling. The pattern was always the same. Day one was travel, broken by tomato-egg-and-onion sandwiches on a picnic bench outside Killarney, then watching the turns in the road until they came to the narrow boreen with the grass mohawk that led to the sea. Then hours spent cleaning the mobile home before bringing in their things from the car and tucking them away into the tiny rooms. Days two through six and nine through twelve were taken up in following the shade along the shingle beach, lifting their striped deckchairs and swapping places with one sun-worshipping family after another every thirty minutes or so, with smiles and excuse mes and thank yous and an index finger holding the place in their books. Or, when it rained, reading side by side on the couch in the mobile home, taking turns to make tea and comment on the likelihood of it drying up. Day thirteen was given over to cleaning the mobile home as thoroughly as if they were trying to sell it to a germophobe, and packing everything ready to leave first thing in the morning. The end of the box of cereal and a half-pint of milk would be all that was left in the little kitchen and her mother would buy them fish and chips for dinner, to be eaten sitting on one of the big flat rocks that separated the beach from the road. When she got older, Laura worried that they might be prehistoric graves, but never enough that she forwent their comfort for the spitty little stones of the shingle.

Day seven was postcard day. In the morning, they would drive the twenty minutes to Dingle and potter around the shops, where they swivelled the postcard stands as if they weren't all variations on a theme. They took their selections to their usual table in the window of the ice cream parlour. Laura writing one to Helen and one to Annie, while she spooned her Knickerbocker Glory, and her mother had two scoops of rum and raisin and a white coffee, while writing the kind of careful update every teacher sent to the school for the staffroom noticeboard. Then it was into the post office for stamps, and the postcards directly into the mouth of the postbox, and they would look at each other as if they were finally free to enjoy the rest of their stay. They walked down Main Street and Green Street and Strand Street, their arms brushing companionably, all the while wondering if they should do the boat tour to see Fungie the dolphin. They always did – day eight – and it was always both spectacular and a little sad to see him leaping out of the water, lazily at first, and to the side, but then, as the boat turned for shore, in front of them, as if desperate for them to stay. They never took photographs: her mother never wanted to risk the camera getting wet on the boat, and besides, she said, weren't the ones taken by professionals better than anything either of them might capture?

Small, Laura thought. Kitty O'Brien lived a small life. Over the years, there were times the littlest thing set her off. The Hoover bag left unemptied, a teabag left on the draining board for later, a film ending spoiled or a TV programme accidentally deleted. In that disproportionate anger, Laura could see her mother trying and failing to stretch to meet the world around her. She looked again at the photo her mother had sent. Beside Cor, under the blanket, was a bump that might have been her mother's leg. One person's small life was another's safety.

She closed the drawer of the dressing table.

'Be honest,' she said to herself in the mirror. 'You were hoping to find your old postcards. Like some lovelorn teenager.'

She nodded to herself. Yes. Yes, that was exactly what she had hoped. That she would find their friendship in a drawer, dusty but waiting and available to them. They had said they would write and likely meant it at the time. She certainly had. But in the gap between what a person meant and what they did was every story ever written. Without the structure of school, their friendship, if it was to survive, had to be pursued and coaxed and eased over the inevitable peaks and troughs. It had to be wanted.

They had wanted something else more. Freedom. A fresh start. To be different people. You couldn't be a different person if someone else was behind you telling everyone that actually you used to wear dungarees and cry at *My Girl* and call yourself a smoker even though you never inhaled, just blew the smoke back out again the way actors do.

There were precious few chances in life to become someone entirely new.

Precisely four, by Laura's reckoning: when you left school, if you moved country, when your first child was born, and when your last surviving parent died.

Those were all the chances people got to start over and they came at a cost – usually to someone else.

Downstairs, Helen and Annie were moving around one another with all the ease of two tabby cats in a shelter. Annie would lift the lid of a pot to check whether the spinach was sufficiently wilted, then a minute later, Helen would lift the same lid. Annie would move a chopping board out of her way, then Helen would move it somewhere else. Annie would use a spoon, then Helen would wash it and put it away, only for Annie to take it out again a moment later. It was like watching a comedy sketch.

'Can I do anything?' Laura said.

If it had been Annie on her own, she would have started opening presses to see what they had to work with, but Helen's claim on the house made her shy.

'We're falling over ourselves,' Annie said.

At the same time, Helen said, 'We're okay, I think.'

Relieved, Laura went to bank the stove in the living room. It was warming nicely and would be a pleasant spot with a glass of wine after dinner.

She wandered over to the French windows and looked out into the garden. The ground was thickly covered and the trees held up their snow-covered branches like film stars gesturing in fur stoles. If her mother were here, she would insist on closing the curtains 'to keep the heat in'. Incomprehensible that anyone would prefer to look at curtains instead of nature's show. Stranger still that she had come from that body, drew half of her whole being from it. The relative strength of her father's genes was a yardstick to which she clung to a greater or lesser extent all her life, depending on her degree of irritation with her mother. Or, more accurately, her mother's degree of irritation with her.

Are you listening to a word I'm saying?

Do you think this is a hotel?

If I have to say it again … the threat unspecified and looming.

Enormous, impenetrable statements, delivered at volume and accompanied with the back of a hand or a wooden spoon or a hairbrush.

What might she have been like if she had grown up in the cool calm of this house?

Outside the window, the trees offered only their elegant frozen shrug.

They ate in the kitchen, at Annie's suggestion. After clearing up and loading the dishwasher, they returned to the living room. By unspoken agreement, they avoided the pair of easy chairs in the window, instead sitting at the dining table. Their faces were flushed in the flicker of the stove, with the remainder of the wine between them, and a box of teeny-tiny Marcolini chocolates Helen had brought from the duty-free at the airport.

'I think you might be the one person I know who could make airport chocolate last nearly a week,' Laura said, selecting a cube of chocolate so dark that the lime shavings and sea salt stood out like an IKEA print.

Helen pretended indigation. 'Airport chocolate! I hardly think so.'

Annie got up and left the room, coming back shortly after with a slab of Dairy Milk Tiffin, the kind they had agreed once upon a time was the best of all the chocolate.

'For old times' sake,' she said, and they all took a piece, even Helen.

'The last time we sat around eating chocolate and drinking was that weekend at the end of the summer before we all went off to conquer the world,' Helen said.

The statement cracked and oozed between them.

'I was thinking earlier about that weekend. I remember it being awkward,' Laura said.

'I can't say I noticed,' Helen said.

'I think we were awkward in ourselves, rather than with each other,' Annie said, ever quick to smooth away a hint of conflict. 'We had stopped being one thing but weren't quite another.'

'Besides, we all wanted such different things,' Helen added. 'I mean, I actually thought I was about to start an acting career.' She laughed a bitter-chocolate laugh.

'We all thought that,' Laura said. 'Didn't Jack promise as much?'

'Turned out that wasn't a promise so much as a throwaway comment I wasn't meant to take seriously.'

'Every eighteen-year-old takes everything seriously,' Annie said.

That was as close to criticism of Jack as Annie would go. Loyalty was her strong suit, no matter the circumstances.

'*What do you think you'd bring to the table?* were his exact words.' Helen broke off another square of chocolate and held it between her fingers. 'I did so badly in the exams because I thought I'd never need them. Having to repeat the year felt awful. End-of-the-world mortifying. But it was the only option.'

Laura knew that Helen had gone off to boarding school to repeat the Leaving. Her mother had told her so when she came home after that first term at university. Laura had assumed that Helen had decided she wanted to go to one of those impossible-to-get-into drama schools instead of beginning directly on a set. She had no idea that Helen had left out of shame. Although, Helen – back-then Helen – didn't really do shame. Likely she arrived at her new school as full of confidence and cock-of-the-walk as ever. *Outward confidence,* she thought suddenly.

'I think we're always more awkward in our memories than we really were,' Annie said.

'Not so for men,' Helen said, breaking off another square of chocolate, even though the first was untouched on the table beside her glass. 'In my experience, they remember themselves as better than they were.'

'Your *experience* was legendary alright,' Laura teased. 'It was one drama after another. Although to be fair, they weren't all boy-related.'

'I can't think what you could possibly mean,' Helen said, half hiding behind her hand.

Laura looked at Annie. 'The time she failed her biology test and made us all walk out of class in protest against the teacher.' She raised her eyebrows and nodded.

'The time the school play ended and she cut all her hair off,' Annie obliged, and Laura drummed her palm on the table with delight.

'YES! Didn't even have the decency to do it before the play, given she was playing a man,' Laura said.

Helen had retreated entirely behind her hands, her shoulders shaking with laughter.

'The time she slapped some boyfriend or other in the middle of a party,' Laura went on. 'I don't think he had even done anything, but maybe that was the point. *Experience*.' She affected a pursed Kenneth Williams mouth.

She knew the mood had shifted before Annie said anything.

'The time she left without saying a word.'

Helen took her hands down and looked at Annie across the table. 'We all left,' she said. 'We were always going to.' She turned her attention to Laura. 'You were right earlier, when you remembered that last weekend being weird. We were all getting ready to leave and pretending nothing had changed. All that endless adrenalin and butterflies. Like waiting for a starting gun to fire and life to begin. Of course it was awkward.'

It was true and yet was somehow also dishonest. Annie was right. What were they all playing at? Sitting here together and talking as if who they were then had more power than who they were now and who they had been in between.

'There are ways of leaving,' Annie said, and Laura could hear the shake in her voice. 'Plenty of people manage to stay friends without exclusivity or living in each other's pockets. You dropped us. You decided you were finished with us and you dropped us. Simple as that.'

'Well, you certainly showed me, didn't you, Annie? You missed me so much that you moved into my house, into my life.'

'How dare you! Jack is my friend.'

The anger was right there between them. As if it had been waiting in the wings, engine running, ready to bulldoze everything. To destroy the good along with the bad.

'Stop,' Laura said. 'Both of you. Stop it this minute. This isn't helping anything and you both know it.'

'I couldn't even come home after repeating the Leaving,' Helen said, not taking her eyes from Annie's face.

'That was hardly our—'

Helen's phone vibrated across the table, startling them. Laura picked it up and saw the hospital number. She handed the phone to Helen, then held her other hand firmly and nodded her to answer.

They listened as it became clear that Jack had had another stroke, bigger and more catastrophic, and was fading fast. Even if the roads had been clear all the way, there wouldn't be time to get there. Instead, they switched to FaceTime, a nurse holding the iPad near to his face so that Helen could talk to him.

'We'll give you some privacy,' Annie said, the effort audible in her voice.

Laura stayed where she was. Squeezed Helen's hand and hoped.

Helen reached out and caught Annie's hand, too. 'Please stay,' she said. 'Please. For him.'

And so they stayed. The three of them in the low light of the lamp and the flickering fire, their eyes on Jack's face as it filled the screen. Helen said goodbye, then gave Annie the phone to do the same, and the two women – Jack's two women – held hands and breathed together as one day became the next.

When it was all over, Helen raised her glass. 'Here we all are finally,' she said. 'The dead dad club.'

ONE TRUE THING

Jack stopped breathing and time didn't stop. It never did, Annie thought. Relentless as it was.

Unforgiving as it was.

Cruel, stifling, immense, pinching as it was.

Formless fog with electrified edges as it was.

Frozen river as it was.

After her father died, everything felt temporary to Annie. She and her mother and her brothers lived with their heads cocked to one side, waiting to hear his boots in the hall. Only the scaffolding of school held her upright and moved her forward, class by class, term by term. The certainty of the bell every forty-five minutes and prayers over the intercom at the start and end of the day. Of Sister Eucharia's ruler tapping a bare knee so that the culprit would roll her school skirt back down to regulation length. Of tests at Christmas, Easter and summer. Of progress.

Did time move where her father was? At the funeral, the priest had talked about Jesus preparing a room in his house for her father and she had to swallow back a hysterical laugh at the image of a feather-duster Jesus, in gown and sandals and crown of thorns, dressing beds and opening windows and giving the skirting boards a lick of a damp cloth. Months later, while they were walking, she told Laura, half-laughing, half-ashamed. Laura had looked at her and, with perfect seriousness, said that she imagined Jesus would have people to do that kind of thing for him. They laughed until she leaked pee as well as tears.

Helen, too, had a way of moving time. Always on to the next thing, a plan for the weekend or a new crush or something she wanted them to go to town to buy. Always certain that life was there for the taking. Her casual assumption that hers was the most interesting of their lives relieved Annie of the burden of being looked at, and it wasn't until Annie's mother's death, years later, a lifetime later, that she saw suddenly how Helen's relentless momentum hadn't always been the best thing for her.

Annie's mother died and time again lifted and carried her onward, with no pause that might let her find her feet in the slippery new world of grief.

'People have been very good,' she said over and over when asked how she was and everyone was happy for the chance to turn the messy specifics into more general conversation.

It was true for a little while. People were very good for a few days or a few weeks, even. But then their patience wore thin. *How are you doing?* reverted back to *How are you?* with its normative responses ranging from *grand* to *grand altogether,* to the bad-day standby, *up and down, sure you know yourself.*

Every time someone asked how she was, what she really wanted was to pinch them hard and then scream.

Her brothers had come for the funeral, bringing with them a constant commentary of gratitude that their mother's suffering was at an end. They engaged in self-satisfied verification of what Annie had already organised, in between thinly veiled conversations about what might happen to the house. Michael took charge of the undertakers and orders of service and announcements in the papers and on RIP.ie. John developed an unhealthy interest in the virtual condolences book and spent his evenings scrolling through messages trying to place people.

'Wasn't there an Ian Creedon in school with you?' he would demand, and Michael looked up from his work emails and made a show of thinking. 'Minor championship season, eighty-nine.' Said with an air of triumph, as if recalling the date of an obscure battle.

When you go back to finish your nursing, they said to her repeatedly, as though Annie's life had merely been paused and she could slip smoothly into the place her twenty-one-year-old self had vacated all those years ago. How nice for them to believe that she had lost nothing in the intervening years. That she had had nothing taken from her. How nice for them to joke about how they themselves would love the freedom to go back to college, if not for their children, their responsibilities.

Every conversation led inexorably to their burdens, familial and financial.

She wanted to ask Michael why he was so keen on selling what he evidently believed to be a magical house, as full today of fairies specialised in routine tasks like putting on a wash or replacing milk or cleaning the fucking toast crumbs off the fucking countertop as it was in his childhood.

They were well-meaning half-strangers and she was glad when they left. Their parting assurances that they would call her the next week might have been intended to maintain a relationship, but it could, in other lights, be read as a decision timetable of the kind they were accustomed to generating at work.

She chose not to worry about it. Not when the quiet in the house was the relief of cold water cooling a burning throat. She looked around her and thought she had only herself to please. She could have toast for breakfast, lunch and dinner if she liked.

The days passed and the house echoed with seemingly endless calls about returning the hospital bed and safe disposal of the remaining morphine and informing various social welfare departments that she was no longer entitled to a carer's allowance. *Sadmin*, people called it, a term cruel and accurate. Every phone call undoing the administrative structures of caring severed something else.

Clearing her mother's room one day, she found a notebook

dating back to the early weeks and months after the diagnosis. It was full of her mother's tiny neat handwriting. *7.30 Get up, brush teeth (with toothpaste from the red + white squeezy tube!), put on clothes laid out on chair (dirty clothes go in basket!).* Then *12.30 Make sandwich (two slices of bread, butter, then ham OR cheese OR jam). Eat sandwich and drink two small glasses of water.* And later, *19.00 Lock front door (turn key once in direction of holy water font, then try handle to make sure) and put key on hook beside kettle (in kitchen).*

The same handwriting she had seen for years in every note for school. *Please excuse Annie from PE today as she has an upset stomach.* And *Annie was absent on Tuesday because we had morning Mass said for her father.* And *Annie will not be taking part in the school ski trip.*

Always polite, always organised.

Annie flipped through the pages. At some point her mother had started assigning each day a number out of five. *3/5 – lost glasses and couldn't read paper. 5/5 –* the day her friend Elizabeth came for lunch – *Elizabeth talked about her knee operation and didn't mention my thing once!*

She didn't flip any further. Didn't want to find the day when her mother had stopped grading herself.

Time passed. A hateful fact Annie ignored by the simple expedient of leaving the calendar in the kitchen unturned and living in a kind of semi-permanent February Wednesday. It was easy to avoid people. She could, it turned out, slip out of her life with comparative ease. All she had to do was have her food shopping delivered and let her grey roots extend their arms and gather in the brown and go to the graveyard less and less and then not at all. She spent her evenings watching her mother's soap operas, a surprisingly intensive endeavour that ate up the evening hours and left her wrung out and ready for bed by nine o'clock.

One mid-morning, the doorbell rang. Annie looked down at her pyjamas and fleece and decided they could pass as loungewear.

As she opened the door, Jack swung around to face her and his brown waxed jacket and tucked-in Burberry scarf were so exactly the picture of the Dr Danny Furlong she had been watching on the screen that she burst out laughing.

'I think I'd better come in,' he said, his face creased with concern.

He saw the funny side when she pointed to his frozen image on the screen. 'When you've been dressed by a professional, you learn to trust their taste,' he said, with a sweeping gesture from his head to his walking shoes.

He was going out for the day, he told her, and would appreciate both her company and her driving skills.

He was kind enough not to mention her dishevelled appearance, or her neglect of the graveyard.

Thirty minutes later, she was in a clean fleece and jeans, tucking her wet hair into a hat while Jack moved the large paper bag with Susan's café sticker into the back seat.

'It's a bit of a drive,' he said. 'Off you go. I'll be the satnav.'

She put her foot down on the clutch and found space, before realising that Jack's sleek green Lexus was an automatic. Her spirits stirred; she had always wanted to try out an automatic.

Ninety minutes later, they arrived in the deserted car park of a historic lakeside walking trail. Ten minutes later again, they were each equipped with an audio guide and a map of the trail's key points of interest: the bronze Celtic symbols, twisted story trees, and islands in the middle of the lake. Jack counted to three and they pressed their start buttons at the same time and walked along in companionable silence. Annie kept the volume low, catching the occasional line and nodding each time Jack raised his eyebrows in interest or surprise at whatever had been said.

'Fascinating,' he said, when they stopped for lunch. He was unpacking Susan's box onto the picnic bench in the lee of a small hill that looked out on to the lake.

Annie watched the mist rolling across the lake towards them. It thickened as it closed in. It would, she realised, curl in below them, literally pulling the world from beneath them. 'What will we do if it catches us?' she asked.

Jack considered the lake. 'Sit tight and wait it out.'

'Don't give me that time-passes crap,' she said. 'Even if it's true, I'm not able for it.'

'What should I say instead?' he asked, handing her a paper plate with a napkin, sausage roll and wooden fork.

'People think that because she had Alzheimer's, that I had already done my grieving and her actual death is no more than an administrative tidying-up,' she said, picking apart the sausage roll so that the flesh lay pink and exposed on the plate.

'People are bastards,' Jack said, and it made her laugh.

'The only way she would let me flush a tube or change a dressing was if she thought she was training me how to do it. Years of having student nurses working under her, I suppose. *Like this?* I would ask, and she was so patient with me then.' She flicked the pink flesh from the plate, sending it sailing into the ditch. Let some intrepid bird have a feast. 'I watched a video on YouTube a few days ago. A ballerina, Marta Cinta Gonzalez, her name was, with barely a thread of memory holding her to the world. She listened to a piece of music and began to move her arms and hands as though she were dancing again. She cried. The voice-over said it was happiness, but it looked a lot like devastation to me.'

They sat and ate in silence for a few minutes, the mist holding steady over the lake.

'Tell me one true thing,' Annie said.

Jack didn't hesitate. 'We learn to live in a world without someone,' he said. 'That's all the wisdom I have.'

Helen cried, a delicate hiccupping and shoulder susurration that was largely silent. Laura took her hand. 'He was a gentleman, Helen. I'm so sorry for your loss.'

Annie had always admired Laura's facility with social situations. But a person could only be who they were. 'Jack told me once that we can learn to live in a world without people. I found that comforting,' Annie said.

Laura squeezed Helen's hand. 'We're here for you, Helen. What do you need? What can we do?'

'That's the thing, isn't it?' Helen said. 'There's nothing we can do.' She gestured towards the window and the sudden snowfall that brought joy to the unburdened.

'The nurses will take good care of him,' Annie said.

'Tell me how.'

'All of it?'

Helen nodded. 'Please.'

'The first thing they will do is turn off the radiator in the room and open the window. Then they will give him a lovely last wash with warm soapy water. They might describe each step out loud, tell him what they're doing as they do it.'

It took time, the slow telling of what happened in the hour after a person became a body. The careful steps that represented the race against biology. The final, gentle efforts of the living for their dead.

'What about his clothes?' Helen asked.

'You can choose something and bring it tomorrow. Or, if you prefer, they will dress him in the clothes he was wearing when he was admitted.'

Helen's eyes filled with panic. 'I can't remember what he was wearing.'

'He had on a heavy cream shirt and a dark green knitted cardigan, with a pair of navy cords,' Annie said. She heard a note of apology in her voice and reminded herself she had nothing to apologise for. As the one who dressed Jack in the mornings, this knowledge was within her professional remit.

'One of his Dr Danny get-ups. Oh.' She looked from Annie to Laura. 'He was a public figure.' She made air quotes around the words. 'I'll have to tell … who will I have to tell?'

'The funeral director will deal with all of that, if you like.' Somewhere, Annie knew, obituaries would already have been written, in preparation for when the time came. But that wasn't something Helen should have in her head. 'If you use Bert Crowley in town, he'll give you a good steer.'

'He was always my dad and Dr Danny Furlong both,' Helen said. 'He played that character since I was three years old.' Her laugh was tiny and bitter. 'I never knew if my father was simply a scriptwriter's idea of what a father should be.'

He retired seven years ago, Annie thought. Quite a lot of time to get to know a person.

'Maybe the writers wrote Danny based on your dad,' Laura said suddenly. 'Thirty-five years in the same role. If you couldn't tell where Jack ended and Danny began, you can bet the writers didn't either.'

Bless Laura's tact.

Annie and Laura left Helen in the warmth of the living room fire while she told her family the news. Annie pressed the button on the kettle and took the lid off the cafetière before reaching into the press for the digestive biscuits and the butter dish.

Laura shook her head. 'Grief drinks tea,' she said, and began to scald the teapot instead. 'Do you remember that mad poster your mother had in your kitchen?'

Annie did. It was a graphic listing some of the daily behaviours people engaged in that shortened their lifespan. A fairly routine cardiac ward-type poster that was given in stacks as part of brief, expensive media campaigns to raise awareness. As if people didn't already know that cigarettes and booze and biscuits were treats from the Grim Reaper's pockets. The kind of poster that dated quickly, as science and shame expanded their reach. To offset obsolescence, Annie's mother began to add things as she became aware of them, crossing out anything that no longer applied, adding it back in when the science changed. In the finish, there was more black marker than poster.

'The poster wasn't that bad. It was all the additions that

made it look a bit …' She searched for the right word to capture her mother's belief in the need to control the body. 'Extreme,' she finished.

'Go on. You know you want to.' Laura waggled her eyebrows.

'You'll have to imagine the crossings-out and overwriting.' Annie took a deep breath and began to list things on her fingers. 'Smoky coal. Smokeless coal. Rashers. Ham. All processed meats. Coffee. Red wine. Real butter. Fake butter. Full-fat milk. Low-fat milk. Too much walking. Not enough walking. MRSA. Bacterial diseases. Taking too many antibiotics. Refusing antibiotics. Antimicrobial resistance. Homeopathy. Any and all alternative therapies. Going out too much. Staying in too much—' She stopped. 'I may have generalised a couple.'

'I still think of that poster when I hear Leonard Cohen singing "Who By Fire",' Laura said. She pressed the biscuits together so that the butter oozed out through the holes.

'Remember how mysterious that song seemed when we were teenagers?' Annie remembered. 'Like it held the whole story of life and death. The drama of it all.'

'Now I listen to the lyrics and it sounds like a form I have to fill out,' Laura said.

It felt good to laugh. Even without Jack in the world.

'I'm not afraid of dying any more,' Laura declared. 'Not since having Coraline. The fear sort of transfers. I'm far more afraid of her dying than of me dying.'

Annie nodded. Why did parents always feel the need to say that sort of thing? As if having children put them on a higher plane of existence. As if everyone else was a mere mortal who should be awed at the depth of their primal instinct, when all instinct was was a lack of control.

'Jack did everything on that poster,' Laura said.

'And enjoyed it,' Annie agreed.

'I'm really sorry for your loss,' Laura said gently. 'He was a good friend.'

'You know, he introduced me to people as his dear friend?' Annie's voice wobbled and she breathed deeply, lifting her ribs to shore it up. As though her sorrow were somehow structural.

'I wonder where he is now,' Laura said.

Wherever it was, Annie hoped it had a good wine cellar and a library. He'd be in safe hands then.

ARMS FULL OF OTHER THINGS

'Did you get through to Conor?' Laura asked.

They had gathered around the dining table, with Jack's chair in the bay window emptier than ever and the stove throwing out heat and light and comfort. Annie felt the strangeness of it. The one-foot-in-the-past and one-foot-in-the-present of it. That iPad call might never have happened. Only the snow piled against the bottom six inches of the French windows gave the game away. They were in the after now.

'He kept asking how I feel. But I don't know what to feel,' Helen said.

Strange that Helen, the girl with two parents, had been the insecure one back then, and here again, it was Helen, the woman anchored by a partner and three children, who, again, felt least certain in herself.

'That's normal,' Laura reassured her. 'It takes a while. Often it takes the funeral to make it real.'

Annie thought of her mother's funeral, all God and traditions. She herself trailing her brothers, with no energy left for objection at how generic it all was. Everything the path of least resistance. The minimum effort.

'Conor asked about the arrangements. What the restrictions would mean. Numbers and social distancing and all that.'

'Pass me the iPad and I'll look it up,' Laura said.

While Helen and Laura cross-referenced dates with various iterations of government Covid mandates, Annie thought about the casual assumption that grief took time to become real. *It takes a while,* Laura had said, but the truth was that it was different for everyone.

Annie's grief was immediately present. Jack's absence every bit as substantial as his presence had been. She was now the keeper of all the Annie-and-Jack memories. Of everything they had been to one another. Death transformed biology into psychology.

'Up to twenty-five people.' Helen was making notes in her phone. 'Household first. Then close family. Then close friends.' She looked at Annie. 'Household is you. If only one person were allowed, that would be you. How funny.'

Funny, how? Annie wanted to ask. *You moved into my house, into my life.* But they appeared to have an unspoken agreement to pretend that their bitter words were never said or heard or felt.

'Who else is in the twenty-five?' Helen asked Annie. 'Which of his friends are ... might want to come? Do they get priority over Conor and the children? Should they?'

They began to debate the merits of children at funerals. The healing that might be unlocked balanced against the fact that they had never really known Jack and so might be uncomfortable with the expectation of mourning.

For Christ's sake. A minute ago Helen was all hot and bothered about the limited numbers and here she was giving three spaces to people who didn't know Jack – and likely wouldn't want to be there – purely for the optics of it.

Annie knew better than to venture an opinion. With no children of her own, whatever she said, no matter if she simply parroted what Helen and Laura had already said, her words came with an ineluctable caveat.

Even in the throes of her most successful relationship, when Annie pictured herself in the future, there was no child there with her. It never felt like a decision, more a statement of fact, something fundamental that she had grown up knowing about herself. That she would never have children.

She made the mistake of trying to explain it to her mother

once. It came out as self-indulgence rather than the self-preservation she felt it to be. Her mother made all the usual comments that implied Annie had simply been unlucky in love, as if the desire to replicate her genes depended on her unlocking the next level of life, and drifted into the twilight convinced that it was simply a matter of meeting the right person, when, in fact, another person was no longer even necessary and, had Annie wanted a child, she would simply have had one.

She was unafraid of being alone. More than that, she welcomed it. The pandemic had brought the spectre of loneliness to her door, yes, and she was grateful for Jack and the company he offered, but it was always temporary, with no claustrophobic overtones of 'forever'.

He teased her about it. Ordered wine from the off-licence purely because he thought the delivery driver had a twinkle in his eye when he looked at Annie. Worried, sometimes, that he was preventing her meeting someone. A lot of young people were hooking up during Covid, he had heard it on the radio. She wouldn't give away her independence that cheaply, she told him, and besides, she wasn't young enough for Tinder or bold enough for Covid rule-breaking.

Laura believed her decision stemmed from the decades of caring for her mother, Annie knew. That, having spent twenty years as a carer, she was done with being responsible for someone else's needs. It was true and it wasn't. There was no lie in saying that she could picture herself with a child and know already there was nothing they could add to her life that would balance out the loss of the next twenty years as well. But neither was it a lie to say that even if her mother had remained in the whole of her health, if she was, even now, standing in her kitchen rolling out the pastry for an apple tart, or stretching the phone cord to its fullest extent so she could chat while emptying the dishwasher of the day's load, then Annie would choose just herself all the same.

Her memories were only hers and only for her todays,

however many they would eventually number. There was no future for her remembering, nobody to hold it for her. And she had made her peace with it. She had. With knowing that there would be no do-over. That she was enough in herself and let the rest fall where it would. Annie looked at Helen and Laura, their faces rosy in the heat from the fire.

'All the funerals are live on Facebook,' Laura was saying, 'so anyone who wants to can watch it online.' She swiped to another tab. 'They're advising that you don't have anything here at the house. No wake or rosary. That simplifies things.'

These women, she thought suddenly, held as much of her as anyone alive.

'We'll figure it out,' Annie said. 'Whatever you need. You'll do Jack proud.'

Helen's face crumpled, the determination collapsing soufflé-like. 'I don't … you're sitting there being so kind when I said such awful things. Literally unforgiveable things. Things I didn't even mean.'

'It's a stressful—' began Laura.

'Thank you, Laura, really. I mean it. But I need to say this. I need to apologise to Annie. I felt guilty about not being here and instead of being grateful, I took my inadequacy out on you. We've spent days – months, even – pretending that Covid was the reason I wasn't here, but Covid doesn't explain the last twenty-five years.'

Annie's fingers were opening and closing as though breathing for her. Like a frog, she thought. Breathing through her skin. Another documentary she and Jack had watched.

'Twenty-five years. I can't even—' Helen said.

'Okay, so Covid doesn't explain it. What does?'

Helen sighed. 'I was too embarrassed to be around you both. Mortified that my big life ideas were revealed for the childish bullshit they so clearly were. You had it together. You had a plan. One that was based on knowing yourself well. On doing the work and figuring out what you wanted. I had nothing.'

'Everyone had—' Laura began, but Helen shook her head impatiently.

'*I* was the one destined for bigger and better things. *I* was the one that people would be proud to say they knew-her-when. I was stupid and so, so arrogant. I thought I could do the year over and come home and find everything the same as if I never left. Everyone waiting for me to get things started. But of course time passed and my mother would tell me about your new lives and it all got bigger and bigger and bigger until I couldn't see past it.'

'I missed you,' Laura said. '*We* missed you. We didn't care where you went or what you did.'

It was true. Or they believed it was. It was always easy to ascribe nobler motivations to your earlier self.

'It was unforgiveable not to come to your mother's funeral. I know that. I'm so sorry about Pauline. About the rest of it, too, but especially Pauline. She was never anything but kind to me.'

'My mother's funeral was one day. I think I'm madder about all the rest of the days, to be honest,' Annie said.

'I know. I'm sorry, Annie. I'm so sorry.'

She could choose not to forgive Helen. To grip the anger and the hurt of all those years. Rerun the slights and the lack of support and the moments missed. Remind herself how unfair it was that someone who betrayed you could hand you all the work to do to fix things. Cradle her self-righteousness to herself and hope that it was enough.

Or she could open her fingers and let the resentments trickle away. Free the future to become whatever it would. Maybe they would be in each others' lives, maybe not. Maybe they would be friends, maybe not. Forgiveness didn't require closeness. It didn't require anything except willingness.

She looked up at Helen and smiled. 'Difficult times come in all shapes and sizes. And you lent me Jack when I needed him. Sort of. Thank you for that.'

Helen leaned over and placed her hand on Annie's. It held

the warmth of the room. 'You still store your emotions in your hands,' Helen said.

'I no longer hold on to emotions,' Laura declared.

'Bullshit,' Annie and Helen said together and the tension evaporated.

'You always claimed that and it was never true,' Helen said. 'You were as teenage angsty as the rest of us.'

'Maybe back then,' Laura conceded. 'But no more. Life is too fucking short.'

People only said that when they had narrowly avoided disaster. For those who had had disaster visited upon them, who had opened their front door or their post or their heart or their legs, life could feel very long indeed.

'She's definitely more direct than she used to be.' Helen nudged Annie. 'What do you think?'

'More swearing, for sure,' Annie agreed.

'What would Jesus think?' Helen added.

Annie must have missed a whole chunk of earlier conversation. Laura only brought out the Jesus chat when she felt comfortable.

'Jesus doesn't care,' Laura said. 'He has his arms full of other things.'

Not *his hands full,* Annie thought, but *his arms full.* As if Jesus were tasked with taking down curtains or draping a sheet over a statue. Again, it was easier to imagine a gentle, domestic Jesus than a Jesus in the working world. No doubt that had something broader to say about the modern world or gender roles or the patriarchy, but that was a Jack-and-Annie kind of conversation. Oh, but she would miss him!

A HIGH HEART

Annie found a welcome five minutes alone under the guise of bringing in more logs for the fire. It wouldn't be a wasted effort. Helen might want to go to bed or stay up, and either way they should be prepared.

Their wellies stood side by side beside the back door, ready to go adventuring. That was another of Jack's words. It was never a walk, nor – God forbid – a hike, but always an adventure. Looking at them, she realised it was Helen who would have the task of clearing out the house. Helen who would lift each item, turn it this way and that, and decide its fate. Keep, donate, bin. The three categories into which every life was eventually divided. She had a sudden urge to walk through the house and touch everything, soak up whatever connection or comfort it might provide. She lifted Jack's wellies and brought them out with her, propping them beside the back door.

Outside, she pressed her hands to her hot cheeks. The fading heat of hers and Helen's angry words seemed silly in the cold of the garden. In the absence of Jack. Who loved who most. Who needed who most. As if it could be gauged. As if it mattered.

Underfoot, the snow crunched and submitted, and she walked all the way down one side of the garden and up the other, taking care to plant her feet cleanly. When she stopped and looked back, she could see her footprints, crisp as the creases her mother used to iron into her father's jeans.

If asked, she could close her eyes and describe everyone in the front row of the church at her father's funeral. Her mother's black and white houndstooth coat that had been the subject of much fretting before they left the house: it mightn't look sober enough, but she was hardly going to buy another dark coat, for what? And she couldn't borrow one because everyone else would be wearing their own funeral coat. She spent the day apologising for herself and pointing out the imagined inappropriateness of her coat to everyone that spoke to her, so that a casual observer might have thought the coat weighed heavier on her than her husband's sudden death.

Far more noteworthy were Michael's girlfriend's high heels, which Annie envied right up until the moment she saw her picking her foolish way across the cattle grid at the entrance to the graveyard. Granny Ivy, her too-red wig garish against the waxy yellow of her skin, her own appointment with her maker scarcely a month away as it turned out, leaning over to ask her mother had she no good black coat she could have worn to honour the dead?

Annie had sat with John to the side of the altar while they waited to do the readings. John reading from Ecclesiastes, stumbling over the word and then rushing through the supposed comfort about there being a time for everything. Annie herself read John 14, or it was more accurate to say she recited it, having spent the morning learning it by heart, as an acceptable way of avoiding the faintly powdery hugs of the various relatives and neighbours who insisted on calling to the house before the Mass.

Do not let your hearts be troubled. You believe in God; believe also in me. My Father's house has many rooms; if that were not so, would I have told you that I am going there to prepare a place for you? And if I go and prepare a place for you, I will come back and take you to be with me that you also may be where I am.

She recited it now to the snowy garden, faltering in places, but with the essence of the thing intact. It seemed that time had stripped out the emotion so that it felt like watching a video clip with the sound turned off. Her memories a story rather than something she had lived through. That was a function of time, she knew. Time and living. She could already feel the same thing happening with her memories of her mother. Those days towards the end, in particular, were taking on a dreamlike quality, and she had begun to think of her in general, amorphous terms of scent and warmth, having to work to remember specifics. Reminding herself to conjure up certain memories. Her mother laughing at the Waldorf salad episode of Fawlty Towers. Her mother shopping for shoes and turning towards Annie with one foot in a silver wedge sandal and the other in an old black canvas runner. Her mother singing along to Fairytale of New York – even the sweary bits – while cutting the greaseproof paper for the Christmas pudding.

She had a handful of such memories of her father. The feel of his rough-skinned hand on her shoulder as he left to take the boys to training or to a match. His shout of victory at a late point in a Sunday afternoon match on the telly. His smile as he handed her a furry purple pencil case for her first day at school, the only gift she could remember coming directly from him. His profile as he ferried her to the church for her First Holy Communion, she in pride of place in the passenger seat for the occasion, he saluting everyone they met.

Would they have been friends, if he had lived? If he ate less red meat or drank fewer pints of Guinness, he would have been there in the evenings, increasingly so, as her brothers developed lives of their own. John would likely have stayed home and worked with her father. There would have been a moment when she and her mother were called out into the yard to admire the work van, with its newly stencilled & Son, and Dad and John beaming beside it. Michael would have moved abroad anyway, he was always going to. But with the economy settling and cheap flights proliferating, they might all have gone to see him. Such extravagances were possible on two incomes. With someone at home, her mother's illness might have been caught sooner. Weight gained or lost suddenly was most visible to the eyes that watched a person dress and undress. Her father would have been the one at home with her mother. Taking on the daily care, the appointments and medications and bruises. Surprising her with the cruise she talked about, enlarging her life even if she was always going to be short-changed by time.

And Annie herself? Impossible to imagine herself other than she was. But the possibility, maybe, that after finishing college, she might have joined the hundreds of newly qualified nurses who took their degrees and their energy and their ideas to Australia or New Zealand. Who met and married and stayed there. Who welcomed her parents in some foreign airport; she, cool and accustomed to the heat, her heart warmed and mortified by her father's pink face and unsuitable reactions to things. Who came home trailing teasing, warm-voiced boyfriends whose fondness for sports made them locals wherever they went. The kind of boyfriend her father would have been delighted to parse every kick of the ball with.

Or maybe she would never have gone anywhere at all, but travelled dutifully home at weekends, deferring questions that entirely missed the point of her life and instead using the time to catch up on her sleep, relieved and glad when he went to bed early.

Her imaginary life.

Her imaginary father.

Jack was all specifics yet. She could close her eyes and feel the rasp of the razor against his cheek. See the two inches of winter-sea-grey cashmere sock between his beloved babs and the bottoms of his trousers. Hear the tiny click of his tongue against his teeth when the waitress brought his poached eggs on white toast instead of the brown he always requested. The hours and days after death were the time to revel in the little things that made up a person, yet were, conversely, the time when the world intruded most with its demands for reactions and decisions.

Annie put her feet into Jack's wellies and walked the same path, leaving his footprints beside her own original set, as though they had walked together. As she walked, she cried silently. A skill honed from years of living with her mother, who had ears like a German shepherd.

The tears were – as they always were – self-indulgent and clarifying.

The thing with what-if-ing was that it encouraged a person to think less of the life they had. The life they chose and worked for and valued. All regret did was make a person look at what was there and want only what was missing. Regret swallowed gratitude and made a waste of the past and the future both.

Right now this minute, she had her health and her independence, and if her brothers insisted on selling the house, she would have means enough to buy her own small place. A two-bed, maybe, with wooden floors and bright rugs and a door that opened into a sunlit garden. She had neighbours and friends. She had had Jack, albeit too briefly. A friend, unexpected and welcome, who shared her fears and joys when the world went quiet. Her breath caught a second time, knocking at the base of her throat. *A high heart.* She remembered the phrase from a book she and Jack read aloud during the first lockdown. A small volume in which the author simply remembered the big and small moments of his youth, the mundane and the extraordinary set alongside one another. A memoir in singular memories, of which she had forgotten all but that one phrase: *a high heart.*

She had her love and her grief and her future and only herself to please.

WHEN THE TIME IS RIGHT

In the living room, Helen and Laura had gathered a pile of pillows and blankets, evidently intending to stay up.

'Is it still snowing?' Laura said.

Annie shook her head. 'It's stopped, but it's freezing hard.'

'I love it like that,' Laura said, pleased. 'That crunch like bubble wrap. I'll have to get Cor out in it tomorrow.'

'Mum always loved snow,' Annie said, surprising herself. 'She said it was less overwhelming when everyone else slowed down and felt as unsteady and uncertain as she was.'

'It must have been especially difficult to watch her slip away,' Helen said.

She meant well. Just because it was what everyone said didn't make it any less genuine.

'I remember her sitting in her big chair in the window, hiding from the sun,' Laura said cheerfully. 'Cor would draw pictures in pavement chalk on the ground outside and your mother would give her marks out of ten, remember? They were stone mad about each other.'

Annie remembered the precious minutes when her mother was entertained and safe and she could have a quiet cry in the bathroom before putting on the kettle or a wash or a brave face.

She remembered the night it became clear that her mother would spend the remainder of her days in the bed.

She remembered covering her mother's chair with a blanket, like a widow hiding the mirrors.

'She's such a good kid, even if I do say so myself,' Laura said.

'Maybe I should give you Réiltín,' Helen said. 'I've been wondering what I model for her. Friendships. Balance.' Her laugh was bewildered. 'You know I don't think I've had proper friends since I lived here. Real friends, I mean. The kind where you don't come home from a night out wondering if they even like you. I used to think of you two. How honest we were with each other.'

Gratifying though it was to hear that Helen hadn't left them entirely behind, it wasn't quite true about the honesty. Although Helen had always been the one unconcerned about hurting feelings. Which made her honest, yes, if not the natural person to turn to when you needed comfort. She was likely exactly the same in her job: brisk, efficient, no shielding. *Politeness serves no one when rights are on the line*, Annie could imagine her saying.

'Why do you think that is?' Laura asked, with interest.

'I honestly don't know. I could blame work or life or busyness. That's what people say, right?'

'That's what people do,' Laura corrected. 'Everyone has their own thing going on and you find a pocket of time where you can.'

'That's easy for you to say,' Helen said. 'You two have the groundwork laid years ago, so it's easier to fall back in. Oh God, that came out wrong. Sorry. I can't seem to say what I mean.'

Once the apology floodgates were opened, it seemed everything was a source of regret. The thing was, Helen was right in a way. Once Annie and Laura were both living at home again, it was easier to be friends than to avoid one another. That didn't mean they didn't choose one another, even if that choice was within the confines of what was available to them. As adults, they were a group in themselves. Even without Helen, they were enough.

Yet it was hard sometimes not to look at their lives, both

of them sleeping at night in their childhood beds, their lives revolving in some way around this house, and wonder how exactly they had become stuck.

'I read somewhere that a friend is someone with whom you can think slowly rather than having to react quickly,' Annie said. She enjoyed letting the implications hang there.

'I suppose I deserved that,' Helen said eventually.

'No breaking out the B,' Laura said, and their laughter at their old phrase broke the tension.

'I think we're grown up enough to be able to say *bitch* without fear,' Annie said.

'At long last!' Laura said. 'Either way, knock it off or I'll have no choice but to walk you through the ins and outs of being a single parent.'

'You're not a single parent, though,' Annie said. 'You have your mother.'

'Fuck you very much,' Laura said, laughing. 'But I'll have you know that cannot hurt because it is perfect truth. And sad and all as it might look from the outside, things could be a lot worse.'

'Does Coraline … I mean, is she …' Helen trailed off.

'She has a father, if that's what you're asking. He's even in the picture sometimes. For Coraline, I mean. Not for me. He lives in New York. He sees Cor when he comes home at Christmas to his parents.'

'Once a year, that's it?'

'When she's older, she'll go to him for a couple of weeks in the summer. That's the plan anyway.'

'He never considered moving back to Ireland?' Helen asked.

'New York is where the money is. No, that's not fair,' Laura corrected herself. 'It's money *and* status. Can you believe I bought into that whole idea of success for as long as I did? I was on the subway one morning – Annie, you know this already, sorry – horribly early, going home to change and return to the office after an all-night meeting, and there was this kid in the seat beside me with one of those holographic cards, you remember the ones we used to have, where it shows one picture when you turn it one way and another when you turn it another? And the kid was flipping the card from green to silver and back again, silver, green, and all I could think of was the reflection of the trees in the river at the bottom of your garden, Helen – hand on heart, I don't think you'd crossed my mind in years – and I thought, *when did I last see something green without having to go and look for it?*' She paused and raised her eyebrows. 'I didn't quite go straight to the airport, but I was on a flight home within the month. Of course, I was hardly home five minutes when I found out I was pregnant with Coraline. Gave my mother a bit of a land, but she wouldn't have it any other way. She likes Cor far more than she ever liked me.'

Annie glanced at Helen to see if she had taken offence at having been forgotten, but Helen was looking at Jack's chair. 'Whenever Dad took me to work with him, he would point to me and say "my Helen" to everyone we met. It made me feel so safe to think they already knew I was his daughter.'

This is my very dear friend, Annie. To be in Jack's warmth and favour was a joy all its own.

'Is anyone hungry?' Annie said, and disappeared to the quiet of the kitchen before anyone could answer.

She went to the fridge and took out a red pepper, spring onions and the block of red cheddar. While the tortilla browned in the pan, she chopped everything finely before closing another tortilla on top and flipping the lot. There was comfort in the familiarity of it. In lifting the quesadilla from the pan and cutting it into eighths. Placing the plate under the grill to stay warm while she fried another. Scooping natural yogurt into a ramekin and putting it in the centre of the plate. Pouring three glasses of apple juice. Taking the whole lot on a tray into the dining room. Comfort in the control of her own two hands.

'Very fancy,' Laura said. 'We wondered what was keeping you.'

'It was worth the wait,' Helen said.

'They were your dad's favourite. "Classy bits" he called them. Sour cream didn't agree with him, though, so the yogurt was our workaround.'

Helen lifted her chin and nodded and helped herself to one. 'What kind of funeral would he have liked?' she asked quietly a few minutes later.

'Traditional,' Annie told Helen. 'With a bit of a twist, maybe.'

'Did … had you talked about it?'

'Not directly. But he went to a lot of friends' funerals. Facebook funerals in the last while. He kept up a fairly lively commentary.' She smiled, remembering. If Helen could be generous, so too could Annie. '*Here come the lilies and the labels,* he would say when the wreaths appeared. He had a little bet with himself on whether or not there would be a floral tribute. MOTHER or LOVE spelled out in carnations. He poured himself a half-inch of whiskey for every one he got right.'

'That's so him,' Helen said, her eyes filling up again. She cleared her throat. 'What do you mean *with a twist?* What kind of twist?'

'Atypical music and readings. Out of the ordinary but classy. A poem instead of a reading, maybe. No Frank Sinatra "My Way" or anything like that. Broadly, I think the removal-then-burial Mass is fine. And if anyone suggests lining the road between the church and the graveyard, say yes.'

'Is that the new guard of honour?' Helen asked.

'Covid,' Annie and Laura said together.

'He will miss out on the big public funeral, most likely,' Helen said. 'I'm sure he would have loved the idea of luminaries saying glowing things about him.'

'He absolutely would. Although it would depend on who it was. A lesser minister looking for his own moment in the spotlight, now that would only have annoyed him,' Annie said.

'It'll be easier on you this way,' Laura said.

'When you're ready to start thinking about coffins,

Bert Crowley has a decent range and he won't fleece you,' Annie said.

'What constitutes a decent range?' Helen asked, and Annie remembered again that Helen had arrived home for her mother's funeral when all the planning was already done.

'Everything from solid oak to veneers. When I went in to pick one for my Mam, he even had an American-style one. The kind you see on TV, you know, where the top opens in two halves.'

'I'm so sorry you had to do that on your own,' Helen said suddenly.

'I wasn't alone,' Annie said. 'Laura was with me.'

Bert Crowley had brought her into his nice bland office and disappeared to make tea and by the time he reappeared, Laura was with him. She had told him to text her when Annie came in, she explained. This wasn't something a person should do alone.

'Two-man job,' Laura had said, with a shrug, and Annie had wondered if she knew she underplayed her own goodness around other people. As if everything she did was no more than the next person might do.

'I'll have that lovely willow coffin Bert had,' Laura said. 'Or the wicker, maybe. I'd trust Bert to remember to put the sheet of plywood on top so the lid doesn't collapse onto my face while you're still throwing in the rose petals – great for mulch so be sure and have plenty of them, please – and the first shovels of dirt. Wouldn't want Coraline to see that.'

'You have it all thought out,' Helen said, taking another quesadilla and spooning some yogurt onto it.

'My mother is *very* practical.' Laura rolled her eyes theatrically. 'Seriously, Cor was a raw babe in arms when she sat me down and told me she had gone to the council and bought a second plot next to hers and Dad's so there would be room for me and Coraline.'

'What if you meet someone?' Annie asked, half laughing.

'He'll have to ask will he be buried with your people.' Helen was laughing, too.

'She obviously thinks I'm a lost cause in the romance department,' Laura said. 'Which is fine by me.' She ran her finger around the inside of the yogurt bowl and licked the yogurt off. 'I actually find it pretty reassuring, if I'm honest.'

'I want to be cremated,' Annie said, a little surprised at herself for sharing so readily.

'*Remember man, thou art but dust and into dust thou shalt return,*' Laura said. 'That used to frighten the bejaysus out of me as a child. For longer than I'll care to admit, I wondered if the dust bunnies under my bed were other children who had crawled under there to hide and were never found.'

'Why cremation?' Helen asked Annie, when they had finished laughing, half-horrified, at Laura.

'I'm not sure where I stand on the whole soul business, but …' She felt herself flush slightly. 'I like the idea of joining the air. It's the closest I'll get to being a bird.' She turned to Helen. 'What about you?'

'No fire or wicker, please,' Helen said. She put on a posh voice. 'A lead-lined coffin, if at all possible. Like the British royals.'

Annie hoped Helen could hear the fondness in their laughter.

'I won't care, will I? Honestly, I'm fine with whatever will comfort the children.' She paused. 'So I suppose snacks at the funeral home – good ones, I mean, proper branded crisps. Maybe a popcorn machine. A churro truck, why not? Free Wi-Fi. A bouncy castle out the back.'

Laura crossed to the sideboard and returned with a bottle of whiskey and three tumblers. She poured a measure into each of the glasses and handed one to Annie and one to Helen.

'One buried, one burned, one bouncing.' Laura counted each one on her fingers, then held up her glass. 'Cheers.'

'To Jack,' Helen said. She downed her whiskey, then poured another. 'And to Dr Danny Furlong, too.' She ran her finger around the rim of her wine glass, creating a faint ringing noise. 'When I was in boarding school first, I used to lie awake at night listening to Olive Campbell snoring through her sinuses and thinking of ways I could humiliate him. A teenage pregnancy would be good, but I was eighteen by then so it wouldn't have been the end of the world. Besides, there were no boys. Not even a male teacher. I thought about claiming abuse of some sort. Being locked in my room or beaten with a wooden spoon or touched inappropriately. No court cases or anything, just maybe a visit from the guards to the set. But of course I wouldn't be there to see it, so there wasn't any point.' She sighed. 'I sound like a monster, I know. In the cold light of day I hated myself for even thinking it.' She swirled the wine in the glass. 'You were right to forget me.'

Annie thought of desperate mornings when she held her mother's morphine bottle in her hand and wondered what she would do if her mother asked. 'We've all had thoughts we're not proud of.'

'For what it's worth, since I came home I can't get away from you. There's some story of us around every bend in the road,' Laura said, raising an eyebrow at them both. 'Also, hatred is a total waste of time.'

'That's exactly it! It was such a waste of time, all that hate. I refused to come home that Christmas, and somewhere in the misery of it all – it was me and the nuns and a girl whose parents lived in the Middle East and she had literally nowhere else to go – I realised that I didn't hate him any more. He was quite right when he said he never promised anything. But I couldn't get past it. Held it against him all these years, imagine. You know I went straight to a hotel when I flew in a couple of days ago, rather than come here? Deliberately booked a PCR test later than I needed to. Jesus, the guilt.'

'If you had got here a day earlier, would you have sat Jack down and had a heart-to-heart and a hug and a cry? No? Then there's nothing you can do but let it go.' Laura was definite.

Annie took a sip of her whiskey. 'The rare times my dad came to pick me up at school, I had to stand by the gate even if it was raining so I wouldn't have to see him looking around a couple of times before being able to pick me out. People are who they are.'

'Would it help to know it often takes me several passes to locate the boys?' Helen said. She made a face. 'Even though there's two of them. In a school with no uniform. At this point, I start talking to one of the other parents and wait for them to find me.'

'I've lost Coraline more times than I care to count,' Laura said. 'No matter where we go, the first thing we do is to decide where to meet if – when – we get separated. I lost her at a Christmas fair once and when I found her she was patiently explaining to a security guard that she wasn't lost, but her mum was.' She shook her head. 'Little madam. I was mortified.'

Annie smiled and nodded and pretended it didn't bother her that her experience, her voice, was being subsumed into fun and funny parenting stories to which she had no reply. To answer would be to put herself on the level of her friends' children. To infantilise herself in this conversation among adults. The best she could do was wait for it to pass. It always did, she reminded herself. Sooner or later, all parents remembered they were people first.

'I can't imagine you worrying what anyone else thought of you,' Helen said, when she had topped them all up and put the bottle to one side.

'I spent more years than I care to count worrying about people's opinions,' Laura said. 'The truth is that I am not magnificent. I am not carefree. I am not out there living my best life and to hell with the begrudgers. I came back and had Coraline and told myself I was living on my terms. That other people envied me my free spirit. That they thought of me as magnificently wilful. Breath-holdingly creative. Great-hearted.'

'Jack always spoke of you in those terms,' Annie said gently. '*The sprite,* he called you. Or, if you were trying to persuade him to do something he didn't want to do, *that fairy.*'

Laura raised her glass again. 'To Jack, who, whatever his blind spots, aged into a lovely man.'

Helen took a sip from her glass and cleared her throat before she spoke. 'Expecting to be happy is a child's dream. Once you're aware of the world and your smallness in it and your pure dumb luck, it's a tough ask to believe in your own deservingness.'

'Agreed,' Laura said. 'Yet we persist in a performance of happiness.'

'I had quite a bit of therapy after Rex was born,' Helen confessed.

As if anyone would otherwise use the word *deservingness* with a straight face.

'Psychotherapy? CBT? Interpersonal therapy? Behavioural activation? Bog-standard counselling?' Laura reeled them off. Seeing their faces, she shrugged. 'New York, baby.'

'Inpatient, actually.' Helen flushed again. 'An expensive private place. You know the sort of thing. We would sit there, me and the interdisciplinary team, pretending we were all invested in the idea that my unhappiness was something almost separate to the rest of me. As if it could be pulled out and examined and dealt with on its own. I used to imagine we had it on the table between us, petting it and stroking it, like a little hedgehog, until it curled itself into a small enough ball that we could consider me better.'

'Did it help?' Annie asked.

'It didn't hurt,' Helen said. 'There was no big resolution. No eureka moment when I began to see my life differently. I slept uninterrupted, which, with two babies at home, was nothing to sneer at, believe me.' She wrinkled her nose and thought for a moment. 'Sometimes I wonder if it was just that they kept me safe while time passed.'

'Isn't it funny,' Laura said suddenly, 'how we expend so much effort and energy on what strangers think of us, while those we love deal with us at our worst? They have to put up with our moods and tempers and tantrums, our silences and withdrawal. The sheer weight of having to keep us happy.'

'I'm going to sound irretrievably single and naïve here, I know,' Annie said. 'But is that responsibility not part of the privilege of sharing your life with someone?'

'In theory, yes,' Helen said. 'In theory you're on this lifelong adventure together, but really ninety per cent of a relationship is the mundane.'

There were plenty worse things than mundane, even if Helen and Laura had forgotten, or had never known. Waking alone, morning after morning, with no one to ask you how you had slept. Waking alone in the middle of the night, breathless and sweating monsters, with nothing but the bedside light to convince you of the line between sleep and dreaming. Fielding invitations on high days and holy days, but having always to remember to be grateful, because everyone knew you had nowhere else to be. Accepting invitations to places you didn't want to go, with people you didn't want to go with, because you couldn't stand another day inside your own head. Opening the wine whenever you wanted, then finishing the wine because it was a waste not to and sure why not? Watching whatever you wanted on TV. Spending half the programme wondering if you missed something, and having no one to ask. Having your restaurant order dictated by what you could cut with one hand while you held a book with the other so the people at the tables around you didn't give you dirty-eavesdropper looks. The fear of choking at home. The fear of falling and being unable to get up or to a phone. The fear that no one would notice. The fear that no one would notice. The fear that no one would notice.

But against all that was the picture she saw when she closed her eyes. A future where she sat in a shaft of sunlight, perhaps a breeze from an open door, a dog lazing on a mat nearby, a coffee at her elbow. Whether or not there was someone behind the sunlight was immaterial. All that mattered was that the peace of that moment remain available to her.

'A friend of mine,' Helen began, and Annie caught Laura's eye and smiled. So many of Helen's stories used to start that way. *A friend of mine* ... As though they hadn't known every one of her friends by name. As if they themselves weren't the major part of that group. If not quite a circle, then that Venn diagram had been a generous eclipse.

'What?' Helen looked from one of them to the other. 'What did I say that's so funny?'

'Nothing,' Laura assured her.

Annie leaned over and patted Helen's arm. 'We missed you, that's all.'

'A friend of mine took her children out of school and went off to tour the world,' Helen told them. Seeing their puzzled faces, she added, 'I meant that if it was something Laura wanted to do, then having a child doesn't mean she can't. Sandrine isn't even that free-spirited.'

'How would that even work?' Laura asked.

'She had to register them as homeschooled for the year. Then she used an online service for materials and testing, as far as I remember.'

'Doesn't it defeat the purpose to have to take the same work they'd be doing anyway?' Annie asked.

'I asked her that,' Helen said. 'If she worried it would be a same-homework-different-table kind of situation, but she said they did a week on and week off, or sometimes a week of mornings, and it worked out fine.'

'Can you imagine?' Laura had a faraway look in her eyes. 'Waking up somewhere different every day. No ties. No timetable. Christmas on the beach.'

'Are you serious?' Annie asked, and Laura shrugged.

'I could be.'

Annie went into the hall and got the notebook from her

handbag. Across the top of a clean double page, she wrote: *LAURA – SHOULD I STAY OR SHOULD I GO?* In the 'Go' column, she jotted down what Laura had just said. 'What else?'

'We're really going to do this?' Laura asked.

'It never failed us before,' Annie said.

An hour later, Annie's sides were sore from laughing and the fire was a warm, weary orange.

'Okay, so to recap the last two suggestions,' she said. 'In the "Stay" column, we have the potential difficulty should Laura decide to become vegan while she's away, since we don't know where she might be or how easy that might be—'

'And missing Susan's vegan rolls in particular,' Helen added.

'And Susan's vegan rolls,' Annie agreed. 'And in the "Go" column, Laura's favourite winter boots—'

'With the fake fur lining,' Laura added.

'Laura's favourite winter boots with the fake fur lining will last a year longer because she won't have worn them while she is away,' Annie finished.

'Because, like the Bishop of Llandaff, I'll be mostly found in warm places,' Laura confirmed.

'Who?'

'Not a who, a what. It's a dahlia. You're such indoor people,' Laura said, waving her hand and very nearly upending the wine bottle. 'Like *sunflowers*,' she said, in a tone that was evidently intended to shame them.

'Or cactuses,' Annie added. 'Cacti.'

'Ladies, I believe we've reached the bottom of the barrel,' Helen said.

'Thank you,' Laura said, suddenly serious.

'I always love a good list,' Annie said.

'No, really. Thank you for not saying that I will never do it. For letting me pretend it's really a choice I might make.'

'Never say never,' Helen said.

Laura smiled at them both. 'Not never,' she said. 'Just not now. Come tomorrow morning, I will go back to my daughter and my mother. I'll hug them both and be grateful – mostly – for everything I have.'

Annie tore the pages from the notebook and handed them to Laura. 'Then keep the list,' she said. 'For when the time is right.'

Nobody suggested banking up the fire again. Even Helen became quiet and drowsy, a marked departure from her teenage alcohol-ingestion trajectory, which was as predictable as it was endearing: halfway into her third drink, Helen visibly softened and was liable to say anything. *I think you're so beautiful,* she would say, staring intensely into Annie's face or smoothing Laura's eyebrows or trying to hug them both and spilling her watermelon Bacardi Breezer down both their backs. *So so beautiful.* Half a drink later, she would pull them close. *Mr Power is a fine thing,* she would whisper-shout, before collapsing in giggles. Still later, the doubts crept in. *When I'm older I'm going to shave my head and change my name so I'll be able to tell if people only like me because of my dad or because I'm pretty.* A hiccupy pause. A maudlin tone. *Do you think I'm pretty?* Then later, far later, when all the drinks were drunk and the sugar and colouring and preservatives had swirled their way back through the lower oesophageal sphincter and hoisted themselves up and out with a mighty and inevitable heave, she would go quiet. *My parents wish they'd never had me.* At that stage of the night, some shushing and indistinguishable murmuring was all that was needed to coax her into sleep, and the following morning would see her restored to her hard, bright self.

A story about them around every bend in the road, Laura had said. Impossible to get away from. Yet Annie felt it would be truer to say she had thought about them every day for what felt like a long time and then not at all.

They gathered blankets and cushions and settled themselves for the night, Helen hovering for a minute before taking Jack's chair. Laura, after a quick glance at Annie arranging cushions on the green sofa, tucked herself into the companion chair to Helen's. In the fading light and covered by blankets, they could have been a tableau of Jack and Annie herself last winter.

Helen's voice was a small sigh in the darkness. 'It doesn't feel real. Nobody knows he's gone except us.'

It wasn't strictly true. Helen's family knew. And the nursing team at the hospital knew. But Annie knew what she meant. It felt as though the three of them were alone with the knowledge that the world was a man down.

Death becoming real was a thing that happened over and over and over. When you picked the coffin. When you saw the gaping hole in the ground. When you closed the front door and heard the silence. When you went to tell her something and found her gone. When you happened upon the perfect winter gloves to match her ridiculous purple felt hat before remembering that the purple felt hat was warming another head these days.

There was an art to the administration of death. The ushering out of life and the ushering in of grief. Done right, they were two separate doorways. Done right, no one got trapped in that in-between space, able to see the fresh air beyond the second door but powerless to get out into it.

Annie lay in the darkness and listened to Laura soothe Helen with patient descriptions of energy transformation. She lay quietly and tried to give the impression of sleep. There was little she could add that would help Helen now. In her experience, anything said now would leave an aftertaste of regret and awkwardness at oversharing. Especially with drink on board. She listened to Helen shifting around in her chair, sighing and thumping cushions and shuffling her backside from one side to the other like a dog turning in circles. It was what she imagined having a child would be like, but without the release of an early bedtime. How did people do it? The endless closeness. The vastness of someone else's unboundaried need. All the air already used by the time it got to you.

It was one of her great joys to close the door and know she would be alone until she herself opened it again. To know that when she entered her house, everything was exactly as she left it. Never finding her petrol tank empty, the milk empty in the fridge. Her habits and quirks remained unremarked and – here was the thing – unjudged. Her movements unpoliced. Her whole being answerable to herself alone. Contentment with her own choices made for comfortable nights.

NOTHING IN HER LIFE SHE DID
NOT PUT THERE HERSELF

Annie woke to the sound of Laura clattering around in the kitchen. Laura never liked sleeping in, nor did she understand those who did, which meant that once she was awake, there was sure to be curated noise. The heavy living room curtains were closed but a band of thin light suggested that it was safely morning. Helen was curled in Jack's chair, her head thrown back and her mouth loose and open in an unflattering pose that confirmed genuine sleep.

Annie sat up cautiously. It was a while since she'd had that much to drink. After Jack's stroke, she hadn't bothered much, partly because she needed to be alert and ready to get in the car at a moment's notice. Partly, too, because a glass of wine on her own made her miss him, which wasn't fair when he was still right there with her.

Now she could drink with impunity whenever she liked. How joyless an idea it suddenly seemed.

She slipped out from under her blanket and went upstairs on quiet feet to her bedroom. To what would shortly be the spare room. She changed quickly, sizing up her wardrobe and dressing table. She could be packed in two hours, she thought. One carload would remove all traces of her. Her eyes fell on the mountain range painted into the corner of the room. A clever and easy little project she had seen on social media during the second lockdown, when winter and spring were brushing politely past one another in the doorway of the year.

When she finished, Jack was delighted with the effect and asked her to do the same in his room. It could easily be painted over. She hoped it wouldn't be.

Washing her face and brushing her teeth cleared out the worst of the woolliness. When she returned to the kitchen, Laura had been joined by Helen.

'Do I look a fright?' Helen asked. 'Or do you look particularly together?'

Annie wondered for a second if it was judgement about how she normally looked, then relaxed. Even Helen said things that could be taken at face value. 'A bit of a fright,' she said, smiling. 'Fright-lite, maybe. And it doesn't matter a bit.'

'Breakfast in ten,' Laura said. 'Pitch in or piss off out of my way.'

After breakfast, Laura went to phone Tim, her fellow community gardener with the four-wheel drive. 'The cook doesn't do the washing-up,' she said, and so Annie set to scrubbing scrambled egg from the pan. Glancing out the window, she saw Helen standing beside the sundial, her phone to her ear. Evidently, their public phone call closeness was consigned to a one-night-only event.

As she watched, Helen put the phone back in her pocket and took out a box of cigarettes and a lighter, the kind of cheap, brightly coloured plastic ones that littered the counters of corner shops, smoking ban or no smoking ban.

Annie dried her hands on a tea towel and went outside, crunching her way over to Helen. How did people ever commit crimes discreetly in snowy places?

'Don't tell Laura,' Helen said, turning at the sound of footsteps. 'I have one sometimes and I've made my peace with that.'

Annie mimed zipping her lips.

'I spoke to the hospital and they said I can go in later to … to see Dad. To say goodbye.'

Helen's left sleeve was pulled long so that her hand could hide inside it. No amount of handwashing and patting into shape would resuscitate the cashmere.

'He needs something to wear. In the coffin, I mean. I don't know which of his suits to pick. Whether he had a favourite.'

'Do you want me to choose something for you to take?'

'Would you mind? It's an awful job, I know.'

Annie shook her head. 'It would be a privilege.'

'Thank you.'

Annie held out her hand for the cigarette and took a drag. 'Do you want me to come with you to the hospital? I can wait in the car or go in with you, whatever you like,' she added. 'No pressure to decide until we're there.'

Helen's hug, when it came, was unexpected. Annie, her head spinning from the nicotine, stiffened, then relaxed into it and rubbed her friend's shaking shoulders. Helen smelled different. A mix of Dove soap and hand sanitiser. Yesterday's perfume faint beside her ear, something light and floral rather than the sweet Body Shop scent she used to favour. *Dewberry? Is that even a real berry?* Annie used to tease her.

'What if he doesn't look like himself?' Helen's voice was muffled by Annie's cardigan.

'He will.' Annie pulled back slightly to look at her watch. 'It'll have been twelve hours, give or take. He will still look like Jack.'

Helen nodded. 'I'd better go inside and have a shower,' she said.

Annie turned and watched Helen crunch her way back into the house. She took another drag of the cigarette, enjoying the dizziness. That slight reel that suggested the world had tilted off-kilter. In the dazzle of post-snow sunshine, the grey of the stone was more pronounced, the creeper thin and vulnerable-looking. Was it only yesterday she had wondered what Helen might do with the house when Jack was gone? Only the day before that the idea of Jack gone had been unimaginable? Only the season before that she and Jack had charted the leaves on the creeper journeying from green to yellow to orange to red, then falling away entirely? Only the year before that Jack's vitality had carried them forward while the world staggered and stopped? How strange time was. How fragile it revealed human lives to be. They were all just a cluster of moments, good or bad, then the memory of those moments, then nothing at all.

How many evenings had she and Jack lit the firepit and sipped wine while the sun went down and the world held its breath that another day might dawn? Sometimes, if he was feeling particularly melancholy, he would hold out his hand and they would dance to the gentle music on late-night radio. He spun her in slow circles and told her stories about his Lily, about their life together. Occasionally, if the stories he told had been sad, he would tell her that he very much hoped he would dance at her wedding. What were humans in pain, if not powered by hope?

'You know better, don't you?' she said to the crow who had come to perch on the edge of the sundial.

Crows got a bad rap, she always felt. When asked to choose a favourite bird, people rhapsodised about wrens' tenacity or robins bringing warm messages of love from the dead or eagles' fierce beauty. Penguins got a look in, despite doing the bare minimum to qualify as a bird at all. Crows rarely got a mention. It wasn't that Annie liked them because she felt someone should, it was more that she had a strong suspicion that if she were to be reincarnated as a bird or to wake up one morning as a character in a surrealist novel, then a crow she would be. Brisk and ungainly and practical. Jack, to whom she had confided her hunch, had always maintained his admiration for crows, citing their curiosity and their care for one another. She had rolled her eyes then, making him laugh. Jack himself would be a peacock, he said, laughing. Gorgeously decorative and with no shame.

The crow watched her stub out the cigarette and wipe her eyes, its head on one side, alert to the possibilities.

'What am I going to do without him?' she asked, but the crow, for all its alleged curiosity and care, had no words of comfort to offer.

She would do the same as everyone did without anyone. Keep her eyes on the ground and put one foot in front of the other until it stopped being an effort and she could once again look directly at the world.

Annie closed Jack's bedroom door quietly behind her and stood in the silence. Most of Jack's things were in his wardrobe, freshly ironed from two days earlier. Before. She ran her hand along the rail, setting the shirts whispering softly on their hangers.

She turned towards the bed, closing her eyes against its emptiness. 'What do you feel like today?' she asked.

He would want to be smart, certainly. But also comfortable. She flicked past his two suits. They had got rid of the others when they cleared his wardrobe as part of a lockdown decluttering project. Two good suits were enough for a man at his time of life, he declared. One for funerals and one for weddings. At neither event had he anticipated being the guest of honour so soon.

She took down a hanger that held a pair of dark grey wool trousers. Yes. He liked these for good wear. He had worn them when they went out for dinner for his birthday in early December in the brief festive flash when all the restaurants reopened and it felt as if Christmas might be possible. Before the worst lockdown. Before the stroke.

His favourite belt was on the trousers he had worn to hospital so she would have to remember to change it over to this pair. Next, his favourite pale grey shirt. A tie? No. A tie would need a blazer and Jack had despised what he called the off-duty politician look.

She took out the maroon tweed waistcoat he wore the Christmas Day before last. Her first without her mother. Her first and last with Jack fully himself. They had skipped a formal meal entirely in favour of blinis and champagne in the morning, then a succession of starters throughout the morning and afternoon, until they moved on to the 'chocolate courses' sometime in the early evening. There had been a tiny oily stain on the satiny left pocket of the waistcoat from where his greasy fingers had rubbed the fabric when reaching for a napkin, but he maintained that the dry cleaner had done an excellent job. Annie held the garment up to the light and couldn't see any trace of a stain. She laid the waistcoat on the chair with the trousers.

The worst part – *the very worst part,* she imagined herself telling someone, although who other than Jack, she would be hard pushed to say – was going to the boxy shelves that ran down the right-hand side of his wardrobe, scanning down past the everyday jumpers, the sleeveless cotton vests. All as white as the snow packing the windowsill; Jack threw them out at the first hint of age, insisting that yellowing vests made an old man of him. After the stroke – the first stroke – she had monitored the laundry as carefully as he did himself, holding up each pristine vest in the morning before slipping it over his head. 'No old men here,' she would tell him, as he slapped his hand against his thigh in agitated agreement.

His good pieces were on a lower shelf and Annie knelt to address them. She drew out each cotton garment bag and looked inside. The fourth one down revealed the fine cashmere cardigan she gave him for his birthday. Specially ordered from Puglia, in a thick fisherman's rib and with a shawl collar. More structured than a regular cardigan, yet without the shiny generic formality of a blazer. His face, when he opened it, was pure delight.

'This isn't one for the gardening,' he said, and he put it on straightaway and twirled for her before going to look at himself in the long mirror in the hall.

He wore it on winter Sundays when they made a game of trying new recipes for dinner. The disasters they had! The fish-and-chip pie with the chips cut too thick and half-raw. The beetroot burgers that left their fingers stained dark pink for days, like something out of Willy Wonka. The shakshuka that had to be abandoned when the lid flew off the jar of chilli flakes, rendering it inedible. 'As fiery as Satan's proverbial,' as Jack put it, arranging their backup supper of cheese and olives and crackers on a walnut board.

Annie reached into her sleeve for a tissue, before remembering that that was one more habit lost to Covid. She got to her feet and dripped her way across to Jack's bedside locker, where she always kept a box of balsam tissues. She wiped her eyes and remembered him twirling, smiling. Fixed him in her memory like that. Jack. Entirely, happily himself. Her very dear friend.

Suddenly the thought of her mother's house was comforting. Somewhere to go to escape Jack's bedroom and his empty chair. She could leave and take with her only her fondest memories.

She took out Jack's overnight bag, the worn burgundy leather gleaming dully in the light from the window. She put his shoes into a shoe bag and placed them sideways so that they took up half of the base of the bag. Then she folded his trousers and shirt and placed them in the other half, topped with his vest and underwear. After a minute's consideration, she added the Beatles socks that Helen had sent on behalf of the children for his birthday. That made her feel slightly better about the cardigan.

In the living room, Laura was putting on her coat and scarf. 'Tim says the roads aren't too bad. He'll drop me home and then run you over to the hospital for your car.'

'Forget those networking seminars, you are the most connected person I know.' Annie squeezed her arm.

'I'm at the other end of the phone. Anytime.' Laura hugged Helen.

It was strange to see them hugging. As if they were in a school play, teenagers dressing up to look like women in their forties.

'I'll be back shortly and we can go to the hospital together,' Annie told Helen.

She would be back shortly. And then gone again. As the jeep bumped down the drive, she watched the house recede behind them.

And after that? What then?

All she knew was that there would be nothing in her life she did not put there herself.

That much was true.

And one true thing was all a person needed.

IT'S DIFFERENT FOR EVERYONE

Helen watched as Tim's jeep turned left towards town and the gates began their slow close. They were an object of interest, those gates, when her parents first installed them. Few people in the parish closed their gates at all.

'Soon everyone will have them,' her father had said, when what he really meant was that people would follow his lead. That he was special, ahead of the pack.

He wasn't ahead now. He wasn't anything at all. His fabled presence – *such presence*, reviewers always gushed – proving as ephemeral as everyone else's in the end.

The house felt the lack of him. That sudden shift from her father always being there to not being there. To never again being there. Helen stood in the quiet of the hall and thought that her father's absence changed the house fundamentally, as though a load-bearing wall had been ripped out. Any thought of her keeping the house, whether to live in or holiday in, was clearly ridiculous. If Glebe Cottage was no longer her father's house, then it was certainly not hers.

She texted Conor. *Snow heavy on the ground here. Their snow boots are bulky but they should bring them. They can wear them on the plane.*

Would the snow affect flights in and out of the airport? Surely not, in this day and age. She took out her phone and texted Conor again. *Will you check the airport information for flight cancellations? The airline and the other main ones too? Let me know.*

She looked at the sent message then added another. *Sorry. Not spiralling. Just – hospital soon so will be out of coverage. xx*

How long would it take Annie to get to the hospital, collect her car and drive back here? The snow threw off her calculations. How many extra minutes would it demand? Thirty? Forty-five? Sixty? With snow in the equation, she no longer had a gauge.

What she needed was to remain active. To get moving and keep moving.

Her father's bedroom was so still it was as though the air had died with him. Nothing stirred. Nothing hummed or dripped or rustled or buzzed or any one of the other thousands of noises that Helen would have welcomed. She could blast music, she supposed. Roll up her sleeves and set to cleaning or clearing or whatever it was that people did with the things that were recently useful or precious to someone else. Instead, she all but tiptoed over to the bookshelves that had housed scripts and contracts and files when this was Jack's study, but now held several neat stacks of paperbacks. She remembered Annie saying they had liked to read the same books and leaned in to read the spines. The selection surprised her. If asked, she would have said her father's taste ran masculine. When she pictured him reading, it was a spy novel or a murder mystery he held in his hand, or perhaps the occasional fabric-bound classic. Yet here were slim volumes of poetry and French novels in translation alongside pick-and-mix-coloured debuts and fantasy doorstoppers. Which went some way to suggesting hidden depths without shedding real light on what those depths actually were. Should she take one, read it to remember him? Mawkish, she decided, and ultimately pointless when she never had any such conversation with him when he was alive to take part in it, and now never would.

People complained that their parents persisted in seeing them as the children they had once been, but the same operated in reverse: her parents were forever stuck where teenage Helen – angry Helen – had fixed them.

An image came to her of Jack and Annie, side by side in their matching armchairs, reading cosily on a midweek afternoon. *Why her?* But she knew why. Friendship didn't carry the same baggage as family. That was the trick with making friends, too, you just had to make it easy for people. Be the one to ask instead of waiting to be asked. Annie had taught her that. Annie and Laura.

The bookshelf held a photograph of her mother, placed where her father could see it from his bed. In the photograph, her mother was standing in the sunshine, a hat in one hand, shading her eyes with the other. To Helen, the picture showed her mother's reticence, her caution with herself. To her father, she assumed, it was the source of some happy memory. With him working away for days at a time, her parents never had a chance to tire of one another. Theirs was – if not exactly a long-distance romance – then certainly an instance of absence making the heart grow fond. Impossible to have lived through the unbearable enforced closeness of the pandemic and not thought longingly of a long romantic absence. When the first lockdown ended and people talked with amazement about the statistics on relationship breakdown, Helen was more surprised that so many couples had nitpicked their way through, emerging together, too worn down and weary to do anything except continue along the path they had chosen *before*. She welcomed Conor being less available to her and thus more interesting. Looking forward to seeing one another, sharing the news of their day. She thought of her parents, a constant pair, with their pre-dinner drink ritual, their endless chat. She was always so conscious of not making their mistakes, always peering at them around the stacks of baggage, that she had entirely forgotten to mimic their gifts.

Their pride in her. Without shame or apology, they praised her achievements. To her, to each other, to visitors, to strangers. *Helen did very well in her Grade VI in piano.* Or *Helen has the lead in the school play.* Or *Helen has the opportunity of a place at boarding school next year.*

The way they talked to her as if she too were an adult. Oh, she didn't mean swearing or anything as pedestrian as all that. It was that they didn't censor themselves around her. Politics, emotions, culture, it was all open for discussion. There was no watershed in Helen's house. If she wanted to sit through it, she was assumed mature enough to watch it. How strange she used to find it at other friends' houses, the false sweetness of other mothers and gruff politeness of other fathers. They found her strange, too, of course, and somewhat inappropriate. They became wary around her. *You shouldn't be talking about things that are too grown-up for you,* Elise's mother said once, when she overheard eight-year-old Helen explaining Gorbachev's concept of glasnost to Elise. Helen smiled politely and went back to Elise's – frankly dull – Mr Frosty machine.

Annie's mother, and, later, Laura's mother, were too busy or too tired to care much what they talked about. Mrs Fleming was always at work or just in the door from work, undoing the buttons on her white nurse's uniform as she went wearily up the stairs in her noiseless white shoes. Mrs O'Brien was home early in the evenings, it was true, but she had exams to mark or classes to prepare, or she simply needed a break from teenagers. Said with a smile and an accompanying flap of her hands to whoosh them out the door.

The corollary of treating her like a grown-up was treating her friends the same way. Her mother kept food in the fridge and they were welcome to anything, anytime. Her father remembered the names of their pets, their interests. *How did that project on Iceland turn out,* he would ask, or *Did you remember the name of the song that was annoying you?* It was no wonder Annie and Laura loved Helen's house.

It was her fond hope that when the time came, her house would be the one her children's friends chose. How easy it is to hope for things with no understanding of what they entail, or the myriad assumptions they contain. That they would be allowed to mix easily, socially. That she would be comfortable sharing her space with strangers. That her children's friends would like her. That her children's friends would like *them*.

Conor answered on the first ring. 'How are you doing, Hel?'

'Are we the nice parents?' Helen asked.

'Hello to you, too. We're very nice. Usually, anyway, if not right this minute.'

'No, that's not what I mean. Are we *the* nice parents? To the kids' friends?' Helen could picture him frowning slightly, the way he did when he was really considering.

Attraction was never solely physical, that much was a given, but how much further did the pendulum swing over time? Gratitude, appreciation, teamwork. Listening. Taking you seriously. The sorts of things that made young people roll their eyes. *You wait,* Helen wanted to tell them. *If it sounds awful to you, that's because you haven't grown with someone yet.*

'I would say we're definitely nicer than Marie's parents or Luka's parents,' he said eventually. 'But neither as cool as Dimi's parents nor as fun as Nico's parents.'

So as far as he was concerned, Réiltín and Marie were still friends. A small comfort. 'That seems about right,' she said.

'We're a solid B+,' he continued. 'Dependable without being flashy. The Skoda of parents.'

'Not Christmas Day, but not January either.' Helen tried to match his tone. 'The Easter of parents.'

'And who doesn't love Easter?' he agreed. 'How are you doing?'

'I'm in the house alone and it's all a bit …' A bit what? Lonely? Creepy? Sad? '… nostalgic,' she settled for. 'All these memories bouncing around and echoing off the walls.'

'Can you hang on until later? We'll be in on the late flight. Everything earlier was booked out. Weekenders, I suppose.'

'Of course. I'm just being … Are the kids there?'

'The boys are here beside me. Ré's in her room. Do you want to talk to them?'

Helen imagined her daughter claiming to be too busy to speak to her. 'Let me have a quick minute with the boys first.'

The boys were a rapid tumble of non sequiturs. Who did this in school, who said that. Questions about when they would get home. There was a planned sleepover, a school trip, a party. Helen didn't hear the details. They left the call abruptly, tussling over whose turn it was to wear the coveted TikTok face mask on the plane. Why had they not bought a second? Her insistence on the boys' individuality, she supposed. *God, Helen!*

After a few moments, Conor came back on the line. 'Réiltín is just getting out of the shower and will call you back, she says.'

'Alright.' What other possible answer could she give?

Maybe Réiltín didn't actively dislike her. Maybe it was simply an assertion. A stretching. Maybe she had too many other things going on and didn't have time for her mother. Maybe it was a phase that would pass. Like roller skates and dance class and Pokémon.

She closed her eyes and tried to see her daughter at twenty, at thirty, at forty, but could only picture the same sullen expression and rolling eyes, beneath a variety of generic age hairstyles. A pixie cut at twenty, long and wavy at thirty, a neat geometrical bob at forty. All she was doing was superimposing Réiltín's face on photographs of her own younger years.

Had Annie chosen not to have children so as to avoid this particular minefield? More and more people were deciding against having babies. For environmental reasons, or financial reasons, or simply because women were no longer afraid to say no. Had Annie said no? Had she ever had the chance to say yes? It wasn't the sort of thing Helen could ask after all this time. *Hi, how are you, and could you justify your life choices, ideally in a way that makes me feel better about my own?*

Her phone buzzed and Réiltín's real face – in a rare

photograph she had permitted her mother to take last summer – displaced her imagined future-daughter.

'Dad said you wanted to talk to me.'

No *hello*. No *sorry for your trouble*. No *how are you doing, Mum?*

'When I was your age, your Papi Jack used to love people thinking he was glamorous. If the phone rang, he used to say it was "the papers" looking to do a profile on him and he would give this little rueful smile as though he would really rather be sitting at the table playing Switch with me and my friends.' Her voice cracked and she cleared her throat to hide it. 'He was quite a big deal here, you know.'

'Like famous, you mean? Will he have a big funeral?'

'It's a bit complicated with restrictions. It might be a small funeral and then a bigger public memorial later. We're trying to figure that out at the moment.'

'We?'

Helen got up and walked over to the French windows. Outside, small patches of snow were melting in the sun and Helen thought for a moment of stirring sugar into mugs of hot chocolate for herself and Annie on winter Fridays, holding the spoon barely under the surface of the liquid and watching the sugar dissolve. 'Me and Annie and Laura. My oldest friends. I guess Annie was your grandad's friend, too. She was living here with him, remember?'

'Gross!' Réiltín sounded horrified.

Helen laughed, as though she herself hadn't worried about that exact thing. 'Not like that, Ré. She was his carer since he had the stroke. But they were friends before that.'

'I haven't heard you talking about her before.'

How to explain the kind of drift that was next to impossible for the social media generation?

'I suppose not. It's funny because once upon a time we were really close. As close as …' She tried to think when Réiltín last had a best friend – any friend – to the house. 'As close as two people could be. Without a romantic element, I mean.' She added quickly, 'Not that there would have been anything wrong—'

'I *know*, Mum. *God*.'

It had slunk by without her noticing, that moment when she transformed from Mama to Mum. When Ré transformed her. The constriction appearing, perversely, to give her daughter more space. It did a lot of work, that narrow 'u', its arms braced against the 'm's on either side.

The silence stretched between them and the words were out of Helen's mouth before she had quite decided to say them. 'Are you happy, Ré?'

'Are you allowed to ask me that? Like, straight out like that?' Réiltín said. 'What if the answer is no?'

Helen's heart wrung itself. 'Then we would deal with it,' she said. 'It would suck and we would deal with it.'

'Are *you* happy, then?'

Helen thought for a minute. 'Sometimes,' she said carefully. 'Not always, obviously, and not right now, because of my dad dying and being away from you all and the pandemic and everything. But generally, I suppose I'm happy more often than I'm not.'

She let the silence stretch again. Réiltín would be lying on her bed, the phone on speaker beside her. Nobody under twenty-five seemed to hold a phone to their ear any more.

'That sounds about right,' Réiltín said eventually. 'Being happy sometimes, I mean.'

The noise that escaped Helen was half-laugh, half-sob.

'*God*, Mum. This is why no one tells you anything.'

'I'm mortifying, I know. Sorry.'

'See you tomorrow morning,' Réiltín said, and, in a minor miracle, switched her video on for long enough for Helen to see her face and her waving fingers.

Outside, the snow had muffled the world and Helen was reminded of the war film that opened with an explosion and showed the first few minutes in silence so that the audience might know what it was like to temporarily hear only the drumming of their own blood inside their head. The boys might like it now they were old enough for proper films. She could look up the parental advisory and see if it was suitable for their age group.

If indoors had been quiet, outdoors was eerie in its stillness and she had the urge to shatter the silence with a yell. She took a breath, then felt too self-conscious to go through with it and let the breath out again in a long, quiet sigh. Sound travelled further over snow and however remote the garden might feel, the reality was never that simple. *What would the neighbours think?* The whip no Irish person could ever outrun.

She walked into the centre of the garden, telling herself that the squeak of snow underfoot would be comforting. Instead, she again had the unnerving sensation of being entirely alone in the world.

Alone and afraid. Nothing between her and the end of her spin at life but whatever unknown amount of time was allotted to her by chance or agency or divinity.

Her father's mother died before Helen was born and his father followed when she was small enough that, to her, he was a voice attached to the smell of Major cigarettes – somehow shameful, though she didn't quite how or why – and boot polish and rashers. Her mother was not in contact with her parents. They were estranged, Helen was told, which, as a concept, seemed at odds with her mother's general lethargy. Her mother had not gone to her own mother's funeral, nor, later, her father's. Across all branches of her family, the women died first, leaving their menfolk to survive, whether pining or thriving.

See you tomorrow, she texted Conor. Then, just in case, *I love you. Mind them for me, won't you?*

I'm afraid, she could add, but he would phone immediately and ask what she was afraid of and if she started explaining she might never stop. She could phone Annie, but Annie was on her way back. Driving. On snowy roads. Helen sent up a quick thought for a safe journey.

Laura answered, crunching and swallowing. 'You okay, Helen?'

'I started thinking about all the things my children will do without me. Exams and parties and college and meeting their partners and getting pregnant and having babies and becoming comfortable with who they are and what they want. That's if they're lucky and I haven't died before they get to all those things. And that's not counting the things they'll have to do when I'm gone, like arranging my funeral and choosing readings and facing their own mortality.' She was on her knees in the snow.

'Breathe, Helen.' Laura's voice was steady. 'Breathe with me, okay?'

'Don't tell me to fucking breathe!' Helen shouted, but she had to suck in air for the shout and it helped.

Laura didn't count or hum or speak. She breathed, too, slow and steady, bringing Helen with her.

'Thank you,' Helen said eventually.

'We are all living in death's mouth the whole time,' Laura told her. 'We only realise when it swallows.'

Helen couldn't help it, she began to laugh.

'What?' Laura demanded.

'"Swallows" sounded so dirty,' Helen said, barely getting the words out.

'You're one to talk, worrying that your children will be getting pregnant without you. I'd be more worried if you were there, frankly.'

By now, Laura was laughing, too, and the sound echoed around the space, as though Helen were surrounded by friends. Her mother had always liked Laura, she remembered. At first because she broke the co-dependency between Helen and Annie that worried her mother, but, shortly, she began to ask where Laura was, if she was joining them, and would sometimes – even when she had one of her heads – make it downstairs to say hello or to show Laura some little change in the garden, something greener or flowering. Everywhere Helen looked, people were gone.

'How do we stand it?' she whispered, not even sure Laura would hear her.

'Oh, Helen, sweetheart. What other choice do we have?'

The third drawer she opened in the laundry room held rolls of bin bags. Helen separated a heavy-duty black sack from its fellows, moved the roll of bags up to the top drawer where they belonged, shut the drawer, thought for a second, then returned them to their new home in the third drawer.

Her father's bedroom felt like his and she hesitated for a moment at her intrusion. But everything he would ever need was in the small overnight bag Annie had left by the front door for the undertaker. Annie had done that job; this was Helen's. Her right and her responsibility.

She could safely ignore all of the medical equipment. Someone else – Annie – would know exactly what to do with it, if not today or tomorrow, then once the funeral was over.

His clothes could go to charity, of course – good quality as they were, any discerning person would be glad of them – but the underwear, socks and vests, she swept into the bag, followed, after a moment, by his pyjamas and handkerchiefs. The books would need a box. She opened the Notes app in her phone and began a new list: *Medical disposal. Cardboard boxes. Charity shop donations.* In the bathroom, she cleared the half-empty bottles of shampoo and shower gel from the shower. She picked up his embossed silver hairbrush and ran the soft bristles across the back of her hand, making herself shiver. How vain he always was about his hair! Maybe that was the result of having someone style it for him for so many years. Whenever they were going somewhere, Helen would be at the front door, ready and waiting, while her mother fussed over something upstairs and her father admired himself in the hall mirror, turning this way and that, smoothing his hair here, puffing it out there. For a second she wondered if she should perhaps keep the hairbrush. But what would she do with it? Use it? Ugh, no. Give it to one of the boys? It was hard to imagine this – or any – brush getting within roaring distance of them. But it didn't have to be about them. Didn't have to be functional. She could keep it simply because she liked it. Because she looked at it and remembered him preening, happy. She put it to one side.

Everything else went into the bag. His razor and spare blades. The cotton wool, cotton buds and anything else that was opened. His aftershave. Helen opened it and sniffed. A new one. New enough not to smell like him. Into the bag it went.

She checked her watch. Annie might be here shortly. She left the bag by the back door and went upstairs to shower and change. The question of what a person might wear to view their father's body was answered by the fact that she had brought one small carry-on suitcase with her and would have to make do with her capsule of trousers, shirt and cardigan. She wished for a moment for a more sentimental mother, one who had held onto some of Helen's old things. Silly, really. What awaited her at the hospital had no room for a reversible Snoopy sweatshirt or a denim shirt or a narrow fringed scarf in the severest black.

IT FLIES ANYWAY

Annie drove with enormous care, her shoulders high to her ears and her hands purplish-white at ten and two on the steering wheel.

'Thank you for driving,' Helen said. 'I'm not sure I would even remember how to drive in snow. At home, hardly anyone I know drives regularly. Except for their holidays.'

'If people don't have cars, how do they do the big food shop?' Annie asked with interest.

'They have it delivered, mostly,' Helen said.

It struck her as funny, suddenly, the atmosphere of polite disinterest in other people's lives that she lived within.

'You know, I've been to countless dinner parties and children's parties and weekends away with various bits of our extended network and not once has anyone asked how Irish people stock their fridges and cupboards.'

'What do they talk about?' Annie asked. 'Wait, don't tell me. Politics. And literature. And cheese.'

'Exactly. But mostly cheese,' Helen said.

'Would you ever move home? Back here, I mean?'

'I ...' Helen thought of the Notes app on her phone. The options list she had made out while waiting for Annie.

Option a) return for three or four weeks every summer, opening up the house like an Austen hero. With the children in tow, giving them the gift of an Irish childhood summer. Freedom and bikes and stony beaches with easy cycling distance and sandy beaches within an hour's drive. A fantasy

– a lovely fantasy, granted – and nothing more. No amount of wishing could give her children a 1980s summer. Besides, it would be ridiculous to use a house like this for such a limited time. Borderline immoral, in point of fact. Like the Swedes and their embarrassment at flying, the *flygskam* that had become a talking point at dinner parties recently. Was there such a thing for second homes? If there was, Laura would know.

Option b) live full-time in Glebe Cottage. Take the children out of school and move their lives, their languages, their limits, several degrees west. Renovate the place. Skylights in the darker upstairs rooms, rid the place of the dark furniture. Let the kids have the dog they wanted. Glebe Cottage had always needed a dog. She could work for an NGO. No shortage of those here. And Conor would find something, project management skills were always in demand. Réiltín would go to the same school she herself had gone to. Would, perhaps, finally find an Annie and Laura of her own. The thought of boarding school whispered, then vanished before she had time for relief or guilt. The boys were young enough to assimilate. To throw themselves into Irish and hurling and black pudding and calling it St. Stephen's Day. Or perhaps they were just old enough to never quite fit and to hate her for it.

But then she had thought about the city. The possibility it conferred. The feeling of breathing room despite the grubby air. Easy to fantasise about the freedom her children would have in her childhood home, with its air and water and greener spaces. Easy to forget that, outside the gate, that freedom would be eroded bit by bit by the eyes of others, their words, the reporting, the expectation. Cities expected nothing, except that you not slow down anyone else.

'I think I've been in the city too long to ever live in the countryside again,' she said eventually. Annie didn't need – wouldn't want – the excruciating detail.

'Despite the lure of a big shop every week?'

'Despite that, imagine!' she agreed.

The journey that should have taken forty minutes took nearly twice that. Although the main roads had been gritted, they crept along, the needle of the speedometer never climbing above sixty.

'I feel like Sandra Bullock in *Speed*,' Annie said, rolling first one shoulder and then the other.

Other drivers were less cautious. One van barrelled past them with its lights flashing.

'Jesus Christ.' Helen flinched and watched Annie tighten her grip on the wheel. Once it was past and gone, she let out the breath she was holding. 'We'll turn the next corner and find him in a heap at the side of the road,' she said.

'Gomicide, Jack used to call it,' Annie said. 'You know, stupid people dying because they did something stupid.'

'That certainly sounds like him,' she agreed.

'That's because he said it,' Annie said.

Her voice had that deliberate airiness she used to affect when she was pretending something didn't bother her. *I was well able to find my own way home, Helen, thanks.* Or *Jamie can kiss whoever he likes.* Or *I had no interest in seeing that film anyway.* Echoes of Annies-past filled the car and, for the first time, Helen heard what she must have sounded like, too. *Charlie said he could give me a lift home and I couldn't find you, so ...* And *The cheek of Anthony kissing Michelle Cleary when he was there with you.* And *I bumped into Laura and we decided to go on ahead.*

'I'm sorry for your loss, Annie,' she said, surprising herself. 'I should have said it yesterday. You two meant a lot to each other, I know.'

'Thank you.' Annie risked a quick glance away from the road. 'I'm going to miss Jack. He always made me laugh, no matter how afraid I was.'

'You're not afraid of anything,' Helen said without thinking, then regretted it immediately. Who was she to say?

'I think you'll find the pandemic happened to everyone,' Annie said, with that same airy tone.

'I felt less afraid during the pandemic,' Helen said. 'There was something comforting about knowing that everybody was afraid. That we were all at the same level. I wasn't the only exhausted, worrying weirdo any more.'

'Bracing is exhausting,' Annie agreed, in her normal voice. 'What were you worried about?'

'Getting Covid and not being able to breathe and passing it on to the kids and them not being able to breathe and going to hospital and there being one bed left and having to selflessly say that my child could have it while I went home to die,' Helen said.

'That's very specific,' Annie said. 'What did you worry about before Covid?'

'In the few days before the children's birthdays, I sometimes refer to them as the age they're about to be. It's a little thing and it makes them happy and proud. Then I lie awake worrying that they will die before the actual day itself and the last thing I said to them will have been a lie and their real age will have to be on the headstone and they would hate being trapped in an age I had already basically told them they had outgrown.'

'They're healthy and well, though, right?'

'Yes. But that doesn't stop the endless parade of possibilities.'

Annie's voice was steady. 'We have a way to go yet. Tell me, if you'd like.'

'My children being smothered in bouncy castles and dive-bombing onto hidden rocks and stepping carelessly off the footpath in front of a car. Falling off walls and down stairs. Fading in front of me with sadness or illness or doubt. Being taken, beaten, shamed, starved, savaged, ignored, belittled, disliked.'

'All those worries are about your children,' Annie said. 'That probably makes you a good parent or a good person, at least.'

'Oh, I have plenty worries about myself as well. I just didn't want to seem self-centred.'

They both laughed a little at that.

'There was a time I was afraid to go to bed in case the worry became so huge I wouldn't ever get up again. In case I ... well, you remember what my mother was like. I slept in a chair in the living room and when that didn't work I cut back to working part-time and that worked until it didn't. The worry found me anyway. I used to think it expanded to fill the available space.'

'Like a gas,' Annie said. 'Remember from physics class?'

Helen shook her head. 'I couldn't make head nor tail of physics. I took it because you did.'

'Seriously?'

'Seriously. Physics and history with you, biology and home ec with Laura. That way I didn't have to walk into a classroom on my own.'

'I never knew that,' Annie said. 'You never said anything.'

'Course not. What a dope I would have sounded!'

'We already knew that. I mean, we were all dopes about various things. We were teenagers.'

'So, what about your secret worries?' Helen said. 'Care to share?'

'The usual,' Annie said. 'Life and death and everything in between.'

After her own openness, the vagueness of the answer felt like a slap and they finished the journey in silence.

A lot of the cars in the car park had been there overnight, their tyres embedded in the remaining snow and their windscreens doilied with prettily patterned ice. Annie turned left and reversed carefully into a spot.

After parking, she shut off the engine and turned to Helen. 'I'm sorry. You deserve better than flippancy. I'm so used to telling people everything's fine.'

'Except Dad.'

'Except Jack.' Annie drummed her fingers lightly on the

steering wheel. 'What is it about turning forty that makes you feel both stronger and more afraid? My right shoulder clicks when I turn over in bed. My feet aren't able for heights or heat or heels. Everything could be cancer. All that bodily vulnerability, out of nowhere and all at once. What if all my best years are behind me and my heart is only held together with memories and I get Alzheimer's and lose even that?'

Helen knew. Oh, she *knew!* But she also knew better than to cut in and say so.

'My mother died and grief is this series of horrible little surprises, like the evil fairy at the christening.'

'Jesus, Annie. I'm so sorry I wasn't there. I should have been there.' Why hadn't she been there? It wasn't like she had a handy pandemic excuse then. What exactly was she doing that was so important she couldn't have come and held her friend's hand? But that was the question answered, of course. The term 'friends' no longer strictly applied. There was no category for whatever they were. Nothing between the all of the past and the nothing of the present and so it was less awkward to stay away. *If in doubt, go*: there was a reason it was the cardinal rule for funerals.

Laura went. Of course she did.

And, Helen told herself, she should be glad that one of them was there to catch Annie's eye in the church and nod in steadfast support.

'There's this phenomenon in Alzheimer's – sundowning, it's called, where the confusion is at its worst in the evenings.' Annie sighed. 'There's a metaphor in there somewhere, if I could ferret it out.'

'I'm sorry,' Helen said, as if there were a magic number of times she could say it in order for it to work.

Annie shook her head. 'Listen to me going on and on and making it all about me. You don't need to hear this.'

'But I do need to hear it. I need to be prepared.' Helen patted Annie's hand. 'Who else will tell me?'

Annie turned to face her. 'I was never trying to replace my dad with yours, you know. If anything, I think I might have been trying to replace you.'

They walked carefully across the icy concrete to the door of the hospital, their arms brushing one another companionably. The building was old. Long and low, unlike the new high-rise purpose-built hospitals. The convent to which it was attached had been incorporated into the hospital some time back, but the building retained the gloomy air of a place whose bricks were cemented hard with judgement.

A nurse buzzed them in and led them to the room where her father had last been alive.

Helen watched the door getting closer. Behind that door was her father. Except he wasn't her father any more. He was something else. He was *the body*. Or perhaps *the remains*.

The nurse opened the door. 'Jesus, Mary and Joseph,' she said. 'It's perishing. We left the windows opened since he passed. You'll want to keep your coats on,' she added.

Jesus, Mary and Joseph. Helen hadn't heard the phrase in so long. There were gradations of it, weren't there, according to the gravity or the wonder or the shock of a situation. *Jesus, Mary and Joseph tonight* was all she could remember. The threat no longer intangible but here in the immediate term. Touchable, almost. *Tonight.* Plenty time for dread. The theological equivalent of wait-til-your-father-gets-home. She realised that she hadn't moved, but was stuck two metres from the door.

'Thanks, Clodagh,' Annie said. 'We'll let you know if we need anything.'

Clodagh nodded and left them to it.

Helen's breath seemed to be stuck. She patted her breastbone with the flat of her hand, but her breath remained where it was, crouched, it felt like, behind her clavicle. Playing hide-and-seek with reality.

'Helen?' Annie said.

The blood pounded in her ears in a ringing roar that was nightclubs and mornings-after and childbirth.

'Helen. Breathe,' Annie said again and the warmth of her hand on Helen's sent her breath whooshing out into the open, ragged as a runner at the finish line.

'At my thirteenth birthday, I blew out the candles on my cake and wished that he was dead,' Helen said. 'I thought I wanted to be like you and Laura, but I didn't mean it. *I didn't mean it!*'

'Of course you didn't, pet.' Annie's hand was firm on her shoulder. 'Besides, it clearly didn't work, did it? I mean, that was thirty-odd years ago.'

Helen laughed a shocked bark and felt a little lighter for both the admission and the reaction.

'I can come in with you or I can wait for you here. Or you needn't go in at all. Whatever you want is absolutely fine,' Annie said. 'No explanations or justifications necessary.'

Helen thought of the bookcase in her father's room and Annie's smiley-face notes on her father's washbag. 'You were his friend, too,' she said.

She zipped up her coat and took Annie's hand.

He looked like himself. That was enough to get her as far as the bed, where tiny changes became apparent. There was a slackness to his mouth that didn't quite suggest sleep, and a slight darkening in the curl of his ears that she might have persuaded herself was nothing more than a shadow if she hadn't known better. He was more still than she had ever seen him in life, the stillness broken only by the corner of the sheet lifting and falling in the breeze from the window. But he looked like himself and she was lighter with gladness.

'Clodagh wasn't lying. It's Arctic in here,' Helen said.

'If Laura was here, she'd tell us that the Arctic is no longer as cold as we think it is,' Annie said.

'Consider us told,' Helen said. They shared a smile. 'What happens now?'

'You can stay for a while. Talk to him if you like. Or say a prayer. I can see if there's a chaplain around if you'd like something more formal?'

Helen tried to think what her father would have wanted. 'Conor is better at this sort of thing than I am,' she said.

'Do you want to phone him?'

Helen looked at her watch. It was early afternoon, he would be getting everyone on the train to the airport.

'Jack liked him, you know. Said he was devoted to you.'

Helen considered the word for a moment. Its undeniably canine connotations. 'The thing with devotion is that it can be hard to distinguish from habit.'

'My mother used to say that love was a decision,' Annie said. 'You might not have to make the decision every day but every now and then you have to actively choose it.'

'Mine used to say *it's hard to love someone in close-up, Helen,* and *you have to keep things interesting,*' Helen said. 'But then …' She gestured to Jack in the bed. There was no need to explain to Annie that Jack could be difficult to live with. 'I think we love people on a sliding scale. 'Some days we're at one hundred and other times we're at eighty or sixty or fifty.'

Sometimes, when she and Conor fought about something, she would listen and nod, all the while calculating where she was on the scale. Was there a number below which she would walk out? If so, that number must be lower than forty, which was the lowest she had ever gauged herself to be.

'You know that whole thing about swans mating for life is a myth?' Annie asked. 'They change mates sometimes, after a bad breeding season, or if a nest fails.'

'Christ.'

'Sorry.'

Helen looked at her father. 'Should we say a prayer?' she said to Annie. 'It can't hurt, right?'

They stumbled through a decade of the rosary. With each new prayer, Helen sent the bucket down to some deep memory well and each time it returned full to the brim with phrases she thought long left behind. *Grace* and *blessed* and *amongst* and *the hour of our death* and *ever shall be.*

With every prayer, her father felt further away from her, as though the words were waves pushing the raft of his body out to sea. It made her feel calmer somehow.

'Why is it,' she asked Annie when the rosary ended and an appropriate period of silence had elapsed, 'that we find it so hard to think of our parents as real people? I mean, beyond the limits of who they are to us? Do you think it's easier for artists' children? Their parents have released something essential of themselves through their fingers or their hands or their brain or whatever. Something that says: this is who I am when you're not here.'

'You have Jack's work as a whole other dimension,' Annie offered.

Helen shook her head. 'He always seemed slipperier when he was Dr Danny, speaking someone else's words.'

She hated watching him on television. Hated the claim that other people had on him. Hated the shift in her own popularity when having Dr Danny Furlong as her dad, so exciting at seven and eight and nine, became mortifying at twelve and thirteen and fourteen. *Helen Furlong,* people called her sometimes, pretending they were joking, and oh! she felt like such a loser, every time. And now Danny Furlong was finally gone, and Jack Fitzgibbon with him.

When Annie had gone to tell Clodagh they were ready for Bert Crowley to come and collect him, Helen leaned forward and took her father's hand. Without his heart beating and heating him, his hand was heavy and cold, no longer really a hand at all.

'In my mind, you're wearing that first pair of babs, the pale grey pair you loved first and best. You have a Martini in one hand, a dish of olives nearby, and, somewhere, Kris

Kristofferson is singing about singing the blues.' She cleared her throat. 'Mum is beside you, waiting for you to catch her up on everything that's been going on. Waiting to hear your stories. One forever Friday,' she whispered.

Her phone buzzed with a message from Réiltín. Not a message, exactly, but something she had taken from social media. A picture of a bumblebee, with accompanying text.

According to all aerodynamic laws, the bumblebee cannot fly because its body weight is not in the right proportion to its wingspan. But ignoring these laws, the bee flies anyway.

It flies anyway.

LEAVE THEM OPEN

The road back was slow and silent. The closer they got to the house, the less Helen wanted to get there. The thought of putting her key in the lock, opening the door and stepping into the empty hallway was unimaginable. She had never before come home without knowing that one of her parents was already there, or would be there shortly, with the kettle on or fresh ice in the fridge. Glebe Cottage was all hers. She alone was the keeper of the keys and the memories.

'I don't want to go back to the house,' she told Annie abruptly.

Annie glanced at her. 'I know. I could say you don't have to, but we'd both know that's a lie.'

'Are you coming back, too?'

Annie's voice was careful. 'I thought I might go back home actually.'

'Will you miss it? The house?'

'Yes. But only insofar as it's tied to Jack. I'll miss thinking of him there.'

'No matter what happens, you can't erase a friendship, you know,' Helen said suddenly. 'Whatever effect it had, those little strands will always be there, woven in around all the bits that were you to begin with.'

'The kind of thing that elbows its way in and refuses to leave?' Annie said.

Helen nodded. 'Not as fickle as a weathervane, but not as robust as a sundial.'

'You sound like Laura with the gardening talk,' Annie said.

Helen thought of Laura, her certainty. 'She seems happy, doesn't she?'

'But?'

'What do you mean?'

'Saying someone seems happy is usually the prelude to some kind of judgement.'

'No judgement. A little envy, if anything.'

Annie snorted. 'Get out of it. Laura's life looks like pure chaos to you and you know it.'

'Oh my God, it really does! All those little bitty jobs! But there's something sort of appealing in it, too. Feeling you don't have to explain yourself.'

'I've been fantasising about the opposite – about living in a place where no one knows you and you don't have to explain why you weren't in Susan's on Thursday morning or why you don't have any red meat in your shopping basket.'

'Would you really do it? Move somewhere nobody knows you, I mean?'

'I've been thinking a lot about changes and choices and circumstances,' Annie said. 'My brothers want me to sell Mum's house and give them their share and I think I will.'

'Is it not yours? I mean, I thought …'

'She left it to the three of us. Which means I have some decisions to make I guess.'

Before she had her children, Helen thought, she made her decisions according to what would make her happy in the future. It didn't always work out, of course. Most often, she got to the future she had set out for herself and it no longer matched what her more mature self wanted. She wasn't the greatest predictor of her own happiness, it seemed, but was anyone? Weren't all humans blinkered by who they were at that point in time? Nobody could see around the corners of themselves.

'What would it mean to you to sell?' Helen asked.

'I've been trying to figure that out,' Annie said. 'I have lots of memories there, sure, equal parts happy and horrible, but I'm not sure I want to pay my brothers a ridiculous amount of money to feel neutral about something. A home should bring joy, don't you think?'

'Pity we can't swap,' Helen said lightly. 'I could sell yours and you could live in mine. It always brought you joy.'

'That's not how the grown-ups do it,' Annie said.

Helen nodded. She was right. They weren't talking about shoes bought in a moment of sale madness that could be passed from friend to friend. Glebe Cottage was security for her children's future.

'Where is your joy?' Annie asked suddenly. 'Since Laura isn't here to ask. And don't say your children.' She held up her hand. 'Not because I'm judgy or because I don't have children myself or because it really doesn't look joyful at all a lot of the time, but because it's too easy to hide behind. Where is your joy, for you, just you?'

Ruling out the children left what, exactly? Work. But work was satisfying rather than joyful. Did that count? She didn't swim in the sea or yarn-bomb postboxes or volunteer anywhere. She occasionally picked up a book, but usually to model screen breaks for the children and she never got much beyond the first chapter. She watched television series, but often simply so she could say she had seen them. And besides, who on earth found their joy in television, or, perhaps more accurately, who would admit to it, even in the privacy of a small car on a snowy road.

'Truthfully, I don't know.'

'I don't know either,' Annie said. 'I'm starting to wonder if the whole joy thing is a myth beyond a certain age.'

Helen unlocked her phone and began to tap out a message.

'Laura?'

'Laura.'

Me and Annie are talking: where is your joy?

As soon as she pressed send, she worried that she had worded it badly, that Laura would think they were talking about her, that they were judging and finding her life wanting.

She needn't have worried. Almost immediately, her phone buzzed.

'What did she say?' Annie asked.

'She sent a photo.' Helen held the phone against the steering wheel so Annie could look safely. Three mugs of hot chocolate, heaped with cream and marshmallows, alongside a TV remote control.

'At least one of us has her shit together,' Annie said.

'Who would have thought it would be Laura, though?' Helen asked, and they laughed guiltily.

Outside the car window, patches of green were visible where the sun had penetrated the snow. Helen thought of walking the snowy city footpaths, pushing the buggy heavy with wriggling or crying or silent boys, until sweat trickled down her back and they slept soundly.

'Do you think maybe we get a certain amount of joy and it can get used up?'

'Joy and grief are the two things that don't get used up,' Annie said. 'There's no quota, there's just openness and luck.' She looked out the window and tapped her fingers lightly, decisively, on the steering wheel. 'My mother died in winter and I swear I thought spring would never come. I'm not speaking metaphorically – every day I woke up to gloom and freezing rain and it felt as though winter would last forever. Then when spring eventually came it was so warm – unseasonably warm – as if it was making up for being late. Overnight, everything seemed greener and the verges were creeping out from the side of the road to apologise and the furze was blazing a bright yellow *sorry!* from the ditches and the trees were hugging everything they could reach. It didn't mean anything real. But it meant something all the same, you know?'

Helen knew. Apologies were easier without words.

They drew up to the gates of Glebe Cottage and Annie pulled in alongside so that Helen could enter the security code. 'Here we are,' she said, as the gates swung open in front of them.

'You should take our green sofa,' Helen said suddenly.

'For your new place. Or your old place. Wherever. For joy. You always liked it best.'

Annie nodded. 'I'd love that. Really. Thank you.'

Through the trees, the walls of the house were a soft cashmere grey in the watery winter light. The creeper would shortly come back to life, transforming the house from strangled to vital.

When her parents had parties, the women would exclaim at how pretty it was, how cool or quaint or cosy, while the men muttered about cracks and damp in a show of vague architectural terminology. The masonry was solid, her father would tell them. The house could take the weight of all that growth.

For all she knew, that was one more of her father's fabrications or exaggerations or wishes. If so, she realised, with a little starburst of gladness, she could simply leave it for the next owner to worry about.

'Bert Crowley has a template for the announcement for the paper,' Annie said, putting her warm hand on Helen's cold one. 'He won't rush you. You can take all the time you need.'

It was more kind than true. Death had already come and so the clock was ticking. The only time Helen had was that allowed her by the rituals of death. Removal. Burial. Three days. One ritual after another, leading her through it, then abandoning her at the graveside. People did this every day, she reminded herself.

'Husband, father, actor, friend. A line on each.'

'That's it.'

'Husband, father, actor, friend.' Helen found herself itemising her father on one hand, like a tic she was unable to control. 'Husband, father, actor, friend.' On she went, unable to think of a single thing he did or liked or said. A whole full life and that was all she had? Her tip-tapping finger was going, going, drumming a beat on her hand. *Husband, father, actor, friend. Husband, father, actor, friend.*

'Want to come to mine instead?' Annie asked gently.

'I think I'd like that.'

She reached for the button to close the gates. The falling winter sun caught the upstairs windows, giving the house a blazing, blinded look. Helen withdrew her hand and turned back to Annie. 'Let's leave them open,' she said.

ACKNOWLEDGEMENTS

Greener started – as almost every book does – as an idle wondering, this time about the differences between old and new friendships. You can't make new old friends, as the saying goes, but you can make new friends, which are sometimes exactly what you need. And if you're lucky, of course, they grow into old friends, which is yet another reason to be grateful for living and for seeing the years pass. I'm beyond grateful to have both kinds of friends in my life – none of whom feature anywhere in this book, except here – thank you all for everything.

I read Clare Shaw's poetry collection, *Towards a General Theory of Love*, all throughout the writing of this book. I loved it then and I love it still – it is one of the few books that lives on my desk, within touching distance. What the Frog Taught Me About Love is so rich and yet so precise about the ways we go about loving and being loved, with all the implied control and expectation involved, and I am so grateful to be able to use some of its beautiful lines as the epigraph for this book. Huge thanks to Clare and to Bloodaxe Books for their permission.

Thanks to Elizabeth and all at Northbank Talent Management for their constant support and encouragement, and to Hannah, for her steady steering of earlier drafts of this book.

It's always a joy when a book finds a home, even more so when it's the right home and the right hands. My heartfelt thanks to every person on the wonderful team at Legend Press, and especially to Cari Rosen, for her insightful editorial input. When I wake up in the night panicking about the story, I remember that Cari likes it and that I trust her judgement.

I firmly believe that cover artists are alchemists and a huge part of drawing readers towards books. Their insights and heart are irreplaceable. I'm so glad to have Rose Cooper as the cover artist again this time and grateful for another pitch-perfect cover.

The right writing group is worth gold and I'm lucky to have the right one. Thanks to Rachel and Sylvia, to whom this book is dedicated, who always understand what it is I'm trying to say and help me to see it and say it better. Here's to the next seven years of writing and friendship.

Thanks to the readers, booksellers, book bloggers, reviewers and book clubs for supporting my last novel, Winter People, so warmly – the practical and emotional implications of that support helped Greener to be here too. Special thanks to the loveliest of local bookshops here in Kinsale and Cork, who always make me feel like a real writer and – most importantly – a real reader. Thank you too to our libraries for stocking my books. It is never less than a thrill to visit them on the shelves or, better still, to find them already checked out. In a world that can feel overwhelming, libraries are a powerful force for human growth and human goodness.

As always, love and thanks to Mum, Dad, Dee, Kevin, Kay, Kathleen, Eleanor, John, Barry and Mel. And to the newest generation of Fays and O'Connors – may your love of reading continue to bring new worlds and new delights.

My fondest love to Colm, Oisín and Cara, for each being exactly who they are, and to Ali, our gorgeous girl, who was a little joy in life and whose memory is precious.

And finally, thanks to Scout – dogs are pure gladness, which is pretty much always the kind of friend you need.